Dedication

To Amy and Larry: Details from your lovely, romance
inspired a portion of this story.

A Refuge for Rosanna

Susan Karsten

A Refuge for Rosanna
COPYRIGHT 2019 by Susan Karsten

Contact Information: titleadmin@pelicanbookgroup.com

Scripture quotations, unless otherwise indicated are taken from the King James translation, public domain.

Cover Art by *Nicola Martinez*

Prism is a division of Pelican Ventures, LLC
www.pelicanbookgroup.com PO Box 1738 *Aztec, NM * 87410

The triangle prism logo is a trademark of Pelican Ventures, LLC

Publishing History
Prism Edition, 2019
Paperback Edition ISBN 978-1-5223-9799-1
Electronic Edition ISBN 978-1-5223-9798-4
Published in the United States of America

1

Rural England, 1816

Carriage wheels thundered, breaking the blessed solitude of the rustic road.

Peter's shoulders tensed. So far, his hard-won, hermitlike existence provided the escape he craved. If he kept to himself, no one would ever find out his past sins. Fists clenched, he wavered and thought to hide from view, but a shred of pride and tattered honor rooted him to the ground. The right to live, and to breathe, regardless of what he'd done, still existed. This well-deserved misery would lift someday.

He decided no he wouldn't hide in a ditch, although he might belong in one. His reputation already tattered, nobody's opinion mattered. He didn't matter, either. When the traveling carriage lumbered into view, he planted his feet shoulder width apart, hands clasped behind his back. The vehicle rolled to a stop, the door directly in front of him.

A burly, whiskered coachman leaned around, peered down, and lifted his hat. He scratched his head, clearly lost. "Can ye direct us to, um...ah?"

The door opened, and a young lady peered out. Shiny dark curls escaped her bonnet and framed large, sensitive brown eyes set in a face complete with dimples and bedecked with an enticing curve of a smile. Pretty though she was, something else called to his spirit—was it her sincerity? Yes, she glowed with it.

"Can you tell us the way to Honor's Point?" A dainty shoe peeked out from under the ruffled hem of her skirt. "It appears we took the wrong road." The young lady's foot shifted, stepping into air. The next instant, she fumbled in the doorway, a squawk of alarm escaping her lips.

Peter leaped forward and tightened his arms around her as she landed against him. She weighed no more than a feather. Her closeness and hints of lilac perfume raised a surge of attraction in his veins.

"Thank you. I might have been injured," she whispered. She then bent in a failed attempt to loosen the hem of her dress from her heel.

The plume on her bonnet tickled his nose, and he sneezed. She glanced up, her luscious lips, so close, beckoned.

A faint surge of recognition pulsed. *What was her name? Rebecca, Rosanne, Rose? Something with an R.* He'd seen her in London, surrounded by pinks of the *ton*. She'd attended the Banting ball in London little more than a month ago—the last ball he'd ever go to. Even in her rumpled and dusty state, she appeared as delightful as across the candlelit ballroom.

Please don't let her recognize me, he prayed. *As much as I'd like to meet her, it's impossible now.* Discovery terrified him.

She pointed to her foot. "Would you be so kind? My hem is caught."

Keeping silent, he braced her weight against his thigh, and extricated the snagged hem as requested. Setting the woman down with tender care, he checked her stability before retracting his light hold on her waist.

She tugged at her short spencer jacket, and passed

gloved hands over a lavender gown, smoothing away the wrinkles. She tilted her head. "We are searching for Honor's Point. Perhaps we took a wrong turn, or missed a turn, or...are we off course? The coachman was sure he knew the way." She gazed at him, her brown, doe eyes waiting in innocent expectancy.

He swallowed. "No, ye be on the right path, Miss. Yer almost there." Peter mimicked the local villagers' accent, as he dragged his gaze from hers and fixed it on the ground. He winced at the bad impression he'd made. She'd think him a rustic nobody—and she'd be correct. He tugged his forelock, slumped his shoulders, and gestured forward. "Take a right at the next drive, and it's nigh on a quarter mile to the house."

To avoid further conversation, he affected a limp and hastened to the path skirting the field. He whistled a tavern tune to suit his general aura of shabbiness. As a gentleman, he'd have helped the young woman back into the coach. But he dared not risk detection. As a common villager, he wouldn't be expected to do the pretty.

He desired no encounters like this, no matter how intriguing. On a scrap of land that was once part of the Honor's Point estate sat the cottage where he lived in rural solitude. The only shred of the property left to him now.

A fair distance from the road, he chanced a look back. No longer in sight, the distant, faint rumble of carriage wheels indicated the vehicle continued on its way. Alone again, he ceased the uncomfortable limp, straightened his shoulders, and headed home.

He looked down at his coat. Limp from too many pressings, and frayed spots at the cuffs, it reminded him of his reduced circumstances. At least his self-imposed exile involved no tailor fittings, no dancing to society's tune, no invitations, no debt-collectors—and no shame. Neither did it allow him to pursue the attractive young lady who'd fallen into his arms.

~*~

Belatedly, Rosanna called to his retreating back, "thank you." She clambered back into the carriage Uncle George provided for the trip. With its well-padded squabs, it gave superior comfort compared to a rented coach, and since he wanted to do this, she'd not quibble. Guilt and gratitude warred for prominence when she thought of her uncle. He'd taken good care of her affairs in the aftermath of the sudden loss of both parents to an epidemic.

However, she objected to Uncle George's philosophy that all young ladies should be married—the sooner the better—to men chosen by the relatives of the young females. Even ones like her who wanted nothing to do with marriage, especially loveless, arranged ones. His kindnesses, however, outweighed the mischief done by his numerous efforts to arrange a match for her.

Settling in, she straightened her skirts, clucking over the torn hem. Where was that workbasket? She'd pin up the hem quickly. It wouldn't do to arrive at one's new property with a torn dress. While she worked on pinning the awkward tear, memories of the indignity of falling into a man's strong arms soon gave way to recalling her battle to arrive at the estate called Honor's Point.

She'd won the right to leave London, and set up

her own establishment in the country, away from society. The death of her first love, Clarence, permanently broke her heart. Why must guilt spoil and adulterate her accomplishment of achieving freedom from the pressures of the marriage mart?

No man ever raised a flicker of interest within her. Not after Clarence. If a man to love and respect would have ever crossed her path, a decent interval after Clarence's untimely death, she wouldn't have needed to flee convention.

Once she had experienced love, it had been impossible to accept anything less. She didn't hate the *idea* of marriage, just being forced into one for money, property, or bloodlines.

After months of negotiating, she'd finally convinced dear old Uncle George to agree to her plan to purchase a secluded estate using her own inheritance she'd received when she'd turned one and twenty. She planned to help other less fortunate young ladies attain refuge from forced matrimony. She was one of the blessed few to successfully refuse to be leg-shackled into a marriage of convenience. Convenient for the man, she was sure.

Hem pinned, thoughts turned to what Barton would say if she'd been awake when Rosanna toppled right into the arms of that strange man. The strength of his hold lingered in her memory. He must be a local farm laborer, perhaps a tenant—except he exuded an appealing dignity.

Rosanna stowed the basket, grabbed her parasol, and thumped the roof of the coach, signaling the coachman to proceed.

At the lurch, fiftyish Barton cracked open one eye and let out a yawn. "Did we stop?"

"Yes, we got directions from a local. Barton, we're almost to our safe haven. It'll be wonderful." Rosanna allowed her enthusiasm free rein. She wanted everyone to be happy.

Taciturn, Barton reached up to tidy her smooth black hair, put on her bonnet, and tied the ribbons under her chin. "Indeed."

Preoccupied so long with the acquisition of the estate, and the move from London to Honor's Point, relief cascaded over Rosanna as the arduous journey neared its end. She mulled over her motives, and hoped she'd thought of everything. Buying this property outside the small village of Woodvale caused her relatives and advisors to question her wisdom.

She'd always struggled to be taken seriously, so what did it matter if they thought her a fool? Why did people think all pretty women were stupid? Standing up to them required all the determination she could muster.

A seed of doubt rested within her heart—doubt she admitted only to herself. Since the plan met her needs and fulfilled her dream she forged on, trusting all to work out. She'd been through an ordeal in gaining Honor's Point, the sanctuary she longed for. Perhaps her last niggle of uneasiness would leave when she at last gazed upon the reputed natural beauty of the estate.

2

Once through the gates, Rosanna craned her neck, eager to view the house. "We're here, Barton!"

The driveway's gradual elevation increased the property's exalted quality. Thick woods gave way to massive overarching elms on either side. When the chaise first emerged from the heavily-wooded section, the dusty carriage windows revealed a ring of surrounding hilltops.

Through the breaks in vegetation, a hilltop manor house came into view as Rosanna's carriage rounded the last bend. The land leveled off, and the vehicle stopped where the gravel drive looped in front of the large house. Elegant exterior stairways arched left and right, then curved back toward the massive door. The impressive entrance gave balance to the facade, and favorable proportions lent majesty to the mellow stone manor house.

Dozens of servants stood assembled on the steps, waiting to greet the new mistress. "It appears they received the note we sent ahead indicating my arrival time."

Barton sniffed. "That's an understatement."

Relieved to emerge from the coach and stand on solid ground again, Rosanna turned in a slow circle. She reined in her excitement and folded her hands in prim fashion. It wouldn't do to give an impression of giddiness. This moment held importance and she must begin as she meant to go on. Her success depended on it. After a few deep breaths of the wonderful, fresh country air, she accepted the butler's escort to the foot of the steps. He bowed before joining the ranks of waiting staff members.

"Thank you for this fine welcome. I am Miss Cabot, the new owner of Honor's Point." She paused and indicated the woman behind her. "And this is Miss Barton, my lady's maid."

The butler stepped forward and gave a pretentious bow. "Miss Cabot, we are all at your service. I'm Perkins. Allow me to present the staff."

Taking time to smile and interact with each servant, from the tall, reedy-voiced butler, who introduced her first to the housekeeper, Mrs. Good, down to the lowliest, scrawny scullery maid, Rosanna fulfilled the expected duties and traditions attendant upon a new mistress arriving at a grand home.

Since she didn't plan to ever marry, she meant to build a rewarding life here at beautiful Honor's Point.

A few servants wore doubtful expressions on their faces, perhaps disliking the idea of a single lady as their new mistress, a bit askance, she guessed. But Rosanna intended to extend grace to win them over. "Thank you all for the splendid greeting. I'm certain I can count on your help learning about this exceptionally special estate." She moved toward the imposing entrance.

A few servants unloaded the bags and trunks.

Mrs. Good reminded the kitchen staff to prepare a hearty tea for the travelers.

Perkins scampered ahead to open the door.

Pleased to put the time-honored ritual of greeting

the household staff behind her, Rosanna and Barton entered the hall before ascending the stairs in the wake of Mrs. Good, the housekeeper, to freshen up after the trip.

A nimble footman followed behind with their travelling cases, which held essentials.

Once alone in the large suite of rooms, Rosanna threw out her arms. "Barton, isn't it lovely? Aren't you thrilled to be here?"

"It's much more clean and peaceful than London, but I hope the staff accepts us."

"Don't borrow trouble, Barton, they're probably very kind."

"Perhaps so."

"Don't be a wet blanket. Our arrival is the fruition of the first phase of my plan. It's hard to believe we're here. I may require you to pinch me."

"You don't need a pinch, but I will help you change out of this travel-stained gown. Turn around, dearie." She commenced unfastening the hooks and tapes that held Rosanna's lavender-sprigged muslin dress together.

Rosanna stretched her arms over her head to facilitate removal of the dress. Clad in only a chemise, she opened her case and fished for a dressing gown, which she donned and wrapped around her waist. "Ahh, freedom. The French Revolution at least brought about our current comfortable fashions. Much better than those cage-like corsets and such."

"I agree. Can't imagine travelling in panniers or a stomacher. There was even something called a rump-pad."

"Sounds nasty."

"I've not eaten for hours and you know my

clockwork appetite. As soon as we've washed and changed shall we hasten to the dining room?" Barton moved toward the door. "I'll be back to help you."

"Take as much time as you need."

Barton moved toward the door. "I hope I can find my room."

"I'm sure a maid will be lurking around to guide you. The staff seems efficient."

In no hurry, Rosanna relished the moments alone. Travelling took its toll. Even so, energy began to return, buoyed by the simple fact of being in her new home. Hugging herself, she moved to the window to admire the view—more of the thick verdant woods and hills she'd passed on the road to the estate. Though thrilled to have arrived, she tamped down her exhilaration by reminding herself that moving to Honors Point consisted of only the first step.

True satisfaction would be found when she started the next phase of her plan.

3

A tour of the spacious house occupied Rosanna the next morning.

At the end of the tour Mrs. Good opened a door off the main hall with a special flourish and stepped back. "Your study, Miss Cabot. I hope it meets with your approval."

Surprised, Rosanna hesitated.

Mrs. Good's eyes held a twinkle of pleasure and she fluttered her hands toward the door. "Go on, go in."

Rosanna entered the room. "A lady's study—how special to have a room of my own." The room's color scheme of hyacinth blue, white, and gold, its tasteful and delicate furnishings, and French windows with a rose garden view, combined into a feminine and useful room. Rosanna stood in the center of the room and took a slow turn around, trying to take in the many delights the space offered.

So many homes held lavish studies for male heads of household but nothing for the ladies besides escritoires in the corners of their boudoirs or against the walls in common rooms.

This was the sort of room for whiling away the hours, making lists, planning, writing letters, and simply living—mistress of her own domain without society's pressure to wed. Pressures she'd had enough of to last her a lifetime. Why people put up with society's tyrannical marriage arrangements, she'd never understand. She placed a hand over her heart. "It is beautiful, and it shows excellent foresight that such a room was included when the house was planned and built."

"So glad you like it. The staff went over this room with extra care for you, Miss Cabot." Beaming with satisfaction, Mrs. Good clasped her work worn hands in front of her ample bosom. "I purposely saved this room for the last on the tour."

"Having my very own study is so inspiring." She ran her hand across the glossy mahogany desk. One more confirmation this was the place for her. "Thank you for the tour. I'll be in here should anyone need me."

She wasted no time in putting the study to use. Seated at the writing desk in the quiet, charming room, she opened the various compartments and drawers, withdrew a pen, ink, and a piece of stationery and got into position to write. But the pen remained still. The ink on the pen, suspended above the paper, dried. Sentences formed in her mind, only to be rejected. The dry ink didn't matter, since glib words and phrases vanished like vapor. She realized an inherent problem. How was she to share her planned harbor from undesired marriages with others?

Palm pressed to forehead, heart sinking, she tussled with the dilemma. A large obstacle loomed. How could she not have foreseen this? How foolish to think the plan would go off without a hitch! All those hours of convincing Uncle George to allow this move, and now this roadblock. Offering aid to other young ladies would be more complicated than simply penning an advertisement.

According to Rosanna's original plan, when a young lady fleeing a distasteful, forced betrothal or an undesirable arranged marriage learned of Rosanna's services, they would see a discreet advertisement in the *Times*, and arrange sanctuary here at Honor's Point. Notices placed in newspapers, however, would also be seen by the very people from whom the young ladies wanted to flee. This presented a severe dilemma.

Rosanna's head sank until her forehead rested on the desk. She considered the setback from all angles. The crisis appeared to be insurmountable. None of the meager solutions that came to mind solved the flaw. Any announcement of the refuge would reveal its existence and defeat the purpose.

Thanking the Lord she'd not confided the defective plan to anyone save Barton, she suppressed a groan, took a deep breath, and stared out the window while massaging her neck. A walk might clear her mind and perhaps the fresh air would blow a solution into her head.

Rosanna retrieved her bonnet from the table in the front hall.

Perkins let her out the door. He followed her out onto the top step.

The parkland around the large house was landscaped to capitalize on the hilltop setting. Paths diverged from the house in four directions. "Where do the trails lead?"

Deferential, Perkins gave an intriguing answer. "Each one leads to a spectacular view of hills, and woods, or patchwork fields."

She tied her bonnet ribbons, eager to be on her way—to walk off her anxiety and perhaps concoct a solution. "How lovely, Perkins. Is there any danger on the property, of which I should be aware?"

"No, Miss Cabot. Nary an intruder, incident, or accident of any kind has befallen a lady here. Honor's Point is safe." He handed her a parasol and placed a shawl around her shoulders.

She thanked Perkins and set off, loneliness ratcheting through her heart. "I've no one to consult with. I alone must think of a way out," she murmured as she walked toward the convergence of paths, reveling in the fresh air, even while wracking her brain for an answer to the puzzle.

The warm breeze coming off the hill, and the scent of summer flowers combined to restore her spirits within a short time. A sensation of relaxed freedom washed over her. The blessed solitude without the requirement of a maid at her elbow at all times was a refreshing novelty.

Energy flowing, she selected one of the four paths. Her chosen route meandered down the main hill, and then passed into the woods. Within the cover of the trees the path grew less tame. Before she knew it, the path took her to the edge of a ridge.

To her left rose an outcropping of large white rocks in the distance. This must be one of the boundary markers the estate's steward mentioned. Rosanna planned to walk out on the other paths soon, each one leading to a corner of the property.

From this ridge, through a cluster of trees below the rocks, she could make out the roofline of a structure. It appeared to be a small dwelling—a cottage perhaps? Besides the dower house and gatehouse at the foot of the drive, she was aware of no cottages on the property, other than the tenants' homes, which were in the opposite direction. She would ask the steward about it the next time they spoke.

She backed away from the precipice and sat on a convenient tree stump near the path. Bowing her head, she thanked God for her safe arrival at her own place of refuge, for peace of mind, and for an answer enabling her to offer sanctuary to other young ladies. Reinvigorated, and with a lighter heart, even without, as yet, any resolution, she rose and walked back to the manor house. Due to her exertions, she anticipated a reviving cup of tea.

Perkins appeared as if by magic to open the door before she'd barely touched the steps.

She shed her bonnet, shawl and parasol. "Thank you, Perkins. I had a lovely walk. The beauty of the property is unrivalled. Please send tea to my study."

She spotted a letter on the silver mail tray. Lifting it, she examined it. The front of the envelope featured a feminine scrawl. In a murmur she read, "To Miss Rosanna Cabot, from E. M." Who was E.M.? None of the few people who knew her direction had those initials. Perplexed, she entered her little study. While waiting for a servant to bring tea, she tore open the letter.

Dear Rosanna ~

Perhaps you recall the last time we met. It was at the Banting ball. You remembered me and our friendship at the academy. Those idyllic years seem so far off, don't they? Even though that ball was over a month ago, our conversation stayed with me. You said you were about to buy a property and move away to the country. The name Honor's Point stuck in my mind and after much difficulty, I was able to find its location through a discreet and helpful reference librarian.

My situation is dire. I must presume your permission to visit. I heard some whispers you've escaped the arranged marriage a relative planned for you. Your kind friendliness to me allows me to assume and plead you will give me aid toward the same end. My parents are pressing me fierce to accept a revolting codger as husband. This was while also attempting to affiance me to a hideous first cousin. In fact, I run for my life as soon as this is posted.

With much hope and trust, your friend,

Elspeth Mordant, London.

Elspeth Mordant. The young lady with the flowing red hair at academy. Never had a prayer been answered so visibly and so quickly. Tears of joy welled in Rosanna's eyes. *Let the tears flow. This is amazing.* A possible refugee landing almost right in her lap. Such an express answer—a clear sign that God listened to her prayers. This needed contemplation.

A maid tiptoed in, white-knuckled hands clutching a fancy, enameled tray. "Miss? Here's your tea."

Rosanna snapped back to the present. She'd fallen into a daze, hands limp in her lap, staring out the window with a wide smile on her face. *What the little maid must think.* "Oh, dear me, I was woolgathering. Don't be afraid, dear. I'm sure I met you on the day of my arrival, but your name escapes me."

"Me name is Dot, Miss."

"Dot. I shall make sure to use your name so I remember it. Well, Dot, I would dearly love a spot of tea. Please put the tray over here." She indicated a table in front of two cozy armchairs in an alcove.

"This fine?" The tray's contents rattled as the nervous maid set it down. Her hands flew to her red cheeks.

"That's perfect, Dot. Ooh, some of cook's delicious bread, with butter and jam will suffice. Thank you for bringing the tray so promptly. I shall enjoy my repast." She smiled and the relieved maid curtsied on her way out.

Indeed, the food tasted delicious, but only distracted her for a few moments. Thoughts of establishing the refuge returned. After almost giving up on the idea, Elspeth had found her. What to do now? To start, she would prepare for a guest. Her plan could be enacted, and at least one young lady in want could be helped. A friend—who was also a wonderful, suitable guest in dire need of Rosanna's refuge.

4

Barton began to scold the minute Rosanna entered the room. Any louder, and her voice would qualify as a screech. "Is it true, what Perkins told me? That you went out alone? I am severely opposed to that."

Interrupted by the outrage poured out on her by the lady's maid, Rosanna's pleasant musings ceased. "Please. You are hurting my ears."

The irate companion stood her ground with hands on hips and a martial gleam in her eye. She inhaled, then lowered her voice to a shade above a whisper. "Fine. To think, a refined young lady such as you, out gallivanting alone. The good Lord knows what might have happened. You promised not to go out unescorted."

Rosanna turned her attention to Barton's words "Now, now, Barton, I'm not a child anymore. It's surely acceptable for me to stroll about my own property. Is it not?"

Barton's worried brows descended from their heights. "Best to be careful."

"Oh, my. This isn't London. I can manage without a chaperone on rare occasions. Please don't read me a scold today. Join me. I'll share my freshly-brewed tea with you as well as some excellent news."

"Fine. No more scolding this time, but don't think I shall forget, nor shall I stop caring about your safety.

What news?"

"First, let me ring for a second cup." Rosanna jingled the bell, making Barton wait for the tidbit. "Once you have a cup of hot tea, I'll tell."

Barton took her hands off her hips with reluctant compliance and made herself comfortable on one of the chintz-covered chairs near the tea table.

Rosanna stood and moved over to the French doors, to drink in the delightful landscape. Near the house, a petite terrace was surrounded by a hedge of roses and farther out, gorgeous local hills were sprinkled with numerous shades of green foliage. She glanced over her shoulder, leaving the luscious sight, to study Barton's posture. Keeping bossy Barton in suspense for a minute or two more wouldn't hurt.

Dot answered the bell and scurried off to get another china cup, saucer, spoon, and plate as instructed.

Barton patted the other chair. "Please come and sit, Miss Rosanna. The water will stay hot, and I'd like to hear the news. It will take her forever to return—too long to wait. Tell me now, if you please."

"Before I tell you, I must start a list." Rosanna went to her desk, wrote for a moment, then held up a small, black notebook, giving it a shake for emphasis.

Barton's lips straightened into a pursed line. "You love to keep me in suspense."

"I've started a list of tasks to help me become better acquainted with Honor's Point." She read aloud. "Number one: ask the steward about the cottage I saw in the distance. I shall add to the list as other tasks occur to me." She closed the petite book, keeping it in her hand, and sat in the second armchair. "Oh, Barton, the news is so special."

"Start at the beginning." Barton settled in, avid eyes glowing. "First, tell me, how exactly did you come about the news?" Clearly impatient, she tried a guess. "Did you meet someone on your walk?"

Her encouraging expression made Rosanna want to laugh—the woman did love tittle-tattle. Amused relief coursed over Rosanna, as it appeared Barton's avid interest in news caused her mind to gloss over her opposition to Rosanna going on walks. "No, I encountered no one. It was after I returned from the walk. Let me tell in my own way."

Dot arrived and silently placed the second setting of china on the table, making a bit less nervous rattle this time. She bobbed her way out, as if scared of her own shadow.

Rosanna chose to hold Barton in suspense a little longer and dawdled in preparing the cups of tea. At last, she handed the older woman a delicate china cup and saucer. "Here you are, dear Barton, milk in first, just how you like it."

"You're a dear, always thinking of me." Barton sipped the steeped tea and sighed.

"You are familiar with my plan to establish a refuge here for young ladies fleeing forced marriage?" She took her first sip, watching over the cup's rim for Barton's reaction.

Barton gave a sniff of disapproval. "Don't worry, I haven't forgotten your plan to help others escape the clutches as you did. Are you still set on that questionable idea?"

"Not exactly. The plan had a major flaw."

Sardonic, Barton's eyebrows lifted in a quirk worthy of Drury Lane. "Only one?"

Rosanna pushed an errant curl away from her

cheek, dreading Barton's disdain. "Yes. Only one. Any method used to advertise the availability of my refuge would alert the very individuals from which such a woman would be fleeing."

"Oh, my yes, that's a problem." Barton sipped, peeping over the edge of her teacup.

"I was stymied and forlorn about ever being able to help. My hopes dashed."

"I can readily imagine so." Barton overlaid her words with sympathy.

"All's not lost, however. A letter arrived, Barton. Its contents have sent me over the boughs." Unable to suppress a smile, Rosanna tipped her head back and massaged her temples, relishing the happy outcome. The news was still so fresh, and she was overwhelmed with God's answer to her prayer.

Barton's fingers pleated the long lappet of her lace cap. "So, a letter. Get to the letter, Rosanna."

"Have you ever heard me mention Elspeth Mordant?"

Barton shook her head.

"No? She's a diminutive redhead. Does that ring a bell?" Rosanna sat up and proceeded to cover a piece of bread with jam then nibble the edge, waiting for Barton to respond.

"Hmm. Can't say that it does, Miss. Did you get word of her?"

Rosanna placed the bread onto a plate and brushed her fingers with a napkin. "You must be on pins and needles, so I'll get to the point."

"Finally?"

"Today, I received a letter from Miss Mordant. She's just about the prettiest little thing. We attended academy together. She's one of the Hertfordshire

Mordants. And so...this is almost too precious." Drawing out the moment, she sipped the now-lukewarm tea.

Eyes wide, Barton's cup clattered into her saucer. She leaned closer. "What did she say?"

"She wrote to me, looking for exactly the sort of help I want to provide here. Her relatives sound horrid. She said they pressed both an old man and a close relative upon her as candidates for her hand." Rosanna relaxed back into her chair, having delivered her tidbit of news, and smiled with satisfaction.

Barton's eyes widened. "You must have been mightily upset when you realized you had no way to help pressured and unwilling brides-to-be. But look what God has done."

The still-fresh memory moistened her eyes with grateful tears. "He answered my prayer almost before I prayed it."

"I hope she is able to get here safely and undetected."

"We must make that a matter for prayer as well." Rosanna sent up a silent petition then and there. "Thank you, Barton, for being excited for me. You had doubts."

"How on earth did she come to write to you? It's so amazing." Barton raised her brows. "Miss Rosanna, did you somehow say more than you should? To someone you shouldn't?"

"Here's the letter." Rosanna raised the missive. "She recalled I was leaving London to live in the country and then heard a whisper referring to my avoiding the parson's mousetrap, and she ferreted out my direction. Oh, here it is. I'll read the part where she explains. '...*Your words stayed with me. You said you were*

about to move away to the country to your own property.
The name Honor's Point stuck in my mind and after much
difficulty, I was able to find your direction through a discreet
and helpful reference librarian.

My situation is dire. I must presume on your
permission to visit. I believe I heard some whispers you
escaped the arranged marriage a relative had planned for
you.'"

"May I read it?" Barton held out a hand for the
letter and perused it. "This is too wonderful to be
called chance. This is God's good Providence, clear as
day!"

"I suppose servant's gossip spread a whisper
about town that I was being allowed to reject arranged
matrimony. What with all the rows I had with Uncle
George, the servants could easily have overheard."

"That would account for any whispers." Barton
crossed her arms. "I disapprove of gossip."

"Miss Mordant must be very clever to ferret out
my location. It doesn't appear that any word of my
plans leaked out. You were the only one who knew. It's
more as if she was guided to me and the Lord is
providing what she needs."

"That's what I was saying. It was meant to be."
Barton's chin came down in a forceful nod. "God's
will."

"Yes, yes. That's what it is, Barton. Where did I
put that notebook? Oh, here it is." Rosanna jotted
down the second item on the paper, then looked up.
"Prepare guest room for E.M."

While Barton re-read the letter, Rosanna rang for
Dot and reviewed the two items on her list while she
waited.

"Dot, I need to speak with the steward. If you need

help finding him, ask Mr. Perkins."

No reason to delay. Tapping her foot, she waited to question the steward as she envisioned the mysterious roofline spied on her walk. Eager for the information she wanted, Rosanna sang out, "Come in."

Entering the room with a cloth cap in his hands, the brawny, middle-aged steward bowed and waited for the mistress to speak first.

"Mr. Bramstock, I have a simple question for you. On my walk today, I spied something unusual." So busy prefacing, the query slipped her mind, replaced with intruding thoughts about her guest, Elspeth, and how the situation would play out. "Umm."

Barton pointed to the little notebook. "Miss Cabot, the list's in there."

"Oh. That's right." She opened it, and gathered her thoughts. "Bramstock, what is the building over to the northeast from here? I could only make out the rooftop through the trees."

Bramstock bowed his head and crossed his chest. "Miss, I believe you must mean Mr. Peter's cottage. That's the direction it be. Mr. Peter, a recluse. All he does is walk the paths around hereabouts. So sad." The man brought a clenched fist up to his chest.

Whatever was so distressing, it must be tragic to bring such poignant words out of the stalwart steward. "Thank you, Bramstock. That will be all."

He hunched his head and shoulders in a half bow, and walked out, the picture of sorrow.

However curious this made her, Rosanna did not want to encourage the staff to regale her with gossip by asking numerous questions about the neighbors. They might get in the habit and pry into her secrets. No need for them to learn how or why she came into possession of Honor's Point. Best the secret stayed between Uncle George, the family solicitors, and of course, Miss Barton, and herself.

5

Mr. Bertrand Clough, the local vicar, paid a call at Honor's Point the day after Miss Mordant's letter arrived. He was the first member of the community to pay a visit.

Not sure what to expect when Perkins announced the rosy-cheeked minister, Rosanna served him tea like any other caller.

He took a sip, then balanced the cup and saucer on his black-clad knee. "I'm here not only to welcome you to the neighborhood, Miss Cabot, but to ask whether we can expect your attendance Sunday next?"

Taken aback by the phrasing of the question, she glanced at Barton sitting nearby, and caught a coy smile on her face. No help from that quarter. The question rattled Rosanna. Coming from populous London, calls and personal questions from the clergy were an uncommon experience. But Rosanna had nothing to hide, so she answered, "I wouldn't miss it, Mr. Clough. Why, Miss Barton and I never forego church attendance. That is, if we are well. And we are both very well, thank you."

"Wonderful. It blesses the whole neighborhood when the leading citizens come to divine services. That, of course, is merely a side benefit. It's much more important that we value God and give Him due worship. Do you agree, Miss Cabot?"

"Indeed. Worshipping in spirit and in truth builds up the soul. After all, the Savior is our only comfort in life and in death."

Barton smoothed the sleeves of her dress in a preening motion and chimed in. "We'll both be there, rain or shine."

Barton's unprecedented show of feminine interest in the minister baffled Rosanna. The man was pleasant enough, though quite old, in her opinion—even older than Barton, surely.

The visit lasted the acceptable twenty minutes and Mr. Clough departed, bowing his way out with additional expressions of welcome.

~*~

Rosanna's neighbor to the south, Lady Jessamine Brook, also paid a call later the same day. She was a fortyish widow, and a most pleasing guest. Even on such short acquaintance, she regaled Rosanna and Barton with a few humorous tales of recent and past situations upon which she brought her healing arts to bear.

The faded blonde with her self-deprecating stories showed that she was not afraid to laugh at herself. Lady Brook explained her interest in the healing arts. "I'm amazed what's to be done with simple remedies such as oatmeal or eggs. To think, a sliver can be drawn out with the membrane of an eggshell."

Rosanna found the topic fascinating and her fingers itched to make notes, but feared it would appear rude. She hoped to remember it to write down the remedy later. As mistress of an estate, she must learn a few rudimentary cures.

"The neighborhood's surely thankful for your presence," Barton said.

"You'd think the days of witch-fearing were still upon us, the way most of the cottagers take on when I bring a simple tincture. My, my, some of them act as if I'd poison them or else carry on as though I'm a sort of magician."

After Lady Brook departed, Rosanna reflected on how much she had enjoyed the visit. "Lady Brook's lovely, isn't she?"

Barton again brushed down her sleeves, in a self-satisfied way. "Indeed, I am delighted in such a neighbor. Lady Brook exudes Christian charity and love. And those qualities are what make her charming, even though some would call her past her prime."

Barton's veiled criticism of Lady Brook caught Rosanna's attention. Did a reason exist for jealousy? Interesting—human nature was endlessly fascinating.

~*~

Late one afternoon toward the end of that same week, Perkins tapped on the sitting room door, and entered to announce the arrival of another neighbor, Lord Halburt.

Rosanna wasn't expecting any calls, but she set her notebook aside and Barton hastened to stow away her needlework.

The butler performed a bow.

A handsome young man sailed past him and halted a few feet inside the door. His dramatic stance held the distinct flair of a pose. Burnished gold hair fell without apparent effort into one of the latest styles. A wonder of the Creator's art, his face boasted a noble forehead, chiseled nose, clean jaw, and vivid green eyes. His muscular and noticeably well-proportioned physique, clad in the fashionable garb of the day, edged him toward perfection.

Though accustomed to meeting a variety of men, each one interested in her sizeable inheritance, after moving to Honor's Point, Rosanna expected encounters with handsome, conceited fops to be a thing of the past. She didn't imagine meeting that type here in the country. Thus, the unexpected sight of a posing Adonis caught her with her guard down, and she stared, mouth open.

Barton conveniently coughed. "Water, Perkins, water."

The butler departed.

Lord Halburt approached the ladies to make a lavish bow. Then he stood, resplendent, as if expecting praise.

Rosanna regained her composure and invited him to sit down by indicating a nearby chair. She introduced Barton while her mind whirled, trying to think of what to say and the proper tone to achieve. She wanted to be a good neighbor, yet didn't want to encourage any male callers, however dazzling their appearance. "How kind of you to call on me, Lord Halburt. Such a pleasant neighborhood we share. Your estate is to the west of Honor's Point?" That blather came out of her mouth when she opened it. *Such a chatterbox I am!*

"Yes, the Halburt and Winstead estates have marched next to each other for almost two centuries."

Hmmm. Talk of estates sharing boundaries often

led to thoughts of joining properties through marriage. She chose not to respond, but instead pursed her lips and tilted her head to the side. Maybe he'd think she was odd and leave.

He rattled on, filling her silence. "Enough of old history, though. Quite astonishing the way Honor's Point went on the block. Had no idea Winstead was so far into dun territory."

The man was certainly frank with his opinions. So, she'd be bold as well. "I hope other neighbors or friends of the family don't resent me for being the one to buy the estate."

"No, no, not your fault. Floating on the River Tick for years, he was. The son tried to get things back to good heart, but it was never enough. Too many poor harvests, and it got away from him."

"Best not to speculate." Barton's starchy interjection served to bring the man's flow of words to a halt. "Here's Perkins with the water. Exactly what I needed." Barton dutifully sipped.

Rosanna smiled at her handsome neighbor and noted how often extreme good looks didn't go hand in hand with sterling character. *How gossipy he sounds.* She deflected his interest away from the property to avoid giving rise to questions about Rosanna's arrival as the new owner, and to discourage any prying into her motives for buying the estate. "Would you care for tea? I can order more hot water."

"Why, thank you so much, but not this time, Miss Cabot. I am sure such a fine young lady as yourself is quite taken up with establishing yourself here in your fine home. I'd not like to tire you. Merely the honor of meeting a lovely and fair flower such as you is enough for a first encounter." He stood and bowed over her hand. "I anticipate many more opportunities to bask in your glow, but alas, I must depart."

Intense relief that the flattering man was leaving swept through her, and grateful that he didn't actually kiss her hand, she smoothly withdrew it from his grasp and hid it in the folds of her dress. So many of her insincere suitors had slobbered over both her hand and her fortune. She'd had enough of all that to last her a lifetime. "Thank you for calling on me, Lord Halburt, so neighborly of you."

He laid his hand on his breast. "Surely we'll be friends and see each other many a time. I shall bid you good day, for now." He made another theatrical gesture and departed.

When she was sure he was gone, Rosanna retrieved her notebook and scribbled a new list.

"What are you writing now, my dear?"

"Oh, Barton, nothing to concern you right now. But what does concern me are the words that man was spewing."

"Words? What in particular bothered you?"

Rosanna flipped closed the cover of her notebook and slid it into her workbasket. "Several. I didn't like the sound of 'first encounter', or 'we'll be friends.' Do you understand why?"

"I'm afraid I do, dear. You thought you were done with swarming gentlemen, didn't you?"

6

Rosanna eagerly anticipated Saturday morning and hoped for a respite from visitors. She breakfasted in her room and expected Barton to arrive any minute to help her dress.

The lady's maid entered with a mended robe over her arm. When she finished putting the garment away, Rosanna patted the seat next to her on the settee.

"Sit by me for a time. Let's talk. Do you like it here so far, Barton?"

Barton sat. "Indeed, I do. It's vastly charming and so peaceful."

"Good, I'm glad Honor's Point is to your liking. Since I am promoting you."

Barton's hand flew to her throat. "Me?"

"From now on, you shall be my companion rather than lady's maid, and known as Miss Barton."

Avoiding eye contact, Barton placed a curled finger against her chin. "Are you certain? I'm content as I am."

"Very sure. You'll accompany me to social events, dear, and shopping trips, charity work, and the like. Even here, I must guard my reputation and keep on the right side of the tabbies."

"Oh, yes. No gossip must arise about you, my dear. With an officially designated companion, you're beyond reproach—above criticism."

"Since you'll go everywhere with me, you can't be occupied any longer with the time-consuming task of dealing with my wardrobe—mending, laundering, dressing, and polishing. Those will be the duties of the new lady's maid."

"New maid?" A shadow of concern slipped across Barton's brow. "Are you absolutely sure? I've enjoyed being your maid."

"Yes, of course. But don't you think you'll enjoy the position of companion?"

"Yes, but will a new maid know how to take care of your things?

"Miss Barton, you'll train her, of course. And you and I together will select the new maid. I've told Mrs. Good to find some likely girls from the existing staff. You stay here, I'll go tell Perkins you're ready to interview."

"Right now?"

"Why wait?"

Miss Barton's dazzled eyes went wide, and she brought clenched hands beneath her chin. "I suppose."

"I do. I will also inform Mrs. Good of your new title and position." Rosanna made a hasty exit, having absorbed enough doubt. Scampering down the stairs she hummed in anticipation of her plans.

Perkins sat snoozing on the hall bench.

"Perkins?" She spoke softly.

He shot to his feet. "Yes, miss? May I be of service?" He yanked down his coat and stifled a yawn.

"Indeed. You perhaps recall that I requested some candidates for promotion to lady's maid? Yes, well, Miss Barton is waiting in my rooms to interview them."

Perkins went below stairs to rally the appropriate

female servants.

Rosanna slipped out the front door. With Miss Barton occupied interviewing maids, a chance to investigate another path presented itself. As entertaining as interviews could be, a solitary walk held more appeal today. A companion could be a blessing many times, but for now, Rosanna longed to be alone.

Tying a bonnet's silk ribbons, she descended the steps, and justified her actions because she needed— no, required—a distraction from Miss Elspeth Mordant's impending arrival. The refuge would be established imminently, by virtue of Elspeth's coming, and an odd anxiety roosted within her. She planned to banish the unease with some brisk exercise.

Headed in the direction of the mysterious cottage seen earlier in the week, she tried to remember what Bramstock, the steward, said. Mr. Peters, or Mr. Peter? No matter, she'd find out soon enough. The path wound through gentle, hilly woodlands, rolling up and down, until at length it came out at a clearing beneath the rocky outcropping seen from afar.

A humble stone cottage stood near the far side of the clearing. Approaching without caution, she knocked on the door. After all, she owned this land. She lifted her hand to knock a second time.

A man came around the corner of the house. He stopped abruptly.

It was the same man who'd helped her the day she arrived. The day she almost fell out of her own carriage. He wore a waistcoat over a fine lawn shirt, open at the neck.

"It's you! I mean, hello." She walked toward him, her hand held out. "I am Miss Cabot, the new mistress of Honor's Point, and I have come to call...er, to see you, rather, to find you. No, that's not it. I came to see what this structure was. I saw it from a hilltop." She turned and pointed, "Over there."

"I'm Peter. At yer service." The man performed a modest bow and sidled toward the door of the cottage.

"Oh. Peter. Yes, that's what I was informed. How does it happen that you are tenanting on my property?" She stopped speaking and the words echoed in her own head. They sounded toplofty and unkind, even when said out of innocent curiosity and in a sweet tone. Thoughtless, though, when the steward said there was something amiss. Something sad.

He ceased edging toward the door and seemed to grow in height. His face took on a distinct glower. "I'm no tenant. The cottage belongs to me. Miss." He forced out this last unwilling word as if to mollify her.

To tone down her unintended insult, she carefully gauged her response. "Have you owned it long?" She tipped her head toward the cottage, brows elevated.

"Aye, it's been in me family for years."

If it were possible, his manner stiffened even further. She moved to a different subject. "The terrain here is so conducive to taking strolls, and I've not yet explored the half of it."

"Few ladies venture this far."

He might be scandalized by her solo rambles—that might account for his marked unease. The seclusion of the spot dawned on her, and she realized the impropriety of this interchange. "So, we are neighbors. Very good. I shall leave now. Sorry to intrude." He didn't respond, and she turned to go, careful to project an unoffended air. Raising a hand in farewell, she walked back the way she came.

It took effort not to rush away. Trembling, face hot, and mortified with embarrassment, she forced her feet to keep a sedate pace and soon reached the shadowed shelter of the woods. A corner of the estate must have been sold off in the past. Perhaps she'd research the history of that in the future, when she had time. Once in possession of the solution to the mystery of the roofline, and her question answered, she'd let it drop and stay busy with her own household affairs.

Curiosity still had its hold on her, however, because new questions emerged. Why did such a fine-looking man live in a humble cottage? He didn't sound like a member of the *ton* when he spoke, but he possessed the definite aura of genteel breeding. He dressed not in typical laborers' garb of smock and breeches, but in the rustic wear of a country gentleman. One with pockets to let.

~*~

Dash it all! A diamond of the first stare lands on my doorstep? What a foolish notion to imagine one might escape the world. He'd had his time of seclusion. The appearance of Rosanna Cabot in his vicinity changed it all.

Her beauty and sweetness arose in his mind's eye when he contemplated her. He didn't want to admire her, but to be honest, he admitted thinking of her a few times after their brief encounter on the road. Her eyes, dusky curls, and sweet femininity made an attractive package.

Don't let Rosanna Cabot cut up your peace. He

straightened and went into the cottage to search for his remaining suit of passable clothes. He'd have to get them all brushed up anyway sooner or later. He hated to admit he wanted to be presentable for the young lady.

Drat, who's knocking now? Peter emerged from the small back bedroom to find the door ajar and a man's head sticking through the opening. A man, dressed all in black, stepped into the front room. His austere apparel put one off, but on closer inspection, his rosy cheeks and warm expressive eyes belied the severity of his garb.

"I'm Mr. Clough, vicar of the local parish." He glanced around, as if to get his bearings. "I know you."

"You've got the advantage, then." Surliness mantled him after his encounter with Miss Cabot, and he failed to mince words. Even though the man's collar indicated status as a man of the cloth, gracious words eluded Peter.

"You're the chap my sister used to call Petey."

"Your sister? To whom might you be referring?" Displeased at yet another intrusion into his privacy, it took effort not to scowl.

"Forgive me, I should explain. My sister was once the head nursemaid at Honor's Point. Do you remember Sarah? Sarah Clough?"

A jolt of longing struck Peter's heart. Sarah. One of the few people who had ever taken any time with him during the long years of growing up. His mother loved him but spent most of her days in London attempting to prevent Father's extravagances. Alas, Mother hadn't been able to stem his sire's gambling.

"Of course." A loving presence in his life, especially after his mother died. He'd been ten years old when Mother passed away, and if it weren't for the nursemaid, Sarah, he'd have been completely bereft of any love or affection. Unbidden, his hand clutched his chest in the region of his heart. "Yes, I remember her well." The words came slow. He was reluctant, but willing to acknowledge the special relationship, because denying it would dishonor the memories and hurt even more. However much he wished to sever all connection to the past, the task proved impossible. "She was an exceptional person. So good to me."

"Yes, Sarah is a wonderful sister. She finally married and moved away."

The minister's voice snapped Peter out of his poignant thoughts. He willed his face to show none of the unbidden sorrow coursing through him. "I am living here because I want to be left alone. What have you come for?"

"I see. All right then, I shall be going soon. I came here to pay a call of Christian concern. I do recall my sister telling me that you once received the gift of faith."

Peter's mind reeled with this confrontation. "How so?"

"She said you responded to the Gospel when she shared the good news with you. Don't you remember?"

Peter brushed his palms together in a sweeping motion. "Vaguely. Childishness. I've moved on from all that. Life intervened."

"No matter what has happened in the intervening years, God still exists, you are still his child, and there's no reason for you to stay away from the fold. And no impediment prevents your attending Sunday services. I shall expect you there tomorrow at nine of the clock."

The clergyman bowed from the waist, backed up two steps, turned and went out the door.

Alone again with the click of the latch.

He hadn't expected to have his childish spiritual yearnings brought up and thrown in his face. The minister's bluntness might be considered refreshing by some, but an unwelcome emotion stirred within his heart and mind as a result of the encounter. Bitterness, so well hidden from others, welled toward himself, his father, and God.

Though unready to open his story for all to read, Peter toyed with the idea of coming out of seclusion. That would mean rejoining the society of Woodvale. His weeks of solitude convinced him he wasn't made to be a recluse. Even though he desired to conceal his very existence, it wasn't working. First, the beautiful new owner of Honor's Point appeared. Then, a man of the cloth armed with personal information landed on his doorstep. He stomped around the room and kicked a stout chair leg.

Why did he ever think he could hide from the world? He'd be forced to come out of isolation eventually, if only to save his own sanity. Even though his initial response to loss made him hide away, many more months and years of loneliness weren't a pleasant prospect after all. Living alone forever after his shameful tumble from society's good graces didn't seem feasible anymore. Pride wouldn't help him learn how to live the life he had been dealt.

7

"This way." With hushed tones, the usher guided Rosanna and Miss Barton down the stone-paved aisle to one of the front pews on Sunday—a privilege of the estate. He gave a perfunctory bow.

"Thank you." Rosanna whispered, then genuflected before entering the pew. The familiar scents of old incense and candle wax filled the air while she settled in, arranged her reticule and prayer book, and removed her gloves.

Trained from an early age never to look behind her in church, Rosanna resisted the strong impulse to glance around the arched nave and determine whether the handsome, dark-haired cottager attended worship services. With effort, she dragged her mind back to worship. Holding her prayer book open in one hand, she slipped down onto a kneeler, and with one hand shielding her eyes from the world, she prayed through the suggested prayer before worship. The beautiful language of the Book of Common Prayer flowed.

...Deliver us when we draw near to Thee, from coldness of heart and wanderings of mind, that with steadfast thoughts and kindled affections we may worship Thee in spirit and in truth...

The phrases rolled on, one after another. Peace soon took hold of her. *So blessed.* Being here in the village church, with its stone-paved floor and hand carved woodwork, seemed so right. After her travails, to come out on the other side unscathed gave her a mantling sensation of God's caring love.

Certainty dwelt within her that she resided right where God wanted her, and gratitude welled— bringing an unexpected tear to her eye.

The service began, and she listened with rapt attention to the beautiful liturgy and sermon delivered by Mr. Clough. He preached on Psalm 87:6 – "All my fountains are in Thee," and exhorted the congregation to look to God for their needs.

The message reminded Rosanna to rely on God alone for refuge and refreshment. Her earthly home secured, she mustn't become complacent about God's plan for her life. She must always reflect Christ to those around her. Invigorated by the worship and the solidity of the ancient church, she bowed her head again for one last prayer of thanks.

The dismissal music played, signaling Rosanna to gather her things and rise. She observed all appropriate traditions such as making the sign of the cross and genuflecting in the direction of the lighted tabernacle. Even though she willingly enacted them, to Rosanna these were mere outward forms, for faith dwelt not within the walls of a building, but in the heart. A heart made forever new by the indwelling of God's Spirit. She squeezed Miss Barton's hand and held it going down the aisle, making their way toward the rear of the nave.

"Aren't the colors pretty?"

"Hmm?" Rosanna drew her thoughts down to earth. "The colors?"

"The windows are casting their hues down onto us mortals. Reminds me of how we can find signs of

God's goodness so easily if we look."

"Excellent point, Miss Barton. One that I would do well to remember and meditate upon."

The minister stood in the archway outside the door, greeting the departing worshippers. As Rosanna and Miss Barton approached, he put a staying hand on the arm of Peter, the dark-haired cottager.

"Wonderful. Miss Cabot, Miss Barton, I'd like you to meet…" His words were cut off by a high-pitched scream from halfway down the aisle.

"Jessie! Get Jessie! Someone's fainted!"

Rosanna turned and glanced back into the sanctuary to discern the source of the shouting. She and Miss Barton reversed their steps to join a cluster of people.

A man dashed out, then re-entered with Lady Brook, who moved like a ship under full sail. She made for the center of the hubbub, a pew halfway from the pulpit.

Concern laced the air as the remaining parishioners gathered in a clump at a discreet distance from the collapsed churchgoer. Murmurs rose as seconds ticked away.

Lady Brook knelt down next to the prone woman. Withdrawing a silver vinaigrette case from her reticule, she administered the remedy by waving it under the woman's nose for a moment or two. She stood up, extended a hand to the fallen one, and assisted her to rise. Arm around the woman's shoulders, Lady Brook said, "Not to worry." She patted the plump village matron whose face blushed red. "A simple fainting. Stuffy air, combined with incense, the heat from candles, and over-zealous kneeling, perhaps." She gave a reassuring smile to the onlookers.

Rosanna followed and reached the door in time to watch Lady Brook escort the light-headed fellow-parishioner outside and guide the woman to the Brook coach for a ride home. Her glance flickered to Peter—the somber, handsome man's presence drew her like a moth to a flame. She forced calm upon her features but when, with one eyebrow raised, he gave her an almost imperceptible bow, her heart sped.

Clutching Rosanna's arm, Miss Barton gave her opinion. "Lady Brook's a wonder."

Rosanna turned so as to address her response to the cluster of nearby gawkers. She spoke in a clear voice. "Yes. She's so generous and obliging. Lady Brook's full of good works of the best sort."

A murmur of approval rose from the crowd.

Rosanna went on. "My, she certainly has a healing touch." She made a point to overtly commend the amicable older woman, in case there were any doubters around. "Lady Brook's knowledge about the medical arts is vast, and a blessing to the community. Praise the Lord."

She turned back to the minister, and disappointed but not surprised, found Peter no longer standing ready for the formal introduction. Interrupted as they were, he had departed during the commotion. Quite the elusive man.

The minister said, "I am sorry, Miss Cabot, it seems your neighbor has slipped away."

"Oh, la. Don't think a thing of it. Miss Barton, my dear companion and I, are very happy and found the worship to be fruitful, indeed."

Miss Barton linked arms with Rosanna before adding her two cents. "That was a fine sermon, sir." She drew out the word 'fine', and beamed approval.

Arm and arm with Miss Barton, Rosanna walked down the church steps. She reflected that a formal introduction would provide much more conventional footing between herself and her nearest neighbor. Their interactions so far not only stood on awkward ground but teetered on the edge of outright impropriety. First falling into his arms and then their bumbling encounter at his cottage, she couldn't decide if she was more embarrassed or humiliated.

Such a risk must not happen again. Even though her solitary walks did her spirit much good, she reluctantly accepted the wisdom of keeping Miss Barton close at hand. If not on every single walk, at least at most other times. Being an unmarried female landowner, she must guard her reputation in this small town. She admitted, however, that if society's class strictures had no influence on her, she would like to see him again. Just to satisfy her curiosity.

8

Rosanna sang as she puttered around her bedroom. "The earth and its fullness with which it is stored. The world and its dwellers belong to the Lord." She splashed warm water on her face and hurried through morning ablutions. The day dawned bright—Monday mornings, always so full of promise. Life and vigor hovered within her, pulsing to be unleashed.

Maybe this day her guest would arrive. She patted her face with a linen towel and gave thought as to how to refer to Miss Mordant. "Refugee" didn't have a nice ring to it, but "guest" was the best term for the situation. After all, not all guests were invited, some came of their own accord.

Grasping the hem of her voluminous white nightgown, she yanked it over her head. She got into her shift and pantalettes. Getting her dress fastened, however, would require some assistance.

Expecting Dot, who'd been chosen as Rosanna's new maid, to appear soon with hot chocolate as per her orders, she approached the wardrobe to select what to wear for the morning. She decided on a butter yellow gown with ivory lace trim around the modest neckline. Something about the country made her want to wear yellow, a color she never wore in town.

A warning tap preceded the entrance of the maid, who entered, bobbed her head, set down the cup of chocolate, and stood silent, visibly nervous.

Rosanna added extra gentleness to her request. "Dot, please do up my stays and gown."

The girl did well enough with the complicated closures, and before long, Rosanna went downstairs to the dining room. She selected a plateful of food off the sideboard. Eggs, bacon, and coffee—enough to hold her until lunchtime, since she planned to be busy with Mrs. Good.

After eating, she made her way to the kitchens, soon arriving at the door to the housekeeper's adjacent rooms. The housekeeper had her proper due in that she, of all the servants, laid claim to a sleeping room and an adjoining alcove for sitting.

"Mrs. Good, are you there?" Rosanna rapped on the door in the hallway near the kitchen and pressed her ear toward the wooden door. "It's me, Rosanna."

The door opened, and the rotund housekeeper tried to curtsey, but it came out as a bow with one leg to the side. "My stars, Miss. How may I be of service?"

"I'd like to discuss the preparation of a guest room for a young lady. She will be here at least a fortnight, possibly much longer. What room do you suggest?"

"Something on the first floor, supposing she's quality?" Mrs. Good gestured to a map of the manor, which hung tacked on the wall near a makeshift desk in her sitting room. She leaned close to it, hunched over, and perused the diagram for a moment.

"Yes, our guest is of the finest quality. In fact, an exemplary young lady of sterling reputation." There. That should stanch any doubts or questions.

Mrs. Good stood erect again, tapped the map with her index finger, and then gave a suggestion. "I suggest the Lilac Room, Miss. Please come in."

Rosanna stepped further into the tiny alcove to peer at the floor plan. "The Lilac Room—I recall that lovely chamber from our tour. Is it prepared for company?" Rosanna hoped it was, on the chance the guest arrived soon.

"Yes, it's mainly ready, Miss Cabot, but needs airing. I'll see to it straightaway."

"That would be most excellent, Mrs. Good. I will come along with you so that I may learn even more about my new home. The Lilac Room." Rosanna allowed the words to resonate. "Such a pretty name."

"Yes, Miss, follow me." Mrs. Good picked up her key ring and held it up. "In case the door's locked." She preceded Rosanna through several halls and up a flight of stairs.

"Here we are." Mrs. Good tried the knob and pushed the door open. She stood back out of the way and gestured for Rosanna to go first.

Rosanna stepped in and stopped, drinking in the exquisite room. Struck afresh that she owned such a treasure of a house, she took a deep breath before whirling slowly right where she stood. Stunning shades of lavender and green were arrayed everywhere in tasteful display. She noted a delicate marquetry-inlaid escritoire placed between two windows that framed views of the surrounding hills.

Even though she'd seen the room briefly on her first tour of the house, it still awed her. "Oh, this is perfect—so special." Hushed in the face of such beauty, she gently stepped further into the room onto a lavender carpet edged in cream. "Any London guest will be more than satisfied here. Who decorated this room?"

The housekeeper's smile vanished. "Lady

Winstead, who once was mistress here, Miss."

Rosanna vaguely remembered that as the family name of the former owner. "Lady Winstead? Is she living?"

"No, she's been gone these past twelve years." Mrs. Good stepped over to the bed and removed the spread and the pillows. Next, she opened each of the three windows. Fresh air flowed in on a cool breeze, its clean scent welcome in the stuffy room.

Rosanna moved around the room checking for dust. Finding none, she turned back to Mrs. Good. "The room is clean, that tells me the house is well run."

Mrs. Good beamed with satisfaction. "Lady Winstead was sickly at the end, but in the past, she put her all into the house. Even when she bided in London, she'd send back things for Honor's Point. She loved to decorate the rooms, several more have a floral theme."

"More?"

"More guest rooms she decorated."

"Remind me, what others are there?" Rosanna found this bit of history fascinating. She'd only peeked into the rooms on her earlier tour.

"The Camellia Room, mostly in white with pale green—that's the next room down the hall." Mrs. Good tilted her head to the right. "After that you have the Cornflower Room, all in blue with touches of gold. They say there's some mystery about the rooms."

"A mystery? How fascinating. What is the story? Is it true?"

"Can't recall what's been said." Mrs. Good's lips clamped shut.

Rosanna suspected the woman knew more. "Tell me whatever you remember of it, no matter how small a scrap."

Mrs. Good folded her arms. She cast her eyes to the ceiling and twisted her lips into a pucker before speaking. "I can't say true or nay, but I remember something about Lady Winstead ordering a small chest built. The estate's carpenter was so proud of his work, he showed it to all the servants one day."

"And what makes this chest part of a mystery, Mrs. Good?"

"Let me think. Perkins told him to remove the box from the kitchen, so's it didn't get greasy. And the box—so very pretty—we never saw it displayed again after he gave it to the mistress."

"I understand. Your story is an example of how mysterious rumors may start. If such a box were still here, someone would have seen it."

"Yes, Miss, and I never did see it in the house again."

Servants' gossip ran rampant, whether in town or country, so Rosanna changed the subject. "Thank you for sharing the history of this tale of mystery. Let us talk about the house and its beauty. Since you've told me the background, I shall want to see all the guest rooms again. Do you have time to show me today, what with getting this room ready?"

"I shan't be a minute." Mrs. Good shot out of the room, and Rosanna heard her instructing a housemaid on further preparations of the Lilac Room.

While she waited, Rosanna strolled to the window. The views from this hilltop manor never ceased to dazzle her senses. She admired the patchwork of fields arrayed over the rolling hills, and came to rest on a certain roofline which showed through the trees of the woods to the northeast.

The cottage owned by the dark-haired man named

Peter. Something about him captivated her. For comparison's sake, Lord Halburt, the exceedingly handsome neighbor, never crossed her mind. But the cottager named Peter popped into her thoughts often. Attraction landed where it would and fell hard. However, she didn't need to act on it.

9

Rosanna shook her head, ousting the reclusive dark-haired neighbor from her thoughts. Viewing several more beautiful rooms in her new home would perhaps provide the necessary distraction—enough to blot out the memory of Peter's twinkling, dark blue eyes.

Mrs. Good stuck her head through the doorway. "Miss, I'm back. If you're ready?"

Turning away from the window, Rosanna smiled. "Lead on, Mrs. Good. Viewing the other special rooms again will be a pleasure. I was in a hurry last time and probably didn't give them their due."

The morning passed in swift fashion, first examining the white and green Camellia Room, then ending the tour in the blue Cornflower Room. Both were lovely, and Rosanna planned to leave them as they were, now that she'd learned their history.

"These are some of the prettiest rooms I've ever seen, Mrs. Good. I believe Lady Winstead and I would have been bosom friends if we'd ever met."

The housekeeper's humble face came alive at the words of praise about her dear, departed mistress. "Yes, miss. She was a treat, and a good lady."

If any of Honor's Point's rooms required redecorating, it wouldn't be these. Rosanna had no desire to dismantle such historic and beautiful décor.

Each special flower-themed room stood testament to the loving care given to the decorating by the home's former mistress. The creative artistry and excellent taste employed in the furnishings and color schemes touched something deep within Rosanna's nature-loving soul.

"Perhaps some new drapes? Replicas, of course. The sun has done its work on these. See how they are faded?" She held up a corner for the housekeeper's inspection.

"Yer right, miss. Your fresh eye picked that up. I've never noticed."

"I'll inquire whether the shop in the village can order replacement fabric."

"The town will be pleased with custom from the manor again."

"Since the staff has maintained the rooms so well, further refurbishing appears unnecessary." Rosanna allowed the corner of the drape to fall out of her hand when her ears picked up a sound. "Stop. What's that?" She cupped fingers to her ears and cocked her head toward the drive. "I hear wheels—perhaps my guest arrives?" Lifting her hem, she flew to the window.

A carriage bowled up the drive.

She turned. "Mrs. Good, that's sufficient for now. Thank you so much." Rosanna restrained herself from dashing off. "I can find my way to the hall, you may proceed with final preparations of the Lilac Room. If I am not mistaken, my guest has arrived, so please make sure the room is ready." Holding visible enthusiasm on a tight leash, she went below, setting foot on the marble floor of the large main hall.

Perkins swept open the door.

A female crossed the threshold. The woman's veil

obscured her face, but the gleam of red hair through the gauzy draping announced her as Elspeth.

"My dear." Rosanna moved forward with both hands extended and took the arriving guest's hands in her own. Leaning in close, she whispered, "Don't say anything yet." She guided the guest toward the stairs, but turned back to give more instructions. "Perkins, order a tea tray brought to the morning room in one half hour, please. I myself will escort my guest to the Lilac Room."

"Yes, Miss Cabot. May I send up the trunk straightaway?"

"Since the footmen are right here, yes. That would be fine, thank you. But I'll take the bandbox. Travelling is so dusty, isn't it?" Rosanna and Miss Mordant proceeded up the grand staircase, ahead of two liveried footmen hoisting a trunk.

Once the Lilac Room's door closed behind the exiting servants, Rosanna and Elspeth spoke at once, followed by a spate of nervous laughter.

Rosanna took a calming breath, one hand over her heart. "I've been on pins and needles waiting for your arrival. Don't worry, no one, save my trusted companion, Miss Barton, is aware of the reason for your visit."

Elspeth lifted her veil. "Thank you so much for forgiving my forwardness in inviting myself here. I had no other recourse."

"Of course." Rosanna indicated a pair of armchairs. "Let's sit." She did so, and continued talking. "Your arrival is providential. I'm ecstatic you're here. You coming here is the best thing that could have happened."

Elspeth sank into the other chair. "I truly had

nowhere else to turn. The family was pressing me hard to accept a suitor. I'd like to be able to say he was a dastard, but he really wasn't. Forty years older, though."

Rosanna's shoulders rose as she gave a shudder. "Oh, dear. Shades of my own past."

"When I refused that one, they dangled my hideous first cousin in front of me as a threat. Perhaps you recall my cousin, Ferdinand?"

"Oh, my. Not him. I do believe he was at a ball I attended last season. He's...interesting. Black hair? And a pale complexion?"

"So, you know who I mean. I don't object to him merely upon his looks. It's his character. He's a worm." Elspeth sniffled. "How could they do this to me?" She reached up to remove her hat. Her silken red hair gave off a subtle gleam.

Pity wrenched Rosanna. "Save the rest of your tale for over tea. For now, I want to tell you how utterly impressed I am that you found me. You'll find it hard to credit this, but offering refuge to others needing to avoid odious marriages was my plan when I first got here."

"That's so perfect, it's nearly unbelievable." Elspeth's hand flew to her throat. "The Lord is so gracious."

"Establishing such a safe haven has been put on hiatus due to an unforeseen problem."

"Tell me what happened with your plan."

"The details can wait, but suffice it to say, I faced the death of my dream when I realized that any publicity would also inform the ones who were forcing marriages on ladies. There went the required secrecy as to the place's existence."

"A terrible stumbling block."

"Then your letter came. A true Godsend." She patted Elspeth's shoulder.

"Oh, my. That's wonderful to learn. I'm so thankful you are welcoming me. I wasn't sure of my reception. I had no time to wait for a response to my letter. I needed to flee." The diminutive redhead's relief to have arrived was palpable and her words trembled with checked emotion. Elspeth reached out and clutched at Rosanna's hands, a tear tracing a path on her pale cheek.

"You are welcome. I vow God's providence is so marvelous." Rosanna indicated a pitcher and bowl. "Please avail yourself of the washstand."

The guest washed her delicate hands, then her face. Sinking onto the stool at the dressing table, she efficiently tidied her silky hair. Wavy tendrils had slipped out of the low chignon she wore.

A rush of sentiment swept over Rosanna and she choked back a sob. "Don't mind me—all at once I'm overcome by your dash for freedom. It reminds me of my own escape not so long past."

"You, too? I overheard a small bit of rumor, but how did you get out of it?"

"Once you descend for tea, we'll trade stories. I'm sure you'll want to change your dress. Travel is so hard on one's gowns. I shall send in a maid to help you. She can show you the way to the morning room. One thing before I go, though. Your name. It's too memorable— too distinctive. Should word reach London, you might be forced to return."

Elspeth's blue eyes blinked back tears. "Thank you for thinking of that. I'm so overwhelmed, I can't see straight."

"I suggest we tell everyone your name is…what's short for Elspeth? I know, Ellie. And we will simply remove the last syllable from your surname and call you Miss Moore. Ellie Moore—ah, that sounds excellent. Do you like it?"

"I love it. It's in essence a new identity. Now, none of the servants or neighbors can spread word of my arrival." The redhead repositioned a hairpin with an emphatic jab.

Before Rosanna left the Lilac Room, she put her arm around Elspeth's shoulders and gave an impulsive squeeze. The instant flow of rapport warmed Rosanna's heart. The way her plans prospered made her float down the stairs. So pleasant to have a friend in residence—a friend to help fill her life's voids.

10

In the morning room, Rosanna sipped tea and nibbled cucumber sandwiches and cakes with her guest. Mundane tea drinking struck her funny after the momentousness of Elspeth's arrival. She wanted to laugh, but things of import must be discussed.

"From here on, I will be calling you Ellie or Miss Moore. Do you think you can remember to answer to those names?" Rosanna clasped her hands under her bosom, embarrassed she needed to introduce subterfuge into the mix.

Worry flickered across the redhead's forehead. "I suppose it will take some amount of getting used to."

Rosanna observed the fleeting anxiety, and acted to forestall it. She gave a mischievous smile. "Perhaps I shall overuse it today, Ellie, to get you accustomed to it. So, Ellie, how was your trip?"

With an answering smile and relaxed shoulders, soft spoken Ellie began a rundown of the travel. "It was arduous, I must say. Disguising myself as an impoverished widow was an inspiration. It got me through without much awkwardness. Thick black veils work wonders." She gave a shudder. "I can only tremble to think of how I'd be treated on a public stage travelling as a maiden unescorted."

"Your widow's weeds hid your distinctive coloring, Ellie. I barely perceived your hair color through the gauze, but I knew to look for it. People tend to turn away from grief, too. Very clever of you, Ellie."

Thus encouraged, Ellie finished the tale of her travels with more energy in her voice. "When the stage brought me to Woodvale, I hired a cart and driver for the short trip to Honor's Point. That about sums it up. I feel as if I'm dreaming and can scarce believe that I made it here."

"I understand why, Ellie. Your escape is nigh to a miracle. Do you think you'll be bored here, Ellie? So used to London, and all of its entertainments?"

"No, I won't. I never cared for the social whirl. My interest is in literature." Ellie released a shy smile and tipped her head to one side, glancing sidelong at Rosanna. "With no one pestering me to appear in society, I shall indulge myself in some scribbling of my own."

"Excellent. Writing is a noble pursuit, Ellie. I shall have your room stocked with supplies. I must write that down." Rosanna smiled encouragement and held out the small platter. "Another cake?"

Ellie dabbed her lips. "No, thank you. I've had enough for now. These are the best fairy cakes I can recall having, though."

"I retained the excellent cook who'd been here for decades before I arrived. If you hear me rhapsodizing about someone named Hannah, that'd be her."

Ellie stared into her teacup for a long moment. She raised her finely arched eyebrows in an inquiring expression. "I feel I should regale you with the remaining sad details of my recent life, if you really want to hear it."

Rosanna had a dozen questions but wanted Ellie

to tell the tale her own way. "Let's move over to the settee in that alcove. Farthest from the door, and with much drapery to muffle sound."

Ellie clutched the neck of her spencer jacket as she followed Rosanna to the alcove. "Are your servants nosey?"

"No more than normal—best to be safe." Rosanna angled toward Ellie. "It's been harrowing for you, hasn't it? Are you sure you can talk about what happened?"

"I want to. It's so good to have a supportive ear. I've been so alone with no one to confide in. I'm the youngest in my family, and you may recall my only sister died. Oddly, after she was gone, it seemed as though my parents couldn't rid themselves of me fast enough."

Rosanna tamped her curiosity with a neutral yet encouraging remark. "Hmmm. I'd always heard how people dote on the baby of the family."

Ellie's fingers pleated her dress. She began to talk in a soft voice. "You'd think so. But no. From the day I turned eighteen, it's been nothing but them angling, and pushing me toward this, that, or the other arranged marriage. At first, after my come-out, there were suitors dangling about, so they gave me some room for my inclinations. But since I didn't care to marry any of them, my parents began to take matters into their own pushy hands."

Sickened, Rosanna spoke from experience. "How unpleasant such maneuvers are."

"It dawned on me over time that I was like a card to be dealt in some scheme. My dowry proved attractive, but in addition, large payments would also be paid to my parents for their assent to any marriage."

"Unusual, but not unheard of." Rosanna responded, then leaned back to listen.

"I don't quite understand the logic or legalities of it all. But back to the events. When I accepted none of the offers, including their favorite candidate—old enough to be my grandfather, they began to push forward my cousin Ferdinand. He, of the frizzy black hair, pasty skin, and bushy mustache."

Rosanna grimaced at the mere recollection of Elspeth's cousin. Even seen across a ballroom, he was worthy of a cringe, hard to imagine having him foisted as a marital candidate. "Frightful."

"It was dreadful. I overheard them planning to get a marriage license and arrange a ceremony to surprise me. That's when I gathered my courage and made a run for it."

"Quite a horrid story. I admire you for not sitting still for it."

"Thank you. What about you? What happened to you to bring you here to Honor's Point, Rosanna?"

11

Rosanna glanced at the door, to make sure it was closed. Talking about her trials didn't come easy to her, but after Ellie told her own tale, Rosanna could be brave too. She spoke in a hushed voice. "Where shall I begin? I am grateful to have my own fortune and that my parents willed it so I could not be forced into a marriage not to my liking. But my good outcome to a common dilemma is quite rare."

"So, having your own fortune solved it?"

"No, it took a lot of gumption as well. My relatives, especially my Uncle George, got it in their heads that I needed to be married." She grimaced, remembering the struggle. "I resisted mightily and the final agreement between me and Uncle George was hard won. He didn't appreciate my refusal of all the men he put forward as suitors."

"Your uncle brought suitors? With me it was my parents." Ellie's face turned white and she clenched her hands in her lap. "I was some sort of bargaining chip to them. Finding a husband with the most advantages for them was their sole aim. Sorry, I didn't mean to intrude my woes again."

"Quite all right." Rosanna patted Ellie's hand. "That must have been horrible."

Ellie urged, "Please, go on."

Even though Providence had blessed her outcome,

painful chagrin flowed over Rosanna as she recalled the trial and she wiped her eyes. "Even though I am crying," she laughed lightly, "It feels remarkably good to confide in you. I've been through my struggle all alone, as well."

Ellie nodded. "We shouldn't be surprised. Everyone else is marriage-mad, casting all caution to the wind."

"So true. But back to my saga. I don't want to paint my uncle as a villain. Uncle George wasn't all bad. As my advisor and official guardian, since my parents' deaths, he dutifully brought forth various marriage candidates who were worthy enough by his way of thinking. Not one of the gentlemen who circled around me with Uncle George's permission and approval were very appealing to me, however."

Ellie wrung her handkerchief. "None? Me, either. Especially my cousin. He was not to be tolerated."

Rosanna's heart went out to Ellie. "For me, there'd been a variety of pimply popinjays, foppish fortune hunters, and callous care-for-naughts. The last straw was a rotund candidate who happened to be forty years older than me. Uncle George didn't see that as a problem, but I did."

"One of mine was forty years older, too. Maybe it was the same man."

Rosanna snorted with laughter, then closed her eyes a moment, savoring her freedom. "We can laugh now that we are safe."

"I must pinch myself to make sure it's real." Ellie gave herself a mock pinch. More giggles.

Gathering her wits, Rosanna continued her tale. Now that she opened up, she wanted the comfort talking would bring. "When I finally put my foot down in no uncertain terms, Uncle went off in a huff."

"Angry? Was he furious?"

"No, more embarrassed over failing machinations. A few weeks later, he came to me with an ultimatum."

Ellie raised a hand to her throat. "How terrifying."

Puffing out her chest, and deepening her voice, Rosanna acted Uncle George's part. "Rosanna, I'll get right to the point. Your presence in my home will not be a good influence on my girls. With Phoebe's come-out next season, I don't need the gel getting any ideas about rejecting perfectly adequate suitors."

Rosanna's imitation sent Ellie into a bout of chortling. "Oh, stop. I'll lose my tea. You could be on the stage."

"Thank you. Where was I? Oh, yes. When he mentioned my 'presence in his home,' that caught my attention. I folded my hands and looked up at him." Rosanna acted out her part. "Alerted by the wording of his remarkable statement, I requested he elaborate."

"What did he mean?"

"I asked him how he could continue as my guardian if I wasn't in his home. It turned out that because of the unshakeable estate plan my parents set in place for me, and since I'd already reached my majority, I possessed some autonomy. This freedom saved me from having to acquiesce to an arranged marriage."

"You were blessed. Your parents must have loved you to put such a stipulation in place." Ellie sipped her tea, and then placed the delicate cup back in the saucer. "What happened next?"

"I vaguely understood the contents of my parents' will, but quite a while passed since I'd heard it read. So, I requested more clarification before Uncle began additional lectures. I asked him to verify that there was no requirement that I live in his home according to the provisions of the will or guardianship."

Redheaded Ellie gasped, and her blue eyes sparkled. She rubbed her palms together. "This is a wonderful story. What were the stipulations?"

Rosanna slipped into her imitation of Uncle George's deep voice again. "I have been reviewing the testament and have found a clause that would seem to allow you to live elsewhere. Harrumph, with a companion, of course. Since you intractably opposed my assistance toward a match, I don't believe your presence in London is either desirable, nor required by the terms."

Switching back to her own voice, she went on. "Quick to suppress my delight at the implications of Uncle's words, I gathered my wits enough to gain control over the situation. Aware of Uncle's predilection for praise, I poured the butter boat over him."

Ellie clapped her hands in glee. "That was clever."

"Thank you. Yes, I thanked him for finding such a wise and excellent point. I told him, as much as I appreciated his efforts at a match for me, my thoughts on marriage remained the same. To soothe him further, I reminded him that since Clarence's death, I hadn't an interest in any man."

Ellie face lit up. "Clarence? Who's Clarence?"

"That is a story for another day. Back to me attaining my escape from the marriage mart. My uncle is an excellent and honest businessman who turned a modest inheritance of his own into a tidy fortune. I tapped into his acumen and asked him to locate a suitable, secluded home, away from London, for me to purchase."

"He helped you even after you refused to follow his advice to marry? Your uncle sounds like a kind and just man. It's almost hard to believe compared to how my own parents treated me."

"Yes, he helped me find this place, Honor's Point. I appreciate that he did not ultimately force me into a distasteful marriage." She couldn't help but smile.

"Dear Uncle George." Eyes twinkling, she resumed her imitation of Uncle George's deep voice. "Rosanna, there's an estate for sale belonging to Lord Winstead. The heir proved unable to dig out from under his father's disastrous mound of debts and it's on the block. It's a secluded property of renowned beauty—yes, now I recall. The property is known as Honor's Point. I shall put my man of business on this right away. Make some preliminary plans to vacate these premises and wait until I inform you of the particulars."

"He sounds like a treasure of a man to do all that for you." Ellie enthused, wrapped up in the account of Rosanna's travails.

"He is a dear—imperious uncle though he may be. That didn't bother me, however, since I was used to him. I never thought I'd miss him, but I do. Now that you are here however, I'll be too busy to long for anyone. It'll be such a lark."

Ellie's brow furrowed with sincerity. "Thank you again for allowing me to stay."

"With my plan in ruins, this place of safety would have sheltered me alone if you hadn't found out my direction and summoned the courage to come here. Having gotten away from forced marriage myself wasn't enough. I wanted to provide others with a safe haven. So many young ladies have nowhere to turn. The thought of a repugnant arranged marriage is so distasteful, is it not?"

Ellie gave an emphatic shudder. "Disgusting, in fact."

"Ellie, you of all people, understand what I've been through."

A tap came on the morning room door, Perkins opened it, and intoned, "Miss, are ye home to Lord Halburt?"

12

Before Rosanna's lips even formed a response, Halburt swept past the butler and entered the room, bowing from the waist and sweeping one arm out to the side.

Rosanna found herself short on patience with this intrusion. "Do stand up, sir."

Halburt straightened and removed his gloves before flicking back his coat tails and taking a seat. He chose the chair closest to the young ladies and posed his legs in a studied display of his masculine perfection. "Thank you for receiving me. I was out riding and decided to visit my fair neighbor."

"Tea?" Rosanna indicated the tray with a nonchalant wave of her hand, hoping to show herself unaffected by the good looks of the intruder.

"Ah, that would be a treat." Halburt locked his avid gaze on Ellie and his brows quivered. "Who might we have here?"

No time like the present to establish her guest's identity in the neighborhood. "May I introduce Miss Ellie Moore. Miss Moore, Lord Halburt."

Halburt hopped to his feet, scooped up Ellie's hand, and bent over it while performing another deep bow. As he straightened, he scanned both women's faces.

Rosanna wondered why. Did he expect one or

both of them to fall at his handsome feet?

"Miss Moore. Moore. Would that be the Yorkshire Moores? Or perhaps the Northumberland Moores?" The nosy neighbor asked, but his interest rang false to Rosanna's ears.

She wasn't sure Ellie wouldn't be overawed by their guest, either by his fine looks or his title, so she interjected before Ellie could respond. "No, just Miss Moore from London, Lord Halburt."

"Miss Moore, what a pleasure to meet you. To have not one, but two of the loveliest young ladies in Christendom veritably fall into my lap brings such light to my humdrum existence."

Into your lap, my eye. Rosanna sought to veer talk away from how lovely she and Ellie were. "Oh, come now. I've heard you're a master at estate management and quite competitive with your yields and flocks. How is that humdrum?" She smiled, then turned down the corners of her mouth so as not to encourage the fop's attentions.

"Yes, I suppose you are right. Not humdrum then, shall we say, earthbound. That's it. Nothing as exalted as Miss Moore here. Why, she resembles a Titian angel."

Ellie ventured a mild sally. "Oh, la, you're exaggerating. Surely your farms are much more interesting."

"My farms are indeed a treasure. One does so value one's property and the heritage of one's estate."

She widened her eyes toward Rosanna, who caught the look and suppressed a snicker.

Ellie proffered, "One quite does."

But he turned to her now. "You must tell me your secret, Miss Cabot."

Rosanna's strongest desire was to either yawn in his face, but he wouldn't notice, or, get him to his feet somehow and guide him out the door. "I have no idea to what you are referring."

"Your secret to such great beauty. You're magnificent. London beaus must be blind to have let you escape their clutches."

She hoped the unwelcome Adonis would retreat, so injected a mild tone of displeasure into her words. "Hardly. I've not heard of an epidemic of blindness in London, nor in any other quarter. You're surely jesting."

But he was oblivious to her hints. The visit wore on, with Halburt paying court to Rosanna, then turning his attentions to Ellie, and back again. His polished flirtations caused Rosanna a struggle to attend—not to let her eyes glaze over at his foolish, obvious wiles and flirting. Perhaps she'd find his company amusing on a later occasion, after she got over being peeved at his intrusiveness. Would the man never leave?

He lifted a quizzing glass, and turned an arch, affected gaze on Rosanna. "Miss Cabot, do you ride?"

She suppressed a sigh, irritated and starting to dread yet another man pitching himself at her. Denying the temptation to lie, she answered without warmth. "Indeed, riding is among my favorite pastimes."

"Well then, tomorrow at nine? Can you prepare by that hour? The best time of day for a ride about my property. You'll want to see Halburt Arms, no?"

The man could put a twinkle in his eyes and a winning tone in his voice, she'd say that for him. Why did he have to ask her? Better that he leave Ellie alone—especially this early on in her stay. She didn't have her bearings yet. "That would be charming. I'll be ready, with my groom at nine tomorrow."

Hiding a yawn behind her hand, Rosanna again wished he'd depart. Now would be the perfect time for him to leave. Why did he sit there, gazing at her between sips of tea? Waiting for a response of attraction? For evidence of a tendre forming? If so, he'd have a long wait. It would take much more than Lord Halburt's handsome face and form to draw her into any sort of liaison.

"So, Miss Cabot, have you discovered anything of interest here in your new home?" With a heightened level of intensity, Halburt leaned forward and watched her face.

"Of interest? Why yes, many things. Where shall I begin? Perhaps I should tell you of the especially delightful rooms here in the house. Are you aware of the talent for decorating possessed by the former mistress of this house, Lady Winstead? She's been gone these twelve, long years and I must say the decor looks as fresh and highly enticing as if done over last month."

"Can't say that I knew the rooms were so exceptional." He glanced around, cursorily. "Of course, this chamber is very nice. Living so close, I never had occasion to stay overnight here at Honor's Point. Tell me all about the special rooms."

In light of such strong interest, the house seemed a safe enough topic to Rosanna. "One floor above, there are three rooms decorated in floral themes: lilac, camellia, and cornflower. Each room is a treat to the senses." She stopped short then, realizing she'd let her inner chatterbox out to play. Increasing his interest in anything to do with her or her home was not her intent.

"Anything else special about the rooms? Legends, trapdoors, the like?" He leaned forward, eager for her answer.

"I am aware of nothing of the kind. What gave you such a peculiar idea?" Rosanna turned her attention to straightening the tea implements.

"Oh, I seem to have heard rumors about something to do with the house. No matter. I'm a fiend for mysteries. If you learn any, please do tell me. I'm like a child in my delight at such tales."

"There is a time for us all to put childhood aside."

"Yes, you are so wise, Miss Cabot. But I'm afraid I am incorrigible with mysteries, legends, treasures, and the like. In fact, I am expecting an answer to my invitation to an important personage any day now. A very significant man."

Rosanna tamped down a sigh yet obligated to respond to this blatant hint. "Who might that be?"

"The great Walter Scott, himself."

"Here? In Woodvale?"

"I've invited him, and am in communications with his secretary, Mr. Purdie. They are planning his itinerary for a visit to England."

"That will be noteworthy. To have a visit from the man who refused the position of poet laureate of England would be quite a social coup."

"I can only hope meeting Walter Scott will be as special as meeting you both." The man stood, bowed yet again, and said his goodbyes. "Ladies, it has been a pleasure. Miss Moore, charmed to have you adorning the neighborhood. Miss Cabot, I shall meet you tomorrow morning promptly at nine."

After he left the room, Rosanna looked at Ellie and

chortled. "Have you ever, in your life, seen such a popinjay?" Rosanna clutched her stomach and tried not to hoot loud enough for Halburt to hear her on his way out.

"Legends, trapdoors, a visit from Walter Scott? What a strange duck he is." Ellie smiled and shook her head. "I think he is nice enough, though. It must be hard not to get a big head when one is so handsome."

"Ellie, you are sweet. You put me in the shade. Here I'm laughing at the poor man, and you look for the positive in him. I'm chastened." Rosanna stirred her tea and thought for a moment. "How good it is you've joined me here. I'm so blessed that you found me. Until you arrived, I didn't admit quite how lonely I'd become."

13

Rosanna woke early the next day, hurried to dress and then descended to breakfast. As a morning person, praise was on her lips as she made her way downstairs. "Exalt the Lord, His praise proclaim." Her voice trilled out before she subsided to merely humming the Haydn tune. She downed a cup of coffee and carried a roll outside.

The peace of the wooded paths which were hers to discover and explore lured her out of doors. Surely, she could get back in time for the ride with Halburt, scheduled for nine o'clock. She entered the woods on one of the paths she'd not tried before. Each stroll provided a fresh experience for absorbing nature's glory. The freedom of these solitary walks filled her spirit and were too precious to relinquish yet. Who could tell her not to walk alone on her own property? Miss Barton tried, but Rosanna retained final say. Surely, just this one time, no one could fault her.

This new path wound downhill, then up again to a rise about one half mile from the hill the manor house sat upon. She nibbled her roll as she walked. The hill's peak overlooked a patchwork of fields lit by the clear morning sun. Her delight grew when she found nearby a simple rope and board swing attached to the limb of a strong oak. Seating herself on the weathered wood, she pumped her legs, and soon soared out and back.

Each forward motion gave her the sensation of flight and she laughed aloud in delight.

She allowed the swing to come to rest, and was about to disembark, to walk the path a bit further, when she heard the rustle of someone nearby. Whirling around, she spied Peter, the dark-haired cottager emerging from the wood, hat in hand.

"I declare, you startled me." Voice high, her hand fluttered at her throat. Shaking, she heard herself spouting prattle again as whenever she came in contact with the man. She pressed her lips into a line, reflecting that awkward moments followed her like ducklings after their mama.

"My apologies, Miss. The former owner allowed free roam to the neighbors on all sides."

She realized her hand was still at her throat, and she dropped it as if it were scalded. "Is that so?"

His tone held no subservience. "I've long been used to walking these woods. Hope you'll continue that policy."

"Indeed, I shall. Such beauty," she spread her arms in benevolence, "is too grand to be hoarded, is it not?"

Demeanor serious, he glanced toward the view and nodded in affirmation before speaking. "I agree, 'tis grand. The land hereabouts is known for its splendor."

"There are two paths diverging from this clearing. Are you familiar? With them, I mean?" She kicked herself with the foot she hadn't put in her mouth. Would she never stop saying such ridiculous things...especially to this man?

At least he didn't let on that he noticed her *faux pas*.

He pointed to each path in turn. "Yes, this one leads to another overlook with a charming view of the surrounding fields. The other wends its way down to a grotto, complete with waterfall."

"Such an embarrassment of riches. Since I've swung high over fields today, I'll choose the other. The one with the falls."

"No doubt you'll be pleased."

It was odd to be speaking to a man, alone in a secluded spot, yet this particular man gave her no unease. Her intuition for detecting cads did not cause one tingle of warning to rise within her. "Would you care to accompany me? Show me the way, so to speak?"

"If you think it proper—seeing that you have no companion again today." He looked around the clearing, then down, as if contemplating the hat in his hands.

"Proper? There's that. But at this early hour, who else will be on any of these hilly paths? They're not used by the staff, and are merely for sightseeing and gamboling, are they not?"

"True. I'd just as soon accompany you along the path, if not for the potential impropriety."

"I've convinced myself it's acceptable for me to walk alone here. Do you think me wrong for that?"

"Not necessarily, simply asking if walking together would be appropriate, both in your sight and in the unlikely chance someone would see us."

She hesitated, distracted by a shaft of sunlight accenting the man's sensitive, yet strong jaw, before answering his doubts. "Let's do. I am my own mistress now and have reached my majority. At this hour, it's almost certain no one will be on the paths to observe us anyway. I simply must view the grotto." She removed her bonnet, for the sun and the exertion of swinging had warmed her.

She shook out her bangs and fluffed them, then stopped abruptly, realizing this might have an unwanted effect on her walking partner. She jammed the bonnet back onto her head but left the strings to hang. Men were known to be silly about a woman's hair, and she didn't want to draw that kind of attention.

He turned away and moved into the shady wooded path.

Rosanna followed behind since the narrow path wouldn't allow them to walk side-by-side. The trail soon opened onto a hilly meadow, and from about halfway down the slope she spotted masses of white flowers ahead. As she neared, she realized it was an orchard in bloom. A gust of wind swept curls across her face. She lifted her voice. "I say, the leaves have turned over and the breeze has picked up. Do you think it'll rain?"

The first raindrop fell before he could answer. He grabbed her hand and they ran to the nearest apple tree. They both crouched down, backs against the trunk. How odd to be taking shelter from the rain with such an intriguing man.

A damp brown dog loped up and settled next to Peter. He patted the animal's head and its tail flopped back and forth. "This is Nellie, my dog."

"Hello, Nellie, nice of you to join us." The smells of spring rain and apple blossoms gave Rosanna momentary bliss. The dry and warm ground under the tree's canopy added to the suitability of the ideal shelter.

The shower soon subsided, and the sun emerged again.

"Look up! The raindrops cling to the blossoms like a glistening cocoon of gems." Why did she have such a propensity for saying such silly things?

He looked up at the sparkly net of droplets above their heads, then at her. "In my experience a special sight like this doesn't come along very often in life."

The reverent tone in his voice and the seriousness of his eyes as he spoke, gave Rosanna pause. Warmth coursed over her skin that had nothing to do with the sun's heat coming on again after the rain shower.

He clambered to his feet and reached out to aid her to rise.

The dog got to its feet as well and waited for its master.

"I've decided I must get back. *Tempus fugit*. I'll have to see the waterfall another day." She stood, brushed her dress, and tied her bonnet ribbons.

"May I escort you?"

"So kind, but I shan't need any help getting home. Farewell!" She turned away and with brisk pace, moved on into the woods, all the while chiding her heart to stop its yearning.

He sounded so nice. But an entanglement with a cottager would be an egregious flying in the face of propriety. That wasn't in her plan, nor did it serve her intention to remain unattached and obscure. She never wanted to marry, another reason not to encourage such an appealing young man—or any man.

14

Rosanna floated into the house and up to her suite of rooms, elated after drinking in the beauty of the woods, the orchard, and the glittering aftermath of the rain. *God's creation is so perfect.* She reveled in owning such a fine and glorious property, while resisting thoughts of Peter, her interesting neighbor.

Miss Barton entered the room after a light tap on the door. "Good morning."

"I had a grand walk this morning."

"You must have. Your voice sounds happy today. Have you forgotten about your ride?"

"No, there's time. Don't worry."

"Get into your riding habit. Lord Halburt will be here any minute." The companion extracted a green ensemble from the wardrobe. She waved it toward Rosanna with a raise of the brow. "I'll help you with the habit. Dot's busy."

"Oh, that. All right, I'll change. But, the walk was glorious." Following upon her unsettling emotions, caused by the proximity of Peter, she submitted to being managed.

Miss Barton laid the habit on the bed, and then turned to Rosanna, efficiently removing her walking dress. "Your walk is why I am here. I told Dot I would assist you to change this morning."

"Her training isn't complete, though."

"No, it isn't. I'm here to remind you that, as your companion, one of my duties is to walk out with you."

"No need—I was fine."

"You very well may be fine, but as I've said, your solo walks must stop. You might be safe here, but a young lady can never guard her reputation too much. Walking alone is beyond the pale."

Barton sounded oddly out of breath—probably due to both her head of steam as well as from all the bending, squatting, and reaching to assist Rosanna into the riding habit.

Rosanna moved to the mirror and, facing away from the other woman, fiddled with her hair, tucking it into the habit's matching shako hat. "Dear Miss Barton, you are sadly out of breath, please sit down and drink some water."

"Don't try to distract me. Walking out alone so early after having only a roll and coffee." She added this to the long list of sins, then clucked her tongue, emphasizing her disapproval. She fastened the final closure and made a heavy exhalation.

Rosanna lifted her chin. "You seem to have all my movements in your sights."

Barton's breathing became even more labored, and startled, Rosanna dropped her scornful demeanor. "Oh, my! Miss Barton, please sit down." Rosanna took Miss Barton's arm and led her to a comfortable seat near the window. She opened the window a few inches, and fanned Barton.

Soon calmed and out of patience with this solicitousness, Miss Barton batted away the fan, and renewed her criticisms. Her dark eyes flashed, and she clutched the arms of her chair, knuckles white. "Rosanna. What makes you think it acceptable to walk alone here?"

Rosanna resisted the urge to release a scold. "Several reasons, Miss Barton. You must calm down."

Miss Barton took a few deep breaths.

Rosanna thought she'd left her circumscribed life behind. She raised her hands to tick off the rationales that made walking alone acceptable. Her words, though measured and tempered by Miss Barton's distress, emerged with a slight edge. "I own this property. It is extremely secluded. I am over twenty-one. Aren't those enough reasons?"

"Please listen, dear Rosanna. I only want your best. My concern is for your reputation in the community here in Woodvale. I grew up in a small village similar to this and rural gossips can be just as cruel and damaging as in London. I don't want anyone to be able to speak ill of *my* young lady." She gave a reassuring smile, and added, "I don't wish to spoil your enjoyment of the new freedoms you've gained, but I have a responsibility to you."

"Rest assured. No one observed my outing today. Well, no one except a neighbor. But he is no concern—in fact, he's a bit of a hermit and wouldn't tell a soul." Even as she spoke those words, she wondered if they were true.

"A neighbor? Not Lord Halburt?" Barton's forehead creased again.

"No, that's yet to look forward to." Rosanna answered wryly with a glance at the clock. "Just a cottager named Peter. I saw him at church, Sunday last."

"Exactly the type of meeting that would give fodder to the village gossip mill. What if he gossips? Say you'll walk with me in the future?" Miss Barton wrung her hands.

"My my, don't look so alarmed. Yes, I will venture out with you or Ellie. I'd hate for you to be worried about me." Miss Barton's passionate persuasion caused a rush of guilt to sweep over Rosanna, and the concession with it brought a returned spirit of peace.

A tap came on the door, Dot entered, and attempted a tentative curtsey. "Miss Cabot, Mr. Perkins says Lord Halburt has arrived." The timid girl bobbed her head as she backed out of the room without waiting for any response.

"Are you comfortable with my riding out with Halburt, Miss Barton? If not, how shall I let him down?" Rosanna would love to do just that.

"You are toying with me. There could be no objection to a ride, with a groom trailing behind, of course. Two people on horses followed by a groom couldn't get up to much mischief."

The very idea of mischief with vain Lord Halburt caused her to cringe.

Miss Barton made shooing motions toward the door. "You just go on."

"I'm glad you're feeling better." Rosanna smiled and stopped at the looking glass. Her bottle green velvet habit looked bandbox fresh as did the matching ostrich plumes quivering atop her jaunty hat. "Thank you for helping me." She left the room and sped down the stairs.

The sight of the perfectly turned-out Lord Halburt waiting in the hall caused Rosanna to stop in her tracks, her mouth falling open. Annoying though he was, she couldn't deny he was a glorious-looking man.

He tapped his foot and slapped his leather gloves into his hands. "Charmed, Miss Cabot. Shall we?"

Responding in kind to his chilly, impatient greeting, she breezed past him. "Let's get out to the horses. We wouldn't want to keep them waiting." She thwacked the side of her thick skirt with her riding crop. *Why did I ever agree to this?*

Ambling along on trails suited for nothing faster than a slow canter, the two riders chatted on the topic of weather, until Halburt pointedly cleared his throat. "How do you enjoy estate living? Is Honor's Point all you expected it to be?"

Puzzled and a bit irritated at his tone which implied a problem, Rosanna answered with asperity. "It's wonderful, and it's lovely. Did you think it otherwise?"

"Just curious about the legends."

"Legend, or rumors? I've heard nothing of the kind—except from you."

His gaze shifted away from direct contact with hers. "There's something, but the memory eludes me at this moment."

How strange. "I shall ask my staff, you needn't concern yourself." Rosanna's stomach began to ache. Whatever was the man getting at?

"Oh, but mysteries intrigue me—it's no trouble— in fact, if you learn anything in the way of a clue, I'd like you to call on me for assistance. I'm something of an amateur enigma collector you see, as is my guest. I'd love to have a puzzle to put before my notable visitor." Halburt's face wore a prideful smirk.

"So, he's coming? As of yesterday, you weren't sure."

"Yes, today I received the long-awaited acceptance to my invitation. Scott and his party will arrive soon. To be certain, this will be the most eminent visitor in these parts for many a decade, nay, a century."

"That will be a feather in your cap." This ride couldn't conclude soon enough to please her. For such a handsome man, he irritated her more than any man she'd known, and something unsettling lurked beneath his surface.

15

Horses have their uses, but my, how they make one smell. As soon as she extracted herself from the presence of her annoying riding partner, Rosanna ordered a bath and sought solitude in her suite. After a soak, she put on a dressing gown and enjoyed a full breakfast on a tray, the roll and coffee a distant memory—one supplanted by the interlude in the rain.

~*~

Some time later, a soft tap on the door brought an end to her privacy.

"Miss, Mr. Perkins sent me to tell you Lady Brook is here to pay a call. He said to ask if you are at home." Dot's voice shook, but less than the last time she'd delivered a household message.

Rosanna gave her a reassuring smile. "Very good, Dot. You may tell Perkins I *am* at home and please tell Miss Barton that I need her assistance."

Miss Barton arrived and scurried into the room, scolding on her tongue. "You've been hiding away up here for quite a while. I was already on my way here, when Dot informed me of our guest. You should change—Lady Brook is dressed to the nines." Miss Barton selected a dress of pale coral trimmed with matching satin bands, and then assisted Rosanna to dress.

Rosanna sat down at her vanity table to smooth her hair and check her appearance in the mirror, turning her face this way, then that. She dabbed Hungary water on her temples as a final touch. "When will Dot's training be complete? I don't want you to work so hard anymore."

"She's quiet, but a quick learner. Any day now, you won't even remember she's new."

"Fine. I look forward to that." Rosanna stood, and shooed the companion onto the dressing stool. "You sit now. It'll only take a moment to fix your bun, it's lost its moorings."

Miss Barton clucked her disapproval, but nonetheless allowed herself to be seated. Rosanna had a gift and love for working with hair, and the loyal retainer never deprived her of the pleasure. A pin here, a strand there, and within a short, few moments the companion's black hair looked much improved.

"Let's go down now. I am ready." Rosanna sailed through the door, assured Miss Barton would follow in her wake. After her rest, she looked forward to her guest.

Ensconced in the drawing room off the main hall, Lady Brook appeared every bit the grand dame. Her purple gown, simply ravishing, adorned with the latest details, appeared to be straight out of Ackerman's, the most popular source of fashion.

The warmth of her greeting belied the grandeur of her mien. "Miss Cabot, I declare you become lovelier each time I lay eyes on you. Oh, and Miss Barton, how are you enjoying our district so far?" Without waiting for answers, she patted the seat beside her and gestured to Rosanna to sit next to her on the divan. "I mustn't delay telling you of a cure I recently learned of. Such a common plant and so effective."

Rosanna sat next to Lady Brook, then responded. "Marvelous you are still learning more."

"Yes, well, I do thrive on serving others with my modest efforts."

"What is the plant, and what does it do?" Rosanna didn't mind adding to her own humble stock of remedies.

"The lowly daisy."

"Daisy? Narrow white petals, yellow center? That daisy?"

"Yes, there's something in the daisy that heals a bruise like nothing I've seen." Lady Brook raised her fingertips to prop her chin in a dainty pose.

"That's amazing. How did you stumble upon this interesting fact?"

"I was combing an archaic medical tome, practically falling asleep, and I kept seeing the term 'day's eye'. Didn't give it a thought—so much in these old books is quite impenetrable—until I came upon a page with a small engraving. Imagine my delight when I put the clues together."

"Clues?"

"The picture, plus the words 'day's eye'." Lady Brook gave an emphatic nod.

Rosanna retrieved her notebook from a side table. "Daisy is, or was called, 'day's eye'? How intriguing. Let me make note of this."

"And further, day's eye is a term which refers to the sun."

Eyes wide with interest, Miss Barton added her two cents. "Amazing what one can learn—almost by accident. In all my years, I've never known a cure for bruises existed."

Gratified, Lady Brook kept up a flow of conversation pertaining to the doings of the neighborhood until a maid brought in a cart and Rosanna served tea. At which time, the chatty guest subsided for a moment in order to sample the best Honor's Point's kitchens had to offer. She selected a pastry. "They know I love anything made with lemon. I must remember to send over some more lemons from my succession house." She quieted to savor the scrumptious, tart treats.

"Lady Brook, what can you tell me of the cottage on the corner of my property? I first spied the unexpected roofline, and subsequently met the occupant." Eyes fixed on her teacup, Rosanna schooled her features to hide intense interest behind a bland façade. She had to admit, to herself alone, the mysterious and attractive cottager, Peter, had everything to do with her curiosity. The undeniable elation she'd experienced earlier while in his company under the apple tree hadn't been merely the outcome of taking in the beauty of creation during her walk. The warmth of their connection left her senses reeling, and her heart in serious danger.

Lady Brook dabbed the corners of her mouth and set down her plate. "How much do you know?"

16

"Know?" Her heart beat faster than normal, but she continued steely control over her facial expression. No need for Lady Brook to get any inkling of her interest when she wasn't even sure if she cared. "I know nothing except that one corner of Honor's Point land appears to have been truncated. A cottage sits upon it, and a dark-haired, youngish man appears to live there." Rosanna ticked the facts off her fingers as she spoke.

"Rosanna, does the name Lord Winstead mean anything to you?" Lady Brook's keen gaze pinioned Rosanna.

"I have heard that name. Let me think now." She paused, casting her look to the ceiling, as if to find the answer there. Her mind worked full speed trying to make sense of Lady Brook's question. "Oh, of course, that is the name of the family who sold this estate. And, I believe I may have heard mention of a young gentleman by that name at one of the countless balls I attended this past season."

"Just as I thought—you aren't aware." Lady Brook took a deep breath and laid her fingers at the base of her throat. "Now, this isn't something you need to feel guilty about, for no one blames you for buying this gorgeous property, but the estate went on the block because of the poor management and squandering of the late Lord Winstead."

"I wondered why anyone would sell such an attractive estate. Uncle George hinted at financial straits but wasn't specific."

"It was so sad. Lord Winstead absenting himself from here, year after year, combined with unfortunate investments, dare I say, schemes. His affection for gaming removed any remaining solvency." The emotion visible on Lady Brook's face teetered on the brink between sympathy and contempt.

Rosanna brought her guest back around to the original subject of her query. "I'd suspected something of the sort, but what does this have to do with the cottage on the corner of my property?"

"I'm getting to that. The current Lord Winstead valiantly traveled through the dun territory caused by his father's imprudence, and arrived at point-non-plus, able to retain nothing of his family estate, save the cottage you discovered. He's been a recluse since he returned to the district." Lady Brook sat back, as if having divested herself of a burden. Her eyes flickered from Rosanna to Miss Barton and back. "I thought you should know."

"You are bamming me! Peter, I mean the occupant of the cottage, is Lord Winstead? I am astounded. Handsome, yes, but he spoke and acted so humble."

"Humble?" Lady Brook's confusion was an echo of her own. "Winstead?"

"He behaved much as a tenant would. He must have been putting on a sort of disguise for me." She hopped to her feet to pace the length of the carpet. "How embarrassing."

"He has been truly humbled, yes." Lady Brook reached for another lemon tart. "Why he'd put on such a pretense is understandable, but strange. After all, he will be living nearby, you'd find out eventually."

Rosanna halted pacing and turned. "Of course, why am I surprised he'd stay, painful though it must be? If it's all he has left, and the estate property is so beautiful I can imagine how it would be difficult to relinquish it entirely." Rosanna recalled the idyllic interlude earlier that morning, and a shiver ran up her arms. "It's so special."

Willing the heat in her face to subside, she went to the window and stared out until she'd regained full composure. She forced herself to sit down with some poise. It wouldn't do for Lady Brook to suspect any discomfiture. *Control and reveal nothing of the turmoil within.*

Casting about for distraction, Rosanna observed Miss Barton's head down and her needle stilled, making no progress on the needlework project, an embroidered reticule. Rosanna scoured her rattled brain for a diversion and landed on a hackneyed topic. "Miss Barton? Tell Lady Brook how well you like it here."

Miss Barton raised her head, cleared her throat, and offered a few words in a tentative voice. "The neighborhood is a fine one. So many congenial folk."

Rosanna waxed on from that opening, cataloguing the excellencies of Honor's Point and hoped her effusions sufficient to deflect attention from the topic of Lord Winstead. She had an affinity for the man, but it would not do for anyone else to know.

Her attempt to change the subject succeeded and talk diverged well away from the cottage and its resident. Something told her she'd get an earful later. She heard her own voice blathering nonentities. "I'd love to meet some of the other neighbors."

On that scintillating note, the door opened, and Ellie entered the room. Lady Brook had not met her yet, so several minutes elapsed while performing introductions. Ellie and Lady Brook were quite taken with each other, and soon engrossed in a discussion of the competing merits of rosemary and chamomile and whether the herbs were as useful as medicines as they were as beauty products.

Miss Barton shot a piercing look at Rosanna and whispered. "See? You must not believe yourself safe strolling about alone. Word could get back to the *haute ton* that you are wandering around the woods." Indignation infused her words, but discretion caused her to stop the flow of invective, for she did not want Lady Brook to realize anything amiss.

"Ladies, I must leave you now. I have two ailing retainers at home to return to. Both my butler and potboy are down. One with the gout, the other with croup." Lady Brook gathered her reticule and repositioned her shawl. "Thanks be, there are remedies for both on a shelf in my stillroom. Enough of that pedestrian talk, however, I do not want to tire you with my medical doings."

Rosanna demurred. "I can only aspire to your medicinal abilities."

"Thank you, dear. Now I'd like to ask whether I may count on you three ladies for a smallish dinner I am planning for the evening after next?"

Rosanna glanced over at Ellie, who lifted a delicate brow, before giving a cautious nod of assent. The poor thing—living in fear as she was. The time had come to nudge her out of the limited scope of the manor. Surely, Lady Brook's invitation brought no danger. It wouldn't hurt to get out.

"A dinner party? That sounds delightful. What time shall we arrive?" Rosanna turned toward Miss Barton, seeking approval. Having only thought of Ellie's reaction, Rosanna's heart sank at the mask of trepidation mantling Barton's face.

"Come at seven. My cook will outdo herself." Lady Brook rose to leave, and the other three ladies did as well, all gathering around the neighbor to bid her adieu.

"This visit has been exceedingly pleasant, I am so glad for such amiable neighbors." Rosanna said what she thought appropriate, but the minute it came out of her mouth, she remembered Peter. *Oh, well, no one else is thinking that, just me.*

The second the door closed behind Lady Brook, two pairs of eyes bored into Rosanna. The questions hung in the air.

Rosanna sat down again, nerves tingling at the expectation of opposition. "My dear Miss Barton, I perceive you have a qualm or two?"

"I've not ever before attended as a guest at a dinner party with my betters." Miss Barton's words were halting, fear was written all over her plain face. "I think I should stay home."

"It's quite unexceptional for a lady's companion to be included in all her invitations, and Lady Brook clearly invited you. You've no reason to be concerned."

"I fear I shall be sadly out of place."

"Nonsense. After all, you're the one who taught me how to go on in society. With my mother deceased since my early years, you, Miss Barton, filled many a gap, including that of social etiquette instructor."

Miss Barton's relieved expression revealed

cautious pleasure at being included in the invitation. "I concede, but only if you're sure."

"Quite sure. Lady Brook exudes a calm graciousness which bodes well for a pleasant dinner party. Also, the neighborhood is somewhat sparsely populated and devoid of anything to draw an influx of strangers."

"I, too, have a concern." Ellie spoke and held up her ink-stained index finger. "Who will be there, do you suppose? Anyone who would possibly recognize me?" She lowered the finger and began to nibble it, revealing her anxiety.

17

"That's an excellent question." Rosanna crossed her arms and thought for a moment, while twirling a curl around her finger. A social invitation brought on unexpected complications. She'd like to have been better prepared for this eventuality, but one couldn't think of everything. "Let's talk this through. Who might be there?"

Miss Barton chimed in, "Lord Halburt, for one."

"Well, I'd never heard of him or met him before the other day, so it's safe to assume he hasn't heard of me either, correct?" Ellie looked at Rosanna for confirmation. "He acted as though he was meeting me for the first time—like a complete and utter stranger."

"That is accurate. I gleaned no signs of recognition at all when he met you." She gave a reassuring pat to her friend's little hand. "Believe me, I watched him closely—like a hawk."

Ellie clutched her hands in her lap. "I am grateful for that."

Rosanna spoke again, continuing the conjectured guest list. "The vicar, Mr. Clough, will probably be included. And his wife, if he has one."

"He does not." Miss Barton piped up. "He is a bachelor." She looked down again, busy with her needle.

"A bachelor is always desirable at such

gatherings." Typical when nervous, Rosanna's tongue wandered into gaucheries—*desirable? Stop.* She couldn't delay any longer, the very topic that made her tongue run away. The time to avoid mentioning the other guest they could expect was over. She took a deep breath and began. "Ellie, you missed quite the on-dit. Lady Brook informed Miss Barton and me that the former owner of Honor's Point, Lord Winstead, is living in a nearby cottage."

"In a cottage? Whatever for?" Ellie said, baffled.

Rosanna smoothed her hands down her arms, suddenly chilled. "So sad. His father lost the estate and the heir only retained one small corner of the property."

"So, the man is destined to live in the shadow of the estate he once owned. A poignant, sad tale. How devastating."

"Back to our presumptions about the guests." *Oh, my.* "I mean predictions, not presumptions."

Miss Barton clucked her disapproval at Rosanna's slip of the tongue. "I should say."

"Lord Winstead will most probably be invited. Lady Brook seemed to be quite kindly toward him." Rosanna concluded her awkward explanation by raising her cup and saucer and taking a sip. She congratulated herself on the relative level of dispassion with which she imparted this information. Relative to her inward turmoil, that was. *No one can think I'm the least bit attached.*

"Back to answer your original question, Ellie. More than likely, no one who laid an eye on you in London will be present. The Season remains in full swing; therefore, society people are still in town."

"True." Ellie said. "That's somewhat reassuring.

My entire life long, this," she touched her hair, "has caused undue notice to fall upon me. Perhaps I should color my hair?"

"Never. Those glorious tresses must on no account be tampered with."

"If you're sure."

"I'm certain. None of the other guests will know who you are, and your new identity will aid your anonymity. Remember, one other thing in your favor is that you hadn't been presented at court or graced your own come-out ball yet. You were barely known in society."

"You're right. It's just that my cousin—my family..." Ellie, eyes down, trailed off with a final word, breathed on a sigh, "—frightening."

Rosanna exchanged a glance with Miss Barton.

"I understand. But we can anticipate what will surely be a pleasant evening. We'll relax and enjoy the dinner party." Rosanna wondered if that were possible with the darkly handsome Lord Winstead present.

"I suppose it's safe to brave the dinner party. If anyone mentions in London an Ellie Moore having attended a country dinner, I'd be shocked. There's less than a miniscule chance attending would lead to my discovery."

"I concur entirely," Rosanna said. "Your situation is fearsome, but you are safe here."

"Thank you, it helped to talk it through." Ellie stood. "I'll look over my gown. I believe it may need pressing."

"Wonderful. I'm sure you'll be pretty in whatever you wear."

"Though I didn't relish attending London social events, because of my family's pressures, one aspect I did enjoy was selecting a new wardrobe. I brought only one evening gown, in my rush to escape. Just the thing for Lady Brook's party." Ellie left the room.

Miss Barton wasted no time before rounding on her charge. "Am I to understand that you met this man in the woods?" Not waiting for an answer, she fumed on, puffed like an angry pigeon. "Charming. Just the sort of thing I've warned you against time and again."

"Yes, well. No harm done. Now I know better. Even here, I must always be on my guard." Such a concession bothered her, however. She wanted peace, not pressure to conform to society's standards. *Why can't I roam free for a bit? Without repercussions or ramifications?*

Miss Barton added the obvious. "And I shall be on guard on your behalf, as well,"

"I only hope it isn't uncomfortable to meet Lord Winstead at an elegant dinner party. I was initially under the impression he was a laborer or tenant farmer of some sort. Now I learn elsewhere—not from him—that he is the former owner of my property." She stared out the window, in the direction of the cottage for a moment, adjusting her mind to the fresh information about its inhabitant.

"I told you. But, no. You must wander about on your own. You've ever been this wayward."

"Miss Barton, spare me another scold. I've hardly been out from under your thumb a few hours of my entire life. Please don't exaggerate."

The companion gave a huff and crossed her arms. "Well, all right, I'll concede that. But if you'd simply taken me along instead of gallivanting alone, this hideously embarrassing development would not hold such awkwardness. You'll need to face the music. Pray he doesn't spread tales and ruin your reputation."

"He didn't seem the vengeful sort. And meeting him now, at a soiree? What will he do? Scorn me publicly?" Rosanna's imagination flew to what it would be like to meet up with Peter at an elegant dinner party.

"It could be bad. I just hope the Lord spares you any shame."

"Indeed, I continually beseech His favor. But, Lord Winstead has his own problems, and I highly doubt he's even thinking of me." Saying these words, however, lanced pain through her temples.

Instead of musing on her heart's tender condition, Rosanna needed to defuse her companion and distract her suspicious mind. "Miss Barton, it's past time for you to finish training the new lady's maid. Your transition to companion will be utterly complete what with this dinner invitation that includes you. From here on, everyone shall be calling you *Miss* Barton."

"If you insist. I am almost through training Dot. She can attend you while you pick your gown for Lady Brook's dinner. Selecting it today will provide enough time if the dress needs any touching up with an iron, or a stray bead mended. You must decide if Dot, my chosen replacement, suits." Miss Barton put her needlework away in a workbag and stood. She brushed a few stray threads off her gown and wiped away a surreptitious tear.

Rosanna stood too and placed a hand on the companion's arm. "You, Miss Barton, can never be replaced. Let's simply say, new lady's maid, and not replacement." Rosanna acted as if she hadn't witnessed the tears and moved toward the door. "Selecting which gown to wear for Lady Brook's party will be enjoyable.

I haven't looked over my gowns since they were unpacked."

"Evening gowns are a pleasure, aren't they, Rosanna?" Miss Barton swept up behind Rosanna and gave a tweak to her sash. "So fancy."

Miss Barton's words reminded Rosanna of something from one of her lists. She held up a finger and waved it gently. "You also have a way with fashion, Miss Barton. And in light of that, we will go to the village tomorrow to select some styles suitable for your new life."

"If you're certain."

"I am. We shall have a fine time. Exploring the village, ordering gowns, taking tea—if there's a tea shop."

Rosanna and Miss Barton ascended the stairs. An agreement had been reached about solo ramblings on the estate, happy plans were laid for the morrow, and a dinner party to look forward to.

While waiting for Dot to answer the summons, Rosanna perused her gowns and evaluated the possibilities. At twenty-two, and Rosanna no longer considered a young miss, society allowed her to wear more vivid colors, which suited her personality and complexion. The requisite white and palest pastel gowns worn as a young lady on the marriage market had not flattered her coloring. But that cloud had a silver lining, since she'd never desired to attach to any of the men at the various society functions.

Back in London, the heady social whirl surely went on, and she had no regrets about missing it. The balls she'd attended during the early part of the current Season did not provide near as much enjoyment as did new gowns.

~*~

Dot's quiet voice, one step up from a murmur, announced the maid's arrival at the door to Rosanna's room. "Yes, Miss?"

"Dot, come in. You look as though you're about to be chastised. This is nothing like that. To seal my decision that you will be my new lady's maid I want you to help me while I select a gown for a dinner party, two nights hence. We'll choose now, so there's plenty of time to press the gown and make sure it fits."

The slight girl appeared about to faint, so Miss Barton snatched a hartshorn vinaigrette from the dressing table and waved it under the girl's nose. She revived and then Miss Barton patted her hand and brought her closer to wait for instructions.

Half a dozen gowns were arrayed across the bed. Two were in shades of bright coral, two of medium greenish blue, and one each of lavender and violet.

"Help Miss Cabot get undressed. These are the gowns she's considering."

With minimal instruction, Dot assisted Rosanna to undress down to her chemise.

"I'll try each gown on, but we won't completely fasten each one. When I stand in front of the mirror, you can hold each dress closed at the back." Dealing with all the tapes, hooks, buttons, and other contraptions would slow the trying-on session to a crawl. The enjoyable process of selecting a gown didn't need to go on for hours.

Rosanna and Miss Barton discussed the merits of each gown. All of the gowns were high-waisted, and of expensive fabrics. Dot made not one comment, but helped in practical ways such as puffing sleeves, and arranging trains.

Having tried the final gown, Rosanna turned away from her cheval glass and selected a vivid coral taffeta evening dress featuring a low neckline filled in with a frothy white fichu. The gown had an embellishment of gold thread in an embroidered ivy leaf pattern down the front and around the hem of the skirt. A filmy white silk underskirt peeked out below the scalloped hem. A necklace of coral set in gold would complete the ensemble. "This one will look just right."

Miss Barton used a gentle tone with the young maid, though her words were pragmatic and to-the-point. "Can you manage dressing Miss Cabot's hair tonight? Even though we're dining at home, it will be good practice for Lady Brooke's upcoming dinner party."

Voice shaking, Dot answered. "Yes, ma'am, I've practiced on me hair." She looked surprised at her own temerity.

Miss Barton departed, and Dot helped Rosanna dress before dealing with her curls. Relaxing while the maid brushed her hair, her mind whirled with conflicting desires. She struggled to convince herself of the appropriateness of her desire to be beautiful at the upcoming party where she would see Peter. God made her, she decided, and she had the right to let her beauty show.

"That's lovely!" She turned her head from side to side, enjoying the luscious hairdo Dot created with a few pins. Thinking ahead to the party, she pictured a perfect coiffure crowning her ensemble.

"Thank you, Miss." Dot stood back, head tilted to

one side.

"You are certainly talented with hair. And that confirms my decision to promote you to lady's maid. Would you like that?"

Dot breathed out her answer. "Yes, Miss."

Rosanna leaned in to hear and added a smile to soften her words. "Dot, you'll have to learn to speak up if you're to be a success."

Spritzing her neck with lilac scent, Rosanna studied the image in the mirror, fantasizing about the reaction she'd get at the dinner party two nights hence. Would Winstead notice? Smacking down the atomizer, she chided herself that it didn't matter. But honest self-examination forced her to admit the reason she wanted to cut a dash at the party. There were two long days to wait. *Lord, why, after all this time, do I care what this or any man thinks of me?*

18

The sheets tangled about her limbs gave further terror to Rosanna's nightmare. Trapped in a mindscape of shifting shadows, around every gloomy corner of a winding corridor hid a malign presence. Each time she summoned the courage to approach, but the wisp of evil vanished. Over and over, the dream played out, resolution slipping through her fingers. She tried to swim to the surface of consciousness, partially waking with her own whimpers.

Half-asleep, and still under the sway of the heart-pounding night terror, she fought awake, sat up, clutched the linens under her chin, and swept her gaze over the dim room. Forcing deep breaths, she murmured a verse, *"greater is He that is in you than he that is in the world."*

Ellie. Her guest's name rose in her throat, the urge to call out strong. But no, it was just the dream. Ellie was fine—asleep a few rooms away.

Too early to expect a maid to appear with hot coffee or chocolate, and sure she wouldn't be able to sleep anymore, she chose the alternative—to rise, dress, and enjoy the sunrise.

But first, robe and slippers found, she slipped out into the hall and, using the servants' stairs, she descended to the kitchens which lay near the foot of this stairwell. Tentative, she pushed at the green kitchen door, and stuck her head in. Ah, the cook was awake at this early hour.

She spoke with a gentle lilt so as not to alarm the woman. "Hannah?"

Even so, Hannah whirled around, wooden spoon clenched in her hand. "Wha? Oh, Miss, you scared the tar out o' me."

"Sorry. A bad dream woke me, and I decided to give up on sleep."

"Wise o' ye. Sleep again, and mayhaps have another nightmare."

"So true. May I please fix myself tea?"

"It dinna seem right, but ye be the mistress. Canister's here." She plunked down a metal container, then a small pot and cup. "Water's hot on the hob. Let me get that." Hannah used a thick rag to lift a sturdy kettle off its hook and poured steaming water into the teapot.

Rosanna stepped forward, and rapidly prepared the brew. She spied a smallish tray and loaded it. "Thank you so much. You're a dear, Hannah. This is just the thing."

She backed out of the swinging door, using her hip to push it, and made the trip back to her room. After placing the tray on a table near the east-facing window, she stirred the fire, added a bit of fuel, and then dragged a blanket off the bed, nestling with it in the chair closest to the tea tray.

"Mmmm." She reveled in the simple pleasure of hot tea in solitude as the sky lit up with gilded apricot streaks. A play of violet gave way to mauve and by the time she'd emptied her first cup, the sun had risen on a field of vivid blue sky.

"More tea, then a list to make." Murmuring, she

acted on her words, pouring another cup. Scribbling while thoughts were fresh, she wrote for a few minutes, then reread, whispering the list. "Order Miss Barton's dresses, visit tea shop."

Reluctant to give up the cozy cocoon, yet eager for what lay ahead, she said a prayer. Rising from the chair, she let the blanket fall while she stretched and recited under her breath. "This is the day which the Lord hath made, we will rejoice and be glad in it."

Flinging the blanket onto the bed, she then crossed the room to reach the wardrobe. Riffling through, she selected a blue striped round gown, one that went on over the head with a minimum of closures—all of which she could reach.

Dot poked her head through the doorway. "Good morning, Miss."

"Oh, Dot. I shall come back up here after breakfast and have you fix my hair, but I'm too famished." She skittered a comb over her curls, put on a lace cap and sailed down to the dining room for sustenance.

To her surprise, Miss Barton stood at the sideboard, making selections.

Rosanna joined her at the buffet and filled her own plate. "You rose early, too, Miss Barton."

Miss Barton's black eyes twinkled. "I'll admit anticipation of today's outing made my eyes pop open quite early, dear."

Seated, Rosanna prayed, took a bite, then set her fork on the edge of her plate. "How very awkward do you think it will be tomorrow night, when we face Lord Winstead for the first time since his true, full identity was revealed?"

"Possibly, quite terribly awkward."

"You're blunt this morning. But I agree and share

your prediction, as well. I have sympathy for him, but am piqued at him, too. Leading me to think he was a tenant—some sort of laborer."

"I needn't remind you that if you hadn't been out alone—"

"Stop. I am well aware. I hereby assure you I do not need another reminder or review of your thoughts on the matter."

"Fine. See that you remember my warnings the next time you are tempted to take one of your solo excursions."

Silence ruled while Rosanna finished her eggs and sausage. She recalled the initial meeting on the road that Miss Barton knew nothing of—having slept through it. No reason to tell her companion about the tumble out of the coach now. Subsequent revelations supplanted any import that interaction once held.

After placing her loosely folded napkin next to her plate, Rosanna addressed a new topic. "So glad Mrs. Good follows the fashion for setting out napkins—do you believe how people would lift the tablecloth edge to wipe their mouths?"

"That's a custom I'm glad to see gone. Hate to think of the greasy stains the servants must have had to deal with on multiple voluminous table linens."

"I shall meet you in the hall in one hour, Miss Barton, and then our outing to the village shall commence."

~*~

Bowling along in an open carriage, with Miss Barton beside her and the coachman on the driver's seat in front, Rosanna kept a firm hold of her bonnet brim with one hand and gripped the side rail with the other. "Beautiful day," she mused.

"Lovely day, indeed. You're sure Miss Moore didn't want to accompany us?" The companion's bonnet had no brim to catch the wind, so she clung to a strap with both hands.

"She planned to write all morning—she's working on a novel."

"A novel? Such ambition for a young lady."

"It does keep her mind off her straits, and she enjoys it."

"She can write one happy ending after another."

"I'm not sure she's writing fairy tales—something tells me her stories might be darker than that."

The outskirts of Woodvale came in sight.

"Oh, good, the village. I like the speed of this light carriage, but oh, the bumps." Miss Barton made a face.

Rosanna glanced over to respond, in time to spot Lord Winstead in the small cemetery next to the church. One glance provided enough to observe the posture of sorrow. Poor man. He did trick her, but had lost so much. She was snapped out of her reverie as the carriage rocked when the coachman stopped in front of a livery.

He hopped down, opened the door, and lowered the steps. After handing the ladies down he asked, "When be ye ladies to return to Honor's Point, Miss Cabot?"

"We plan to conclude at the tea shop after our shopping." She nodded toward a shop with a cup-shaped sign. It read 'Pekoe Shoppe' and looked inviting enough. "In approximately two hours or so, after we visit that tea shop, we will wander over to the livery."

Rosanna linked arms with Miss Barton and strolled down the cobblestoned sidewalk. "Happy I wore half boots with these pesky cobbles."

"Indeed. Here's a mercantile, 'Beaumont's', shall we start here?" Miss Barton deferred to Rosanna's wishes.

"Yes, and don't let me forget to obtain some yardage for Dot's new uniform dresses. She says she can sew."

"Excellent. Then I won't be the only one whose wardrobe benefits from the shuffled positions."

Entering the shop caused a bell to chime, and an apron-clad man, clearly the proprietor, stood up from behind the counter. Chafing his hands together, he appeared to take their measure, and then a smile wreathed his face. "Good day and welcome to my humble establishment milady, ma'am." He nodded to each in turn.

"To be sure, 'tis a fine day. I am Miss Cabot from Honor's Point, and this is Miss Barton."

"Honored." The man creaked a bow. "I'm Beaumont, the owner of this fine establishment. How may I be of service?"

"We've come to purchase dress goods. It appears you carry an adequate selection."

The man stepped aside and swung his arm in an expansive gesture at a wall of fabric bolts. "The best in three counties, miss. The dress fabrics are over here." He bustled over to one side of his display and made another sweeping wave.

"Miss Barton dear, you point out what you'd like to see. I'll refer to my list—to keep us on track, of course—with such vast choices. First, we shall select materials for five day gowns." Rosanna stood back to allow Barton the full pleasure of choosing, careful not to take over with her own opinions.

"So many selections for such a small-town shop," almost overwhelmed, Miss Barton stage-whispered behind her hand. She pointed out the bolts she wanted to examine and, swift to comply, the merchant yanked them from the shelves to form a large pile.

Fingering the weights of Miss Barton's choices, Rosanna inquired of Mr. Beaumont. "Is there a seamstress in this village?"

"My wife—trained in France." As if on cue, a petite woman wearing a modest, yet beautiful dress appeared through a curtained opening. She curtsied prettily.

After introductions were made, Mrs. Beaumont produced the latest Ackerman's edition, and she and Barton consulted it for styles.

While they were occupied, Rosanna made quick work of selecting fabrics for Dot. A drab stripe and a medium brown, thick linsey-woolsey would be both easy to work with, as well as serviceable and appropriate for a maid. Four yards of each, plus four yards of white for aprons went onto a growing pile. She wrote notes and meandered over to a display of wool shawls. One of these for Dot, too, since she would need the warmth.

Turning her attention back to her companion, Rosanna exclaimed over the five choices for day dresses. "Miss Barton, those are perfect. Now for two evening gowns."

Miss Barton's eyebrows flew up. "Two evening gowns? For me?"

Rosanna gently forestalled her quibbles. "You

must be dressed according to my requests, my dear, as you will be accompanying me to many a party in time. Already, you've modified one dress for Lady Brook's party. So choose what you like—sparing no expense."

"Only if you insist." Barton selected two lustrings, one dark claret red, and one of a greenish brown.

Rosanna lifted her eyebrows. "Are you sure, Miss Barton, about this brown?"

"I've ever been praised for how well I look in brown." Barton held the swatch to her chin to prove it flattering. "I do know my own mind, Miss Cabot, and you told me to make my choices."

"So I did. Beg pardon, dear friend. I'm sure you're right. I look so poorly in brown myself. Now come and choose shawls." She patted Barton's hand, soothing her ruffled feathers. "One for day, and one for evening wear."

Selection made, Rosanna concluded with instructions. "Please take my parcels over to the livery. My carriage and coachman are there." She turned to the proprietor's wife. "Mrs. Beaumont, may I send a carriage for you tomorrow at eight? You may bring Miss Barton's yardage then. I trust you to cut the appropriate amount for the gowns."

Mrs. Beaumont bobbed a curtsey. "I'll be there. *Merci.*"

"Please do send my bill along at that time. I'll send payment home with Mrs. Beaumont tomorrow. We shall see you at Honor's Point tomorrow to begin Miss Barton's fittings."

The proprietor followed them to the door and held it open. "Thank you for your custom, Miss Cabot. We are happy to serve you."

"'Tis happy I am, Mr. Beaumont, for your excellent

fabrics and your talented wife. We shall return for more in autumn, if not sooner, to purchase pelisses, capes, and boots for the colder weather."

Over an hour had passed. Gaining the cobbled sidewalk again, Rosanna linked arms with Miss Barton. "So, dear companion, did you enjoy that?"

"Very much. I haven't ever had the pleasure of selecting seven gowns in a single day—nay, a single year."

"And what about Mrs. Beaumont—is she satisfactory?"

"The woman is a gem. So much insight and such good suggestions. She'll be a pleasure to work with."

Rosanna patted Miss Barton's arm. "Don't let me forget evening slippers for you. Mrs. Beaumont can measure your feet tomorrow and her husband can order some—just for you. Make sure to tell her what you'd like."

"You're too good to me, dear." Barton dragged a knuckle under each eye.

"You deserve it. Let's step in here for tea. I am ready for refreshment."

Another belled door, another proprietor clearly happy to see new customers. Ushered over to a bow window, Rosanna accepted assistance to be seated and placed her reticule on a spare chair. "We'd like tea and scones."

The hot brew arrived in a trice, and Rosanna took her first sip as the door's bell clanged again. Lord Winstead halted just inside the door and glanced around, gaze landing on Rosanna's face, which promptly heated.

"Good morning, ladies." He performed a stiff bow, aimed first in Rosanna's direction, then toward Miss

Barton.

An alarming splotch of anger clustered in her breast—he'd made a fool of her. As if from a distance, Rosanna heard herself respond with a dull pleasantry. "Hello." This man threw her into confusion, but why?

"I thought I saw an Honor's Point carriage pass by. Couldn't miss the chance to pay my respects to two such fine ladies, since I was nearby."

Baffled by his flirtatious words, she sat mute.

Miss Barton filled the gap, batting her eyes. "Charmed."

"Miss Cabot?" His gaze skewered her. "I especially wanted to speak with you."

Rosanna opened her mouth to respond with grace, anger fading, when the bell sounded again. Oh, no. That most annoying man, Lord Halburt. Now she wouldn't hear what her mysterious neighbor was about to say. He'd surely not speak it in front of this— intruder. Where did *that* word come from?

"My fine neighbors! So many friends gathered in one place. No doubt there are a few scones left?" Halburt's weak jest fell flat.

"Perhaps you'd like to look in the case. Over there." Peter moved his hand in a dismissive flap.

But Halburt ignored the hint. He stood, as if waiting.

For what? She'd bark before she'd invite the popinjay to join them. Especially since he'd encroached just when Peter was about to say something—surely something more intriguing than what Halburt would spew.

He propped his hand upon his walking stick— clearly a practiced pose—with one ankle crossed in front of the other. "Ladies? Oh, and you too, Winstead.

I finally heard from Purdie—that's Walter Scott's aide. The great man will be travelling to see the Regent and has acquiesced to honor Halburt Arms with a visit to break their travel."

"Walter Scott? Oh, my," Miss Barton breathed out the words on a swell of awe. "I've been reading his *Lady of the Lake*. Will we meet him?"

The man preened as he spoke. "That is entirely possible. He's not asked to be shielded from his public."

"Well, thank you for informing us of your news." Rosanna tried to infuse her tone with a hint of farewell, but he didn't get the message.

"Miss Cabot?"

Please go away. "Yes, Lord Halburt?"

"I was hoping, Miss Cabot…"

Oh, how he blabbered.

"…you would consent to holding one of those famously entertaining treasure hunts your home, Honor's Point," he nodded at Peter, "is famous for."

"I believe I told you I know nothing of treasure hunts, and little of the past owners' practices regarding hospitality in my home. I'm afraid I possess no real interest nor obligation to continue what may very well have been a delightful diversion." She fiddled with her teacup handle, pinky raised.

"Winstead, tell her." He nudged Peter with his elbow, and Peter sidled away, out of reach. "Tell her the fun we used to have."

"Halburt, I shall not join you in pressuring Miss Cabot, but yes, the hunts were amusing. Why do you think it so important to offer one while Scott bides with you?"

"The man is a treasure hunter *extraordinaire*. He's

not only a genius as a writer, but he possesses a serious avocation of locating and collecting historical troves. They say he's on the trail of the missing Scottish regalia."

Rosanna rattled her cup in its saucer, hoping the shop woman would appear to break up this annoying intrusion. "Any treasure hunt I could concoct would not have a worthy treasure at its end—not worthy enough for your guest, I fear."

"Are you sure, Miss Cabot?"

"I'm hardly going to put up one of Honor's Point's historically significant items as a prize for an evening's diversion."

"Even so, perhaps he'll find the Honor's Point treasure I've heard whispers of these long years."

She gasped at the insensitivity of mentioning this in front of Peter. "My Lord Halburt, cease with your plaints. I'll hear no more of this. Mayhap I shall consider it, but not another word to spoil two ladies' outing." With a decisive turn of her shoulder, she ended the conversation.

Out of the corner of her eye, she could see Winstead hustling a protesting Halburt toward the door with a firm grip on the fop's forearm.

After shoving Halburt out through the door, Winstead called over his shoulder. "We gents bid you ladies *adieu*. We must get to the inn because Halburt has to check for a message from his guest. Perhaps the inn holds a treasure." And with that, they were out the door, and the bell clanged.

"My, oh my, how time flies, I fear two hours are almost gone." Barton repositioned her shawl and checked her bonnet ties.

With a pained sigh, Rosanna snatched up her

reticule. "At least those two aren't dogging our steps." She rose, left ample coin on the table, and led the way out, thanking the tea woman for the service.

Ensconced in the carriage and leaving the village, Rosanna spied the graveyard again, and her thoughts flew. Having come away from his grieving, and about to broach something, Winstead stopped when Halburt intruded. What was it he was about to say? An apology? Perhaps—anything to allay the stiff, cool air resting between them like a gray cloud. But should forgiveness come so easily, in light of his trickery?

19

"Oh, no." Rosanna spotted a carriage parked near the front door of the Honor's Point manor house. "Don't let it be Halburt."

From the direction of the stables, two small grooms appeared to open the carriage door and let down the steps.

Rosanna hastened down the carriage steps and moved toward the house, reticule strings twined through tense fingers.

Perkins emerged. The disgruntled butler held the door open. He stiffly leaned forward as she passed, voice just above a whisper, "Miss, you have a caller."

"I see. I presume by the crest on the coach, it's our neighbor, Lord Halburt?"

"Yes, Miss. It's him."

She whispered back, "Could you not tell him that I wasn't home?"

"I tried, Miss. But this partic'lar lord o' the realm would not be gainsaid. He shoved past me claimin' he met you in yon village and your conversation was interrupted."

"It's not your fault, Perkins, so don't look so sad."

"Thank ye, Miss. Is it true?"

Not wanting to openly state Halburt's lie to a servant, she bordered on prevarication herself. "Oh, yes. We were talking in the village tea shop, to be sure.

Give it not another thought."

Once in the hall, she left off her gloves, bonnet, and parasol and moved toward the stairs. "Perkins, there's a package for Dot in the carriage. Please take it to her room. Also, send Dot to my room. Miss Barton and I will be down in a nonce—if our neighbor inquires. He'll need to be patient."

Rosanna untied her own boots, as she awaited Dot. She kicked them off, sending them across the rug and shuddering to a halt against the molding. "That man does plague me. Ooh." She unbuttoned her spencer, took it off, and about to throw it to join the boots, halted when Dot entered. "Oh, Dot. Thank you for coming to help. I'd like to change into one of my white figured muslins. The one with the key border."

"Yes, miss."

"I'll wash off my travel dust while you get it out and check it over. One of my muslins has a small tear near the back of the hem. I can't remember which."

"Yes, miss."

"Perhaps you can find it as well and see to mending it." She turned away from Dot, loosened the round gown, one of the few she could doff on her own, before yanking it off over her head. She sank down onto the bench, clad only in her chemise, and took out her hairpins in front of the looking glass. She massaged her temples, elbows resting on the dressing table.

"Headache, miss?" Dot snatched up the discarded gown, shook it, then draped it over her arm. She busied herself at the wardrobe, hung the dress and located the white one with the key design.

"No, simply tired. My head gets tired from this," she shook her heavy, dusky curls, "weighing it down."

"If we pin in a different place, it will ease the

ache."

"Excellent, Dot. Did Miss Barton tell you that trick?"

"No, miss, I learned that on me own. Have ye washed yet, miss?"

"No, I'll do that now, thank you for the reminder. I have a guest waiting below." Grim, she soaked a cloth and wiped her face and hands, then bent over the bowl to splash up water. Drips cascaded down her arms as she reached for the towel Dot held out.

The maid took the dampened towel and blotted a few drops Rosanna missed. She set it aside, picked up the requested white muslin dress and held it ready to assist.

Fastened into the dress, hair repositioned with pins in new places, Rosanna felt a bit more inclined to think she could handle seeing Lord Halburt again. Twice in one morning posed a trial—but with God's help, a surmountable one.

"Dot, come with me, and sit in a corner chair."

Whispering a prayer for patience, she descended to the drawing room where Perkins placed the visitor. She wouldn't say guest, because guest meant someone invited, didn't it? "Lord Halburt, what a surprise. You must have raced home to beat me here."

"Ah, Miss Cabot, it is a veritable vision you present to me." He clutched the front of his ornate waistcoat with one hand and threw the other over his forehead as if to swoon. "Who wouldn't race—nay, move heaven and earth—to drink in your beauty?"

Ignoring this overblown praise, she sailed past him and walked to the window. "Rain may come this day. Perhaps you'd best get home, so you don't get soaked."

That thought clearly made the vain man gasp, but he recovered with his own notion. "If it rains, I'd merely stay here. Then I wouldn't be caught out in it. Cozy indoors with a lovely lady friend. Nothing to dislike about that."

Itching to wipe the self-satisfied smirk off the man's face, she rounded on him with a pointed question. "Why are you here, sir?"

He tucked a thumb in his waistcoat pocket and struck a pose while speaking. "Why? What man needs a reason to seek out your fair face?"

"Come now. What is it? Are you planning to ply me about the treasure hunt?"

"Perhaps. But I have some other questions, first. Your friend, er houseguest—Ellie Moore—how fares that young lady? I noticed she did not accompany you and that wonder of dignity, Miss Barton, to town. Is she ill?"

"No, sirrah. She had something else to do. Here, at the house." *Why did I even answer this fop? He talks so much, it must be contagious.*

"What occupies that fair maiden? She's mysterious."

"That is none of your affair. I'm afraid you love a mystery a little too much for your own good. Mundane matters kept her home." More to get rid of him than to please him, she threw out a bone. "I will take the time to consider holding a treasure hunt here at Honor's Point. When you pin down the dates of your guest's stay at Halburt Arms, please inform me."

"You'll accommodate me, then?"

"Sir, please don't put it that way. I will consider entertaining your honored guest, if I am able to see my way clear. If I have no qualms or conflicts. I must study it out. Please, no more on this topic." Dealing with this man would add steel to her spine—she needed it. She glanced at Dot, who, with downcast eyes, must have heard this whole idiotic exchange.

"Then, if we can't discuss your delightful plans, before I leave you, I insist you take me on a stroll about the house." The man's voice dropped to a wheedle. So undignified.

"I suppose, but the servants are cleaning, and I don't want them disturbed. We may just peek into some of the rooms."

"Oh, that will be a treat!"

"Dot, please escort me." The man was a child in Adonis's clothing—would he leave soon—please? She led him to her study, and, blocking his entry with her arm across the doorway, allowed him only to poke his head in through the crack of the door. "I have private correspondence sitting out and surely you wouldn't expect me to let anyone to be privy to that." She closed the door with a snap, wishing she could catch his chiseled nose.

"And here is the dining room. Have you seen it in daylight?" She allowed him to enter the room and she stood back while he goggled. *If I didn't know better, I'd think him a poor man, not a wealthy, titled lord.* He reeked of covetousness—a form of poverty, no matter the earthly wealth.

He spoke with reverence. "These panels, these paintings, these cabinets—divine."

Sickened by his lust for material goods, she next took him to the library where he oohed and aahed over the leather ranks in the dim shelves. "Do you read, Lord Halburt?"

"No. But I collect valuable books. Lord Winstead's

father sold me some priceless tomes toward the end." He stroked the spines of a few books, then extracted a cloth from a pocket and studiously wiped his fingers.

"Charming. Now we shall look at the ballroom, and that will be final stop on your tour."

Giving the man no choice but to follow, she swept out.

Dot scurried to keep up.

Rosanna entered the ballroom and stood off to one side of the door.

Halburt came in, gazed around, then swooped over, grabbed her, and capered out on the floor twirling her and prancing like a buffle-headed clunch.

Rosanna yanked free, and lifting her arm, pointed to the door. "Our tour, as well as your visit, is over. The butler will show you out."

"I meant no ill. Say you don't hate me. I couldn't bear that, dear beauty."

"This isn't about hating, or not hating, this is you leaving. Good-bye."

She visualized his tail between his legs as he slunk out. She gave a rueful snort at his impetuosity which appeared to come without an upper limit. She had little hope this was the end of his nonsense. The thought of arranging a treasure hunt at this man's request held no appeal. But she would enjoy entertaining a world-famous author—a once-in-a-lifetime opportunity.

20

Rosanna released an exhalation as Perkins gave the front door a firm latching. "If he appears here un-invited again, please don't admit him, unless you check with me first."

"Sorry, Miss. He barreled in, shoving past me afore I could say boo."

"I understand. Simply do your very best to keep him scarce. Now on a happier subject, please serve a light lunch for three in the morning room in half an hour."

"Oh, there you are, Miss Cabot. I'm so glad you're home." Ellie entered the hall on quiet feet. She wore a simple blue and white striped day dress and raised brows. "Did I hear Lord Halburt's voice a moment ago?"

Rosanna first wrung her hands lightly, deciding how much to say. But then, with a swoop of the arm, she linked hers with Ellie's, and guided her to the morning room. "We shall have lunch in a nonce. Let's visit while we wait, and I will tell you all about my day."

Once in the morning room, Rosanna latched the door and pressed her ear against it, listening. No reason to distrust the staff, but she didn't want to be overheard. "Dear Ellie." She paused, looking for the right words, then moved further into the room. "I'm not sure why, but Lord Halburt's annoying curiosity included several questions regarding you."

"Questions? About me? Why?"

"I don't know. On the face of it, his queries weren't too specific, or suspicious. But there was something that didn't sit right with me. He's annoyingly nosey."

"What did he ask?" Ellie's face blanched and her eyes filled with tears.

"Nothing terribly unusual. Questions such as, what were you doing this morning, and why didn't you go with me to the village." Rosanna wanted to brush it off, and downplay the potential threat of a snoopy neighbor, but in good conscience, had to inform Ellie.

"Ooh, that is worrisome. He is so curious, he might have suspicions about my presence here."

"Perhaps. But let's not rush to judgment. The man is such a nodcock, who could say what he's thinking?"

"It sickens me that such a vain, nosey man can threaten my peace of my mind so. That's why I must hasten to complete my work."

"How is your writing progressing?" Rosanna glanced at the clock and hoped Miss Barton would tarry.

"Fairly well. I am two-thirds of the way through my manuscript. I intend to become the next Mrs. Radcliffe."

"Mrs. Radcliffe? Her books are certainly popular. I've always known you liked to write, Ellie, but I recall you were a poet. Don't I remember you mooning around at academy with reams of poems flowing from your hands at all hours?"

Ellie snickered. "Yes, that would be my

recollection as well. But you see, as a mature woman now, I must write what I most likely could sell to a publisher."

"Must write?"

"I must write so that I can pay my way in life. As of now, I can't access my funds. I won't live off your kindness for years on end."

"You have always been so clever. I am sure you will succeed."

"Thank you for your vote of confidence."

"Contrast your intentions to publish with my disastrous scheme. Here I create a refuge, have no way to announce it, and then I don't even think of the futures of the women who might come."

"Darling Rosanna. Don't blame yourself for those little oversights. How would you have known? You simply wanted to help out of the goodness of your heart. I, for one, am grateful."

"Your coming here is a blessing to me, so enough of that. I suppose covering the old ground of my errors will not get us anywhere. What type of novel are you writing?"

"I am penning a romance. A close reading and study of Mrs. Radcliffe's style provided me with a starting point. I've analyzed what I think are the secrets to her success. My story, therefore, is full of mysterious castles, dungeons, and near-disasters, such as maidens dangling from cliffs and the like."

"The novel—such an exciting development in literary style. Do you have a pen name selected?"

"Not yet. It will be Mrs. somebody, as that is the fashion. Who knows if those authors are married—or even women?"

Rosanna smiled, and laid her hand on Ellie's arm.

"I will think of some pen names for you—it will be fun for me. Mrs. Sanderton? Mrs. Wellstone? My contribution to the success of London's next publishing sensation."

"You've not read one word of my novel but thank you for your confidence. Once complete, I shall have to clear the hurdle of locating a publisher."

"Let's cross that bridge together, Ellie. Perhaps Mr. Clough or even Perkins would consent to go in disguise to proffer your manuscript to the highest bidder?" Rosanna could barely contain her snorts of laughter at the mental pictures thus created.

Ellie's laughter trilled. "It might help to have a man present the manuscript. Even with the success of Mrs. Radcliffe and her sort, a dim eye is still cast upon authoresses. Some even publish under names such as 'a lady' or under male pen names. Back to Lord Halburt. I don't suppose he could have any knowledge of my scribbling penchant, so why was he asking those questions?"

"He is a first-class snoop and a gossip. Perhaps he pokes and pries on a regular basis. I'll find a subtle way to ask Perkins or Mrs. Good for more information on the insufferable man's habits. But it won't do to raise their curiosity about you, either."

~*~

Peter kicked at a loose stone on the path. Eager to unburden his guilt, he found his feet taking him to his old home. Honor's Point, the most beautiful estate in the county, perhaps the entire south of England, drew him like a magnet today, but it wasn't any longer due to a frustrated desire for the property. It was a desire to set things right between him and Miss Cabot.

His reasons for keeping his identity from her appeared sound at first. But in retrospect, he wasn't proud of the unnecessary deception. She'd done nothing to deserve his deceitfulness. Thus resolved, he pointed his boots in her direction.

Safe to presume she'd be home by now, done with lunch, and ready for any afternoon visitors. He planned his words as he strode on—toward an improbable yet important meeting. Why this sense of destiny? It was a simple visit, albeit a slightly uncomfortable one, since he'd be apologizing for his idiotic masquerade.

A good thing, too, to get it out of the way. He'd be at Lady Brook's dinner party with Rosanna tomorrow night—a formal affair, with no chance to convey his regrets in that public setting. Better now.

Allowed entry by a broadly smiling Perkins, he was bade to wait in the drawing room. Ah, there was his once-favorite armchair. To sit, or stand, waiting for his hostess? No idea how long she'd be, he chose the chair, and soon dozed in the warm sunlight streaming through the French doors.

"Ahem. Lord Winstead? Are you awake?"

Abrupt in departure from a fleeting dream about fishing, he leapt to his feet, cheeks warm. "Yes, yes, fully awake. Miss Cabot." A bow seemed in order—perhaps that would raise his level of credibility. As he bent over, arms in perfect gentlemanly position, he berated himself—how could he allow sleep to overtake him like that? Her opinion of him was low enough already.

"Perkins said you'd called, but I was delayed.

Training my new maid. Dot, make your curtsey, and please do sit over there for a time." Rosanna gestured toward the farthest corner of the room, then seated herself in a pretty blue and ivory damask armchair near the window.

Such spirit, and that color she wore—he'd never liked violet before...but it was decidedly exquisite on her. He tore his gaze away, suddenly shy in her presence. He knew what needed to be said, however, and he wouldn't shirk his self-imposed duty. Not after coming all this way. "Mother liked beauty, but comfort stood high in her criteria as well when choosing home furnishings. Do you like that chair? It was one she favored." There, that brought the subject into the arena.

"It's very charming."

Her voice sounded curt. He needed to go forth with his plan. "You've made a good choice with this home. I hope you'll be happy here."

Miss Cabot's fingertips came up, covering her lips for a moment, then she dropped her hand, clenching it in her lap. "Surely you haven't come to comb over that sore subject?"

"No, absolutely not. I am here for a completely different reason. I owe you an apology."

"La, sir. For what?"

Did he detect a tremble? Fear? Or simple embarrassment? "For deceiving you, upon our first few meetings."

"Deceit. That is a sin." Her fingers flew up again, and her cheeks flushed.

What a darling. "Indeed." Lowering his voice, he tried again. "I shan't try to excuse it. You're right. It is a sin to deceive one's neighbor." *One as pretty as you, for certain.* "When you stopped on the road, I was experiencing a wretched day—one of my worst. Having trouble accepting my newly reduced circumstances."

"Oh, my lord, you don't have to tell me this." She fluttered her delicate fingers, still blushing. "All's forgiven."

"But I do want you to understand, I bore no ill motives. The moment got away from me, shall we say? And then, the time you came to my door, and of course, when I came upon you in the woods, I couldn't find the words. I simply let you continue to believe I was some sort of rough cob of a tenant."

"Rough cob, you? Never did I think that. Well, almost never."

He gave a bark of laughter at that. "So kind of you to let me off the hook this way. What can I do to repay you for my misdeeds toward you?"

"Let's cry friends. And if there's ever an opportunity to repay me, I shall not hesitate to seek your aid."

Ah, could she be any sweeter? No, and he'd die before he caused her one more bit of distress. "I shall wait on bated breath for a chance to be your champion."

"How well do you know Lord Halburt?"

Egad, was she asking about that annoying cur because she liked him? "Well enough." There, that was diplomatic.

"I suppose you've known him since boyhood, growing up together, living on adjoining estates."

"I knew of him. But he and his family travelled about quite often, so we were rarely playmates, as one would expect due to proximity. No, we encountered each other infrequently." And he preferred it that way.

"He seems like a curious man."

"Curiously behaved, do you mean?"

"Oh, no. I mean curious such as asking questions."

"Curious is one word for it. Has he been nosing around here again?"

"Again? Not exactly."

"The man can be annoying. I recall him pestering my father, on one of his last and infrequent sojourns here, peppering him with questions about mysteries, treasures, lost fortunes, and so forth."

"Then he has a habit of that. He's been by here, poking, and prodding with questions. So unamusing."

Miss Cabot was generous. The man was something far worse than un-amusing in Peter's opinion, but she was so kind. An urge to enfold this darling woman in an embrace soared through him, and for a moment, he had to restrain his arms from their wont to wrap around her slim shoulders. His lips tingled with desire to touch hers. He stood, to shake off those wayward fantasies, and then moved over to face the far window.

The quiet maid sat across the room with her head down and fingers flying over some piece of stitchery.

He pushed aside the drape and leaned forward to view the sky. Another glorious, early summer day. He turned away from the window. "Looks clear, no clouds. Might I interest you in a stroll around the grounds, Miss Cabot?"

"Yes. I must say, the paths here are a delight. I can hardly let a day go by without venturing out for a walk."

Assisting her to her feet allowed him to hold her hand. So soft. Wait, he dare not drift to those thoughts.

She was not for him. He shouldn't toy with her…or himself. Just be her friend.

"Dot, please accompany me. I don't know where Miss Barton is, but you'll certainly benefit from some fresh air." She turned to Peter with a confiding air. "Miss Barton is more than likely napping. The shopping in the village wore her out. Surprising, since she was used to London."

"The shops of Woodvale are few."

"True, but perhaps it is all the fresh air here that promotes good rest. That, and the delicious light lunch we had when we got home." Fingertips flew up again. "I am sorry, I just start to natter, and then…"

Delighted, he let out a guffaw. "Don't be concerned. I enjoy a spot of chatter. Life can be so serious."

A cloud passed over her brow. He wanted to kiss it away, but didn't suppose he should, not with the maid nearby. And not in any case.

Out in the hall, she handed the maid a parasol almost as tall as she was, selected a chip straw bonnet from the hall tree and tied it under her chin.

He took her elbow, and guided Miss Cabot down the steps, passing Perkins, who beamed before closing the door with a satisfied thump.

Peter extended his arm toward Miss Cabot, she took his cue, and laid her hand on his forearm. "I know a route. We'll start on this path over here, west of the house, and wind our way around to the rose garden on the east."

He glanced back to see Dot about twenty feet behind, walking along, occupied with swinging her mistress's parasol like a plaything. The feel of Miss Cabot's hand on his arm gave him a shiver of pleasure that traversed his body and fizzed through his veins.

"Lord Winstead, I am concerned that my prattle will give you a poor opinion of me. You'll think me more hair than wit. But I do study such things as the Bible, poetry, and now, of course, land management."

She looked up with those velvety brown eyes and he'd have believed anything she cared to say. "I assure you that your intellect is not in question. I find your company to be stimulating." That didn't sound too earthy, he hoped.

She moved her hand off his forearm and threaded it under his arm, and soon their elbows were linked in a companionable way that made his face hurt from smiling. He'd kick himself later for the hope that rose within, but for now, he'd simply enjoy the walk.

Which he did, until a pesky commotion occurred in the form of one of the grooms, who ran up, panting.

Peter loosened her arm and turned.

The lad tugged a forelock. "Miss Cabot, Steward Bramstock sent me after you. He's waiting in the library." Having delivered his message, the groom turned tail and scurried off.

Rosanna faced Lord Winstead, and as if choreographed, he found her hands cradled in his.

Her trusting eyes gazed into his. "I must go back. Something's come awry upon the estate. The steward needs my assistance with some decision."

A pang lanced through his core. This pained him—it should be him who needed to attend to urgent estate matters, not her.

"Dot, we are returning to the house, come along." She smiled sweetly and raised a hand in farewell, turned away and was gone.

21

The appointed hour arrived the next evening, and the carriage wheels ceased their rhythmic crunching on the gravel as the coachman stopped in front of Brook House. The warm brick of the imposing home glowed in the setting sun. The scent of viburnum shrubbery perfumed the air.

Rosanna attempted to suppress the pulsating anticipation coursing through her veins as they traveled the short distance to the Brook mansion. She hated to admit it, but the expectation of the appearance of Lord Winstead caused her inner effervescence. No matter how she tried, the yearnings refused to go away. Yesterday's emergency robbed her of time with him. And the worst was that it hadn't been an urgent matter at all. Taking a deep breath, and imposing steely self-control, she concentrated instead on making Ellie comfortable.

"I can reassure you, my dear, that no one at the party will have any knowledge of your true identity." She patted Ellie's hand to comfort her, but the little redhead was trembling, down to her silk evening slippers.

"Are you sure?" Ellie's voice was a mere whisper, yet serious and intent.

"You want to hide here, but there's no need, with reasonable precautions, for you to become a hermitlike wraith, never appearing in public."

"Rosanna, you especially should understand all too well the type of pressures I escaped. And the ghastly idea of discovery and a forced return to London only to be required to take part in a distasteful arranged marriage makes me quake."

"To the best of my knowledge, you are safe here."

Agitated, Ellie smoothed the front of her pretty gown of willow green embossed satin. A silver netted shawl along with silvery jewelry and hair ornaments completed a stunning toilette. "If you're sure."

"Try to relax. Fear of the unknown is wearing on you. Once we get inside, you'll discover all is well." Rosanna turned to Miss Barton for reinforcement. "Isn't that true, Miss Barton? Tell Miss Moore."

The older woman gave reassurance. "Miss Moore, Miss Cabot and I will take care of you. It's quite sure Lady Brook has only invited a few neighbors. We already know all of them, don't we?"

One of those in attendance would be Lord Winstead. This thought made Rosanna's heart pound, and so to change the subject off this personally volatile note, she commented on Miss Barton's apparel. "That dark blue is perfect on you, Miss Barton. You look so nice."

The companion wore a simple, yet attractive dark blue evening gown. She'd altered and trimmed in satin one of her existing day gowns, since the dresses from the village seamstress were not ready yet.

"Thank you, dear." In high alt, and preening, the companion looked quite regal in her satin shawl and jeweled hairpin borrowed from Rosanna.

Rosanna's nerves calmed as thoughts moved off herself. Loyal Miss Barton, the daughter of a humble clergyman, began in service as a nurse, since she had no relatives to take her in when orphaned. Elevating the woman who had been so faithful and more of a friend than a servant, to a status more suitable to her birth gave Rosanna pleasure and satisfaction. Miss Barton could enter society with her head high.

A groom held the horses while footmen stepped up to assist the three ladies from Honor's Point to descend the carriage steps.

With a sweeping gesture, the butler announced their entry, booming, "Miss Cabot, Miss Moore, Miss Barton."

Followed by her entourage, Rosanna entered the room and performed a proper curtsey to Lady Brook. The hostess, seated near the fireplace, chided. "Lovely, Miss Cabot, but do get up. Just watching you do that makes my bones ache. We don't stand on such ceremony here."

Rosanna straightened, smoothing her coral silk gown.

Ellie and Barton smiled their relief at not having to perform curtseys.

Oh, well. At least she'd learned something at academy. Curtseying took effort and skill. While mannerly and somewhat balletic to see, one also had to make sure to adjust one's curtsey to the rank of the recipient. Any sane woman happily dispensed with the showy maneuver.

The surrounding guests chuckled with amusement at Lady Brook's edict banning further curtseying.

As if magnetized, Rosanna's gaze landed on Lord Winstead, and his eyes locked on hers until she turned and unfurled her fan. So warm all of a sudden.

Was his adjustment to once again appearing in

society quite uncomfortable after his time of semi-anonymous seclusion? So many things she wondered about. The awkwardness that his masquerade as a country laborer was at an end.

He stood in a semi-circle with Halburt and the minister, Mr. Clough. The men began a series of bows, one to each arriving lady. Perhaps they too wished someone would say 'enough!'

Lady Brook took control. "Ladies, please be seated, so the gents can sit down. Frimley, pass the refreshments."

The butler brought over a rolling cart laden with iced lemonade for the ladies and arrack punch for the men.

All greetings complete, the minister sat next to Miss Barton. He spoke first. "Tis a blessing to have three such fine ladies join the congregation."

Miss Barton simpered. "How kind."

Rosanna sank into the nearest chair, relieved for something solid beneath her after the initial contact with Lord Winstead. "Mr. Clough, I am sure it will be a blessing for us as well." She planned to make even more time for spiritual life now that she didn't have the distractions of London and the distraction of the battle to avoid marriage.

Clough turned away to converse with Miss Barton. "Miss Barton, where was your father's parish?"

Rosanna overheard bits and pieces of their animated conversation which showed every sign of continuing on since the two had their heads together.

Halburt, Ellie, and Lady Brook were seated across from Rosanna and well into a discussion of the merits of the local architecture. Ellie did a lot of nodding, while the other two traded numerous comments upon the excellencies of their own ancestral homes, the state of their mortar and shingles, as well as the splendor of their gardens. Ellie may have her ears talked off, but with no strangers present she'd be happy.

Lord Winstead settled into a chair next to hers. Rosanna wasn't altogether sure she wanted to speak one-on-one with him because of the emotions his presence stirred within her. He ended up next to her by default simply because all the others were grouped and conversing. The awkwardness of owning his beloved former estate loomed large in her mind, her nervousness a great contrast to when they were alone yesterday, and easy with each other.

His low, vibrant voice disrupted the obvious silence that had fallen over their part of the room. "You've had time to recover from learning that I am Lord Winstead, former owner of your home? And do you continue to forgive me, in good accord as we parted yesterday?"

"Did I not say so?"

"You did, but I need reassurance."

Was he flirting? Perhaps. No beating around the bush there. "Indeed," she murmured. Within, she tested her emotions. The embarrassment inherent in this situation was a painful touchstone—like an emotional toothache—freezing out her usual warmth and creating a stiff shadow over her true nature.

Stymied, she searched her social repertoire for a way out. No smooth words presented themselves, instead, she blurted, "I think you know 'twas shabby of you to let me think otherwise." He had asked for forgiveness, so why open the wound again? The confrontational remark welled out of the remnants of anger lurking in her heart. It seemed to her now that he almost led her on under false pretenses. But had he? Or had her own stubborn foolishness in walking out alone gotten her embroiled in this embarrassment?

"I had my reasons."

"I'm sure." Incorrigible. He dared to be abrupt with her. In her opinion, he should still act the supplicating gentleman, regardless of who was at fault. Perhaps beg for her forgiveness yet again.

Time seemed to drag because of this inelegant situation. Would their hostess never announce a move into the dining room? Rosanna covertly studied Lord Winstead, superimposing the image he presented tonight over her earlier encounters with him. The man's severe black evening clothes and snowy cravat suited him well.

Yesterday, he'd truly humbled himself. Even to the point of seeking her out in the village, then calling on her at home. The stroll in the garden had been...lovely. *How awkward this must be for him.* Sympathy welled, coming out of nowhere. His voice drew her out of her rambling thoughts.

"Was your meeting with Bramstock urgent?"

"Bramstock?" What did he mean? "Oh...yes. I mean, no. Not urgent, but rather that he'd become impatient for my decision about how many bags of wheat seed to order."

"I see. Unfortunate that our walk was interrupted. I hope attending to such a large estate doesn't weigh too heavily on you."

"So far, no. But it is a large responsibility. Especially with the lack of sunshine this year." The topic too close for comfort—she angled away, feigning interest in a painting.

A vague memory of having seen him at one ball or

another crawled to the surface of her mind. Had he participated in the marriage mart hanging out for a rich wife in an attempt to save his estate? Not that he didn't have every right to do so.

Whether or not he'd been trying for an heiress didn't really matter. She turned toward him with a question. "Did you take part in the London Season this year at all?"

The hunted expression on his face caused another wash of pity for him to sweep over her. He looked stricken—he must have failed in heiress-hunting, hence the loss of his estate. When would dinner be announced? This tension wore on her.

"Yes, I was there. Perhaps we were at some of the same parties. How, ah, amusing that our paths should cross out here in this rustic region." His facial expression clouded over even more.

What was he thinking? Clearly something weighed on his mind. Whatever it was, she wasn't sure she wanted to find out. He looked so blue-deviled, and the easy camaraderie of yesterday couldn't be re-established.

She reminded herself that she wasn't responsible at all for the dire circumstances which brought down his fortunes. She merely bought a beautiful estate in good faith. With those thoughts came another hearty pang of compassion for anyone who had to give up a property as stunning and gorgeous as Honor's Point.

Squire Bredon was announced. A debonair older man entered, and then moved to greet Lady Brook, before avidly kissing her hand. The numbers were now even. Rosanna noticed a flush stealing over Lady Brook's cheeks. Rosanna caught Ellie's glance and raised her brows, smiling. Ellie nodded surreptitiously in return, then lowered her lashes, acknowledging deliverance from her fears.

Turning back to Winstead, who still sat at her side, she decided to throw out a white flag. "As I said yesterday, we must cry friends. I hold nothing against you for allowing me to think you a humble cottager. I forgave you."

"I wasn't sure. Your attitude tonight seemed to belie yesterday's accord."

"So true. With our time abbreviated yesterday when I was called away, I became confused when I saw you again. The somewhat hurtful truth stung fresh again." She watched him as he processed her words. She didn't want the oddness of it all to continue to hang on between them.

He looked into her eyes and smiled in clear relief. His gaze caressed her from head to toe, taking in the silky coral gown. "I failed to mention the sheer loveliness that is you this evening. When you wore violet, I had no idea such loveliness could be surpassed." Lips slightly parted, he clearly had more to say, but the moment passed.

Lady Brook's butler announced dinner.

The group of guests in the room swam back into Rosanna's consciousness as all rose for the procession into the dining room.

She gave Lord Winstead a warm and encouraging smile, he nodded, and a spark passed between them. "I would like it to no end if you'd call on me again tomorrow, Lord Winstead."

22

"It's time for dinner." Lady Brook stood and thus began the arranging of couples by precedence. Lord Halburt claimed the hostess, his and her titles being the highest of each gender present.

Next in precedence came Lord Winstead. "I shall be honored to take Miss Cabot to dinner." He inclined his head, lifting one brow in question. A willing Rosanna stepped up and laid her hand on his extended forearm.

Squire Bredon, with a jolly air, smiled at Ellie and held out his arm. She murmured her assent and they followed the previous couple toward the dining room.

Mr. Clough cleared his throat, "Miss Barton, you are left with no choice. Do me the honor?"

Miss Barton's cheeks colored as she laid her hand on the minister's arm. "Why yes. I am honored."

Rosanna's intuition tingled. Questions later, she fought a smug smile.

The guests entered the dining room and Lady Brook directed them to their seats. "Halburt, you're on my right, Lord Winstead my left. You're next to Miss Cabot. Miss Moore, to Lord Halburt's right. Squire, you're to Miss Moore's right. Mr. Clough, please preside at the head of the table with Miss Barton on your right. There." She sat down with a whoosh of skirts billowing about her and let out a feathery laugh.

Rosanna reached her chair only to find Lord

Winstead there before her, and the heat rose up her neck as he solicitously helped her into her seat. Her arm prickled with delicious attraction when his hand brushed her skin.

"Very good, everyone. Since we are informal, please forgive the lack of place cards. I shall attempt to do better next time." Lady Brook then turned to her left and began to share repartee with Lord Winstead.

Rosanna felt quite awkward. Here she was, sandwiched on her right by Lord Winstead, the source of the most embarrassing situation she'd ever faced and on her left, righteous Miss Barton, by whom she'd been dressed down for happening to meet the man in the woods.

Miss Barton tendered a dinner table topic. "This soup is delicious, is it not, Rosanna?"

The commonplace words helped Rosanna through this rough moment. She responded with gratitude. "Yes, so delicious. Have you tasted the lobster salad? I recommend it." There, not even one quaver in her voice. Feeling stronger, and about to turn to her right and say something neutral to Winstead, she was interrupted.

Halburt, from across the table, made a bid for her attention. Halburt appeared to be asking her something.

"So sorry, I was woolgathering. You asked?" Her right side tingled with awareness of Lord Winstead. Why, since he was just another neighbor?

"I fondly remember the traditional treasure hunts that used to be held at Honor's Point. That was such a treat." Across the white linen expanse, Halburt's eyes gleamed at her. He pointedly waited for an answer.

Why, the man acted like a discourteous child.

What on earth would possess him to refer to events from the Winstead family's years as owners of the estate? Did he not have an ounce of discretion?

"I have no real knowledge of any treasure hunts. Other than you asking about them. Perhaps you can enlighten him, Lord Winstead?" She hated to carry this into his lap, but she really didn't know how else to respond.

"Those are bygone days. Some members of the older generation were prone to creative entertainments back in their era." His frosty tone by all rights should serve to quell the bumptious neighbor, Lord Halburt.

Rosanna's ears burned, so embarrassed for Lord Winstead having to speak about the past when those very days of excess led to the eventual loss of his lands.

Halburt, however, did not recognize a set-down when one smacked him in the face. "I remember those wonderful treasure hunts so fondly. Such a lark they were. If you'd be so kind, Miss Cabot, to ask the housekeeper if she remembers the details of how it was carried out?"

"I'm not sure I'm interested in recreating that tradition."

"You could have a treasure hunt for tradition's sake. That would be a true delight. Perhaps when my esteemed guest, the poet Walter Scott, comes to visit?"

The square-jawed, handsome lord's comical yearning expression looked like a child hoping for a treat. Stifling an urge to laugh in his face, she gave a response that half assented. She mumbled, "As I said before, perhaps."

To avoid any further queries or requests, she applied herself to the beef and Brussels sprouts. Never had she been so glad to see a full plate in front of her.

23

Rosanna's eyes opened. Drapes pulled back, sun shone into the room. A cup of chocolate steamed on a tray next to her bed. Groggy after her late night, she sat up and reached for the eye-opening beverage.

Though soon wide awake after a few stimulating sips, she closed her eyes again. Prayer seemed like the best way to start the day. *Lord, please protect this household, and guide me* ...more thoughts flowed from her mind and heart. It felt so good and so right to pour out her cares to her Heavenly Father.

The duties she carried as mistress of a large estate lay heavier on her shoulders than expected. Though satisfying to have Ellie here, the unanticipated corresponding weight of responsibility set her to worrying.

What of Ellie's future? Though her goal of escaping from the trap of being married for her fortune and bloodlines was accomplished for now, what about next year, the year after, or ten years from now? Should she really encourage Ellie to remain single and alone even if only by tacit approval? Such heavy questions to ponder.

With a start, she sat up in bed, eyes wide open due to her a sudden revelation. *What if I were to marry someday?* How would that play out? Would Ellie continue on in her refuge status permanently?

Rosanna needed to have a talk with her.

It could be a tragedy for the Ellie to live burrowed away here with life passing her by. Not something to be decided by default. Too momentous. When planning a refuge for young ladies fleeing forced marriage, she'd only thought of providing the place of escape, not realizing the liabilities and emotional toll involved. Getting away from a horrid arranged marriage was a good thing, but an entire lifetime hidden away didn't seem right. She'd hate to see Ellie locked into a situation in which she lived all her days hidden from the world.

Not that she found Ellie to be burdensome or unpleasant. No, spending time with someone near her own age blessed her. They must discuss some scenarios for the future. The inconsistency of her own position flirted on the edges of her logical mind. Pushing the errant thought away, Rosanna threw off the covers and scrabbled on her desk for pen and paper to add 'discuss future - EM' to one of her lists.

Flopping back into bed, mind spinning with concern, she pulled a pillow over her head. Lord willing, Ellie's presence wouldn't produce serious problems. Rosanna would get used to the new burdens. Through running Honor's Point, she'd already gained more experience in decisiveness and initiative.

Whatever her own future held was just that—future—and she would know what was right for her. She wasn't accustomed to being a leader or having any bearing on another's life decisions, but she'd give Ellie's dilemma a top priority. Responsibility was beginning to feel normal, but merely providing a refuge had unexpected consequences and baggage.

~*~

Dot assisted her again this morning. That proceeded well. The small decision of choosing a new lady's maid made another step toward becoming confident at running an estate.

Attired in a jonquil day dress, sprigged with apple green, the matching ribbons danced as she skipped down the lavish oak stairs toward the hot breakfast served in the dining room each morning. Rosanna made selections from chafing dishes on the sideboard. Bacon, eggs, ham, and applesauce—she had plans for the morning and ate heartily.

A handy footman glided forward to seat her, and another poured hot coffee.

Her companion arrived and joined her at the table, her plate containing only a piece of bacon. Rosanna passed the sugar bowl. "Here you are, my dear Miss Barton—for your coffee."

"No, thank you. I'm reducing."

"I see. Taking a page out of Dr. Fanting's popular book?"

"Yes. Limiting white foods. Such a late night I haven't had since London. After midnight." She sipped her coffee with obvious contentment.

"Yes, it was quite the affair." Rosanna nibbled her second piece of bacon.

"Such an exceedingly delightful evening last night, don't you agree?" Miss Barton said, after a brief silent prayer.

"Yes, and Mr. Clough is quite congenial, is he not?" Rosanna couldn't resist teasing her staunch companion. She'd detected signs of a tendre, at least on Miss Barton's part.

"He's a wonderful minister, and that's what's important." Miss Barton gave a small harrumph and applied herself to nibbling her breakfast.

Rosanna decided to leave the topic of Mr. Clough's good qualities for another time. "Another thing that's important is getting your new dresses, as is due for your new status as companion. I am so glad we ordered those gowns."

"Mrs. Beaumont can only work so fast. She came as arranged two days ago."

"Were you satisfied with her skill?"

"Very much. I am grateful for the dresses, dear. And can't wait to wear them, especially to church."

Stifling her amusement, Rosanna turned to greet Ellie, who entered the room. "Good morning. This is perfect. The three of us can have a coze about the party last night."

Ellie's plate held only toast. "Toast and coffee. That's the ideal breakfast for me. If I eat more, I feel like a stuffed goose." She observed Rosanna's plate and backpedaled. "Of course, others don't feel like stuffed gooses, silly of me to say that."

"I don't mind, Ellie. I love a hearty breakfast, and I'm not easily offended." She wanted to put Ellie at ease. "Miss Barton eats lightly today as well."

"To be expected after the lavish meal last night. How did you like your various dinner partners?" Ellie sipped at the hot coffee.

Rosanna volunteered an answer. "Lord Halburt behaved quite different than I expected. So enthusiastic and youthful last night. All that interest in what amounts to a childish amusement." She hoped her remarks would deter questioning about Winstead.

Ellie raised her eyebrows and cut her toast into small pieces. "Childish amusements? Oh, you must mean his inane talk of treasure hunts. He seems to have a vast passion for them."

"His looks alone might lead one to expect him to be a paragon in all things. That chiseled profile, the thick hair, and his physique resembling one of those Greek statues, if I may say so." Rosanna looked over at Miss Barton with a smile, fully expecting a set down. Her companion did not disappoint.

"Miss Cabot. Referring to a man's build is thoroughly *outré*. You must refrain from such *risqué* talk. Really. Just because we live in the country, you needn't become coarse." Miss Barton rattled down her cup harder than necessary to emphasize her point.

Rosanna had all she could do to refrain from laughing. She liked to goad Miss Barton occasionally, all in good fun, but she felt a little guilty. "I'm sorry. Don't be angry. It's too beautiful a day for that." Her gaze turned toward the French doors of the dining room. Outside, a perfect day unfolded. "Who wants to walk with me?" She glanced from Ellie to Miss Barton. Giving them time to respond, she dabbed the corners of her mouth with her fine linen napkin, plunked it down next to her plate and pushed back her chair.

Ellie and Barton were each waiting for the other to answer.

Rosanna got the impression neither one wanted to take a stroll this morning. "Ladies, I have been told quite roundly that I am not to walk out alone any more. One of you will have to accompany me."

"That's correct. You must not wander about unescorted, even here."

In Rosanna's opinion, Miss Barton took undue satisfaction at setting a limit for her. Decisiveness was in order. "Since neither of you ladies want to go, I shall take Dot."

Rising, she rang the bell. When Perkins appeared, she requested that Dot be called upon to walk out with her.

"I highly approve." Miss Barton sniffed and lifted her chin.

"I gave you my word. Having Dot along won't be an annoying intrusion. Why, she's so quiet, it will be similar to being alone." Rosanna refused to become aggravated on such a glorious day. She meant to have a wonderful walk, and nothing could keep her from that.

24

"Are you all right, Dot?" The short-legged maid struggled to keep up with her pace. What a bother of a situation. If only Miss Barton hadn't extracted the promise not to walk alone.

"Yes, miss, I'm all right. Just not used to walking so far." The slender young girl flagged, so Rosanna took pity.

"There's a clearing ahead, we'll stop there, and you can rest." She recalled times when her dear mother put her own convenience aside to accommodate a weakness in a maid even staying up all night nursing sick servants back to health. Mother taught kindness to staff as part of being a 'real' lady.

Dot drew a hand across her pale forehead. "Thank you, miss."

Rosanna's heart went out to the wilted girl. They reached the clearing and sat on a convenient downed tree trunk. "Amazing how rough bark can be so comfortable when one is tired." Rosanna enjoyed a few peaceful moments in the quiet, serene spot while the maid caught her breath.

The tranquility ended with the sound of rustling in the brush.

Emerging from the woods, Lord Halburt came into view, briskly brushing himself off. "Miss Cabot! I say, what a surprise!"

To Rosanna's ears, his exuberance hit a false note. With sinking heart, she remembered his estate lay in this direction—perhaps they'd wandered onto the annoying man's property. That would explain his presence. "Yes, 'tis a surprise. Are we near or upon your lands?"

"No, no. You are still on your own fair land. Our shared boundary, dear Miss Cabot, is at least one-quarter mile that way." Using stage worthy gestures, he turned away to point.

Rosanna and Dot looked at each other. Mistress and maid suppressed smirks. The man's silliness invited mockery, even though one must refrain. His stagey poses, dramatic flair, with theatrical gestures and the good looks of a Greek god, made his every move and word seem like something out of a farcical stage play.

Standing and brushing off her dress, Rosanna made ready to retrace her steps to the manor. "So nice to see you again, so soon." Rosanna waved and stepped off with a rapid pace. But his voice speaking from the region of her right shoulder took her aback.

"I'll come with you. It's been a while since I visited at Honor's Point. Other than my two recent brief visits, I can't remember the last time." His pompous tones were loud, and he strode along poking at the underbrush with an elaborate walking stick.

Rosanna picked her way down the path, fuming with irritation. What on earth did he mean by his remarks? He was there two mornings ago. The coxcomb must think he's irresistible. *Lord, when I asked You to give me more patience, this was not the trial I had in mind.* Nor did plans for the day include a visit from this unwelcome, uninvited guest.

She glanced over her shoulder to see Dot ten feet behind, stumbling along in their wake, doing her duty as chaperone, since the need for one truly existed now.

The party of three reached the house and entered the front door which opened at the hands of vigilant Perkins.

Rosanna breezed into the hall, handed her bonnet to the butler, and said a few hasty words of instruction. She nodded to Halburt, and with ire-fueled dignity, ascended the stairs. She paused and glanced back to witness Perkins relieving the noble neighbor of his ebony walking stick and top hat. The butler then stood ramrod straight to convey Rosanna's wishes. "Lord Halburt, Miss Cabot requests you please be our guest in the drawing room." He stepped with a somber gait over to a door which he opened with a flourish.

Dot scuttled past Halburt and followed Rosanna up the stairs.

~*~

Rosanna entered the drawing room a short while later and realized Ellie'd been in there reading. *Oh, bother! Poor Ellie.*

Halburt continued to talk non-stop of everything from the local hunt, to property values, to whether Honor's Point would host any parties soon. His flow of words stopped only when Rosanna cleared her throat to announce her presence. She observed Ellie's stunned expression. "Miss Moore, are you feeling well?"

"I'm fine. Lord Halburt was just telling me about...himself and a few other topics. My, it was so fascinating. I had a hard time keeping up with it all."

She set down her book, rose, and then crossed the room, achieving some distance from Halburt. "I need more light."

Near the fireplace, Ellie's little hands fumbled in a workbasket next to a conveniently distant chair. She sat and busied herself with an embroidery project, head down, getting a needle threaded and finding the place she left off.

The nobleman greeted Rosanna with his now-customary overblown bow and flourish He began a sustained monologue on a set of antique armor he was corresponding with a dealer about, and Rosanna understood why Ellie looked stunned. Halburt was a consummate bore of the first order.

Rosanna calculated how soon she could bid him *adieu* without being considered rude. Why didn't she say good-bye when they'd arrived at the door? She framed words of dismissal and opened her mouth to speak when he began to flirt.

"Do let me add, the sky did seem to become bluer after I stumbled upon you this morning. When I first saw you in the woods, Miss Cabot, I thought I'd caught sight of a nymph. Yes, that's true, so classic, you are so worthy of being immortalized on a Grecian urn."

Her eyes widened in shock at this outpouring of treacle. Did he think she liked him tipping out the butter boat upon her? "Now, Lord Halburt, do cease this undeserved praise, it's too much." Her true self wanted to shove him out the door. Dishonesty in the service of diplomacy still rankled. Her words weren't a lie, but she felt like a deceiver, for not giving him a well-deserved set down to firmly send him on his way.

"Miss Moore, you too are looking fine this morning." He turned his flattery on Ellie, ignoring

Rosanna's request to desist and raised his voice to cover the distance to the corner where Ellie sat stitching. "Finding you here in this room was a treat to my poor lonesome existence. Having a sweet maiden such as you in the vicinity is a balm to me. Such a pretty lady."

Rosanna wanted to burst out laughing at Ellie's expression upon receiving this outpouring. She had the look of prey staring down the barrel of a loaded gun.

Enough of his absurd posturing. Going on the offense, Rosanna stated in a flat tone, "We have enjoyed your visit and will see you another time in the future." Upon that statement, she rang the bell, and said, "Perkins will let you out."

Caught off guard, the man could do nothing but get up out of his chair and bow his way out, filling the air with flowery farewells. "My heart yearns for the next time I shall be blessed by the presence of two such visions of loveliness. Farewell, sweet maidens of beauty."

After Halburt left the room, and the front door closed with a solid boom, Rosanna laughed softly.

Ellie joined in.

It felt so good to laugh after the odd tension the man caused.

"That was peculiar." Rosanna smiled, eyebrows raised, but lips shut to prevent more hoots of mirth from escaping. "Does he have intentions toward one of us?"

25

Ellie hurried with an answer. "He is obviously smitten with you. I do sincerely believe you are the object of his affections."

"No, I swear it is you he is ever so fond of. He called you a treat and a balm after all. I am merely an immortal nymph. Too droll." Rosanna sobered, and her next words dampened the amusement and serious thoughts flew into her mind. "We both came here to leave all that behind, but it's not turning out to be so simple, is it?"

"There's your meeting Lord Winstead, too."

Ellie meant well, but the innocent young lady didn't understood the totality of the situation. Her connection with Lord Winstead wasn't a simple, ordinary event. Proximity to his lost estate had to be painful for him. Embarrassing for him to get caught pretending to be a humble tenant. She wondered whether to confide. "There's that, yes."

She couldn't deny her attraction to Peter. It came as a surprise, after all these years. For so long, no man had been able to scale the solid walls around her broken heart. Not wanting another love after Clarence's death, and numbed by grief, she'd welcomed the single state and expected it to go on forever. Naïve in light of recent events.

The sun went behind a cloudbank and the room

grew dim. Memories welled up. She braced herself for the waves of sorrow she'd experienced so many times.

Instead, she examined her heart only to find a sweet welling of peace. Without the threat of forced marriage hanging over her head, healing filled her soul. The pain no longer remained. Only a faint tinge of sweet sorrow lingered. She decided to tell Ellie about Clarence.

"Do you recall the day you arrived here? That day, I related a small part of my life story. I partially explained why I'd moved to Honor's Point. I mentioned Clarence and that I would tell you that part of the story another time."

"I remember that. I never will forget your dramatic tale."

"Odd how one's life can seem riddled with drama, depending on perspective." Rosanna took a deep breath and ran her hands over her hair. "I want to tell you. This will be the first time in many years I've spoken of my lost love." In truth, this would be the first time telling anyone the full tale. She always hated to contemplate how she'd lost her precious Clarence four years ago. But she needed to talk about it.

Ellie's blue eyes grew round, "Are you sure you want to speak of it now? I'd hate to presume."

"It's time. I'm ready to completely unlock sorrow's cage."

Ellie sniffled.

Rosanna extracted two lacey handkerchiefs from her reticule. She passed one to Ellie and kept one ready in her hand. Thus resolved, Rosanna commenced her tale. "My father, a younger son, was an Oxford don. My parents and I lived in a charming residence, tucked against the college walls and built of the same sandstone. I became acquainted with a student, Clarence Huntsdown, the youngest son of a bishop at the local cathedral parish. Our young love flowered."

"Clarence was quite romantic and full of fun. He did sweet things like dropping a love note out of a third story window so it would land on the path in front of me as I walked by." She leaned against the back of her chair, crossed her ankles, and closed her eyes, remembering. "He confided later that for him, it was love at first sight. He'd spotted me in church the first Sunday after we moved there. I grew to love him too."

Ellie breathed out a soft, "Oh," and swept a handkerchief under each eye.

"A righteous young man, Clarence met his end one night when he tried to stop a malicious attack on another student."

Ellie gasped.

Rosanna wanted to speak of it at last, but her listener might not be ready to hear it. "Shall I cease this mirthless narrative?"

Ellie sat straight, one hand clenched in her lap, the other dabbing at her eyes. "No, I do want to hear your story. It's just so very sad."

"All right, I'll go on. The bullies turned on him and beat him viciously. His life on earth ended when overwhelmed by their brutal assault." After speaking these words, Rosanna lowered her eyes, and her lips moved in a silent prayer.

"How tragic. My heart goes out to you. What a loss. Your first love." Ellie began to sob into her hankie.

Rosanna came over to pat her back. "Now, now. Don't take it so hard. It's so long ago. I've accepted it now. I did my share of mourning, raging, and living in a blue-deviled state. I hope you understand that I am truly fine."

Ellie's questions came out on a cloud of sniffles. "You are? Suddenly, after all this time?"

26

Rosanna patted Ellie's hand for a minute more, then sat back on her chair and hugged herself. She'd never been able to speak of Clarence and their love to anyone after his death, and yet she had told the whole tale to Ellie. A marvelous sense of peace blanketed her. "It is amazing. Yes, I am healed. Coming here to beautiful Honor's Point and getting away from the arranged marriage circus in London has healed my heart. Please don't cry for me."

"God can do so much with our sorrow, if we let him." Ellie's sincere tone spoke of experience in the realm of grief.

Perkins stuck his head through the doorway after a light tap. "Miss Cabot, Lord Winstead is calling. Are you home?"

The jolt of delight that sizzled over her caught Rosanna by surprise. "Yes, but put him in the morning room. Offer him refreshment, and I will be with him shortly." The butler departed, and the two ladies looked at each other, smiling.

"We certainly have an abundance of male callers this day." Ellie put away her handkerchief with a rueful smile. "I have some things to attend to in my room. Including some mending, which I actually enjoy."

"Thank you for listening to my story. It did me

good to finally tell someone after all these years. In God's providence, it was through you that I was able to bring it out into the light of day." Rosanna stood and gave Ellie a gentle hug.

"You are more than welcome, my friend." Ellie left the room.

Rosanna stopped in the hall to check her appearance in a mirror and decided her jonquil dress tidy enough. Hard to believe the clock said only ten o'clock, so much had happened already this morning. She suppressed a fleeting wish that she'd worn a prettier dress, but she'd chosen this ensemble when she'd dressed to suit the walk she'd gone out on earlier.

The walk Halburt intruded upon, that is. When he'd insisted on visiting the house so soon after, she'd had no time to change clothes. Such a contradiction. He looked like a carved angel, but acted like an immature puppy.

She slipped into the morning room, leaving the door ajar for propriety, and stopped in the center of the carpet.

Winstead moved toward her from where he'd been standing near the fireplace.

She lifted one hand over which he bowed. Wariness crept into her senses as an attitude of tension emanated from Winstead. "Shall we sit over there?" Not waiting for an answer, she went over to an alcove window and sat in one of two striped-satin armchairs positioned to take advantage of the breezes wafting in, carrying the scent of lilacs. "What brings you to call?" After these words slipped out, she kicked herself. What sort of impression did that make? So undiplomatic. He looked distracted, so maybe he didn't register the inadvertent tone of challenge in her question. She must be ever more careful with her words.

Serious, his brows lowered into straight lines. "I wanted to see you."

The rattle of the tea trolley's arrival masked her sharp intake of breath. Her mind whirled. *He wants to see me?* There was a serious tone in his voice. This neighbor was certainly more congenial to her liking than the last. Even though this man warmed her senses, she wasn't prepared to accept an onslaught to her heart's affection.

The servant departed, leaving the door wide open.

Dot appeared in the doorway. "Miss?"

"Oh, hello, Dot. Wait for me on that bench in the hall. I'll call you if I need you."

"Yes, Miss." Dot scurried out of view.

"Your household staff is efficient," Lord Winstead said, his tone unemotional to the extreme.

"Indeed." She'd been mistaken, for this discourse hadn't the sound of the suitor. A thread of a thought edged around her mind. What would it be like to be pursued by him? She'd enjoyed her interactions thus far with the dark and handsome blue-eyed man. He also possessed a fine build, and excellent manners.

He placed his cup gently back into the saucer. "Delicious tea. Ah, lemon scones. I remember these well. I believe you retained Hannah, the cook?"

"She's a treasure. I'll be sure to tell her you praised her scones."

This must be so difficult for him—sitting as a caller at his former home. Visiting Honor's Point had to remind him of everything that he'd lost. Her heart squeezed with warm compassion for him. She couldn't do a thing about his loss, other than be kind and charitable in her attitude toward him. That wouldn't be an unpleasant chore. But she sensed the agreeable and easy-to-talk-to man arrived with something uncomfortable on his mind, and she wished he'd get to it.

His words rushed out. "Miss Cabot, I want to make it clear that I carry no resentment toward you for buying Honor's Point."

"Oh, my. That's good to know." A mild response leapt to her lips—suspicions of the source of his tension confirmed.

"I harbor no ill will. In fact, it pleases me that someone so," he paused, "nice came to live here."

"I intend to take care of it to the best of my ability. Between Bramstock, Perkins, and Mrs. Good, the estate runs quite well, and I am learning all about the property." She hoped this remark didn't accentuate his ouster from the estate. Choosing this moment to butter a scone, she prolonged the spreading procedure, taking the time to help get her past this touchy moment.

His face held a slight smile and his eyes locked on hers. "After you so graciously forgave me for my little deception, I couldn't let another day go by without making sure you knew that I have no enmity towards you."

Aware of his every nuance, she drank in the pleasure of his presence. "You had me completely fooled."

"It's not often in life one gets to take on the persona of an entirely different person."

"Did you enjoy baffling me?"

"Enjoy? No, indeed. You arrived at the depths of my despair and humiliation." He lifted his cup and saucer but neglected to take a drink. "I did not relish it.

In retrospect, it was absurd and I sincerely regret deceiving you."

All appetite flown, she took a small bite of the lemon scone, just for show, set her plate down, and then touched a linen napkin to the corners of her mouth. "But I think we've moved beyond that, now haven't we? You've asked my forgiveness for the trick you played on me. Perhaps we needn't speak of it again?"

"Your forgiveness means the world to me. So graciously given."

"I'm over it. It's clear that your pretense wasn't personal. You had no nefarious motives." Rosanna took another miniscule nibble of scone.

"Thank you again for your forgiveness. I shall treasure it and never presume upon it again, Lord willing."

"Oh, la, say no more of it. I can understand your reasons and am only glad for your sake that you are out of seclusion. The dinner party proved delightful, no?"

"Indeed. The vicinity is blessed by the presence of the three ladies of Honor's Point. Lady Brook's dinner parties have never been so well-bedecked in the past."

His lavish, yet sincere compliments touched a chord within in a way Halburt's never could. A flush of warmth heated her cheeks. She wondered again if this visit indicated the beginning of some sort of pursuit. Would she welcome that? Her healed heart notwithstanding, it was a long time since she'd entertained such thoughts. She tucked them away to enjoy contemplating later. The visit lasted for another ten minutes, and he rose to depart.

He reached toward her, and her hand lifted as if

drawn by an invisible cord. His touch was warm and firm.

"Thank you again. Your arrival here was the catalyst for my return to life." He bowed over her hand, and brushed his lips across her fingers, causing a quiver to rush up her arm.

She tilted her head and looked at him through lowered lashes. "You are very gracious, sir."

He released her, clicked his heels, and departed.

She sat back, bowled over by the man's attentions. His personality carried a refreshing frankness. Recollections of the sensations she'd experienced in his presence overtook the day's realities.

Perkins stuck his head in again. "The mail is here, Miss. You have a personal letter today, shall I bring it in?"

27

"Yes, that would be fine. Bring it in here, please." Personal mail arrived rarely now, with no family but for Uncle George and his brood. Her parents had succumbed to cholera the year after Clarence died.

She'd only received one letter from Uncle George. A perfunctory note regaling her about London society in which she had no interest. She hadn't given any of her friends her direction upon departing London because of her initial plan for a secret refuge. With the original idea a failure, due to the insurmountable difficulties in getting it off the ground, she'd written to one or two special friends. Maybe one of them had answered.

Perkins proffered the letter on a silver tray,

Rosanna picked up the envelope off the tray.

He bowed his way out again, closing the door behind him this time.

Dear Rosanna,

Thank you for your letter. Where do I start to catch you up with my news? So much has transpired since I saw you last. I'll be brief. You may recall seeing me at Mrs. Banting's ball? That was my first ton ball. Soon after that, my courtship with an aristocratic man of my father's choosing ended abruptly. Through a series of events, I am now married! To Mrs. Banting's nephew, Lord Russell. He's all that I ever dreamed of—such a wonderful, godly man.

One reason for my letter is to tell you we will be in your neighborhood soon, calling on our acquaintance, Lord Winstead. When we are so near you, we shall call on you as well. God be with you, Melissa (Southwood) Russell.

Interesting. The newly wedded couple was coming to call on Lord Winstead. Perhaps the two men were close friends.

Seeing Melissa again would be diverting. The busy day wore to an end and Rosanna fell asleep and dreamed of a dark-haired man with blue eyes.

~*~

At church on the following Sunday, after a particularly rousing hymn, Rosanna and Lord Winstead made eye contact across the pews. His glance shot desire down to her toes, and back up to nestle under her heart. Guilt welled up that such a sensation occurred during a worship service. She pacified her remorse by inward assertion that she hadn't sought the stirring, rather it came unbidden. A sidelong glance at Ellie and Miss Barton showed neither noticed anything untoward.

They both appeared deep in worship.

Gracious Mr. Clough greeted the group from Honor's Point after services. "Miss Cabot, I'd like to call on you very soon. What day would be convenient?" The man beamed at her from behind his round spectacles.

Her thoughts came back down to earth when Miss Barton jabbed her in the ribs from behind. She gave the first answer she could think of. "Friday. Yes, the end of the week is better for me. Shall we say one?" As she shook the minister's hand, she reached back with her foot and pressed Miss Barton's toe in retribution.

The three ladies nodded and smiled then moved off, trailed by Dot, having decided to walk the mile back home. Before they got around the first bend in the road, footsteps approached from the rear.

Rosanna glanced over her shoulder only to discover Lord Winstead a few steps back.

"Miss Cabot, fine day, is it not?" He doffed his hat and came alongside, matching his longer stride to hers.

Miss Barton and Ellie dropped back, falling into step with Dot about six feet behind the couple.

Her cheeks warm, she smiled up at him. "Tis fine, indeed."

~*~

Her big brown eyes sparkled out from under the brim of a stylish bonnet—dazzling him. He'd battled with himself whether to invite her to go on a walk. He wasn't in a position to woo a young lady, yet he couldn't help himself. The strong draw of his attraction to Rosanna wouldn't take no for an answer. From the moment she'd fallen out of her carriage into his arms the day she'd arrived, he'd been aware of the pull.

"May I beseech your company later this afternoon? For a walk upon the paths, or a stroll in the garden?" How insipid he sounded to his own ears, but there was no help for that. Many a lovesick male trod this foolish ground before him. A few long moments passed before she answered.

"That would be lovely. Shall we say three o'clock?"

His heart swelled with gratitude that even though she'd hesitated, her response didn't reveal any disgust. "I'll be there, Miss Cabot. I must be off. Have to meet with Mr. Clough over Sunday dinner to discuss spiritual matters." Why did he say that? She'd think him a braggart or a nodcock.

"Goodbye." Rosanna's lilting tones didn't sound annoyed, however, so maybe it rang fine to her.

She acted so natural, and unaffected. He liked that about her. She didn't put on a show as many young ladies did. When she looked at him with those trusting eyes—his heart hoped.

28

Departing from Rosanna's delectable company, he reversed course and entered the vicarage grounds through a black wrought iron gate. After closing the gate, Lord Winstead approached the vicarage door, his emotions mixed. He enjoyed his few talks with the minister so far, but the time had come when he needed to go deeper—to confess his sin. An ugly blot kept him from a clear conscience. He needed to deal with his transgression.

Compassionate to a fault, Mr. Clough appeared to be the best person to help him rid himself of a mortifying burden of a sin too heavy to bear alone. Convinced the minister wouldn't be too shocked, and if he was, he'd hide it, Peter forced his reluctant feet to the door and knocked, half-hoping no one was home.

A maid answered and ushered him into a cozy dining room. He discovered the minister already seated at a table with an expectant look on his face.

"So glad you could join me, sit right here." He gestured to a place set across the table.

Peter sat down with rising trepidation.

A mob-capped serving girl backed into the room carrying a loaded tray. She unloaded a tureen, a heaping basket of rolls, and a butter dish. She then served each man a bowl of steaming soup, before leaving the room with the tray tucked under her arm.

"Shall we pray?" Mr. Clough proceeded to ask God's blessing upon their meal and their time together. "Lord God, King of the Universe, we beseech a blessing upon this bounty mercifully provided for us. May our words be edifying and full of grace. Amen."

"Delicious." Peter set down his spoon a short time later. The meals he'd been throwing together of late consisted of nothing near as tasty as this. "Living alone in my cottage has its merits, but cookery isn't one of them." Peter's words set the course of the conversation, preparing the basis to work his way around to the painful revelation he needed to make.

"My small staff takes good care of me. I am grateful." The minister's response downplayed Lord Winstead's reduced circumstances.

Clough's kindness gave him the courage to forge on into difficult territory. "I want to talk about..." The serving girl re-entered the room bearing another tray with two plates of roast beef and vegetables. She set one plate down before each man, bobbed a curtsey and departed for the kitchens.

Peter let his words die away for now, instead addressing the appetizing meal with his knife and fork. What he had to say could wait. Determined to get it off his chest today, a half hour either way made no earthly difference. Besides, the maid would return with pudding before long. He'd bide his time.

~*~

"Ah, a fine meal." Mr. Clough pushed back his chair and moved over to an alcove featuring a bank of broad, low windows.

The arrangement of two upholstered chairs and a divan provided a view of the gardens and the woods beyond. Both men sat.

The minister locked his fingers, elbows on the chair's arms.

Peter leaned forward with his hands clasped and arms resting on his knees. "My compliments to your excellent cook. Thank you." Peter used small talk to ease into the painful topic.

The minister smiled but said nothing.

The silence lengthened before Peter dove in. "I need to unburden myself. There's something on my conscience."

"I see. A peaceful conscience is greatly to be desired. Confession is good for the soul."

"I hope you'll still think that after you hear what I have to tell."

"Your soul's condition is quite important." The minister's calm demeanor showed no signs of stress.

Peter began to perspire and found his breaths harder to come by. "You are perhaps aware I was residing in London for a time earlier this year? Before Honor's Point was sold?" Peter's mouth got drier with every word. He swallowed before continuing. "I did something reprehensible."

The man crossed his ankles, unlinked his fingers, and leaned back, looking as though he heard this sort of thing every day. Maybe he did. "Young man, all have sinned and fallen short of God's glory."

Peter's resolve ratcheted down, but he pushed onward, forcing the words out. "Thank you for the reassurance. It's just quite hard for me to forget what I did and forgive myself, let alone believe God will forgive me."

"Go ahead. Tell me everything. It won't be any worse than things I've heard before, so don't worry."

He shortened the sorry tale of his offense against God and man. "I abducted a girl I was courting and tried to force her to marry me for my own financial gain. I am very sorry for my actions." There it was, flopped out like a bale of dirty laundry.

The minister cleared his throat, and paused, thinking before responding. "What you did was clearly wrong. You certainly know that."

"I do."

"Though you don't need an intermediary, I can guide you. God sees the heart and true repentance. God has given us a Savior through whom we can resolve sin. When we confess our sins, He is faithful and just to forgive us and cleanse us from all unrighteousness. As God's children we are assured that Jesus has fully paid for all our sins. We will pray together." The two men bowed their heads and lifted their hearts to the Lord.

Tears rolled down Peter's face. His sin burden was gone. He was free.

~*~

On his way home, in time to prepare for his stroll with Rosanna at three, Peter's steps floated. His heart soared with grateful relief and firm resolve to walk rightly in his life from then on, no matter how difficult it was. Hard times were starting to feel normal.

29

Rosanna slipped out the front door just as Lord Winstead lifted his hand to the brass knocker. She'd been waiting for his arrival and didn't want a loud knock to wake up any of the resting inhabitants of Honor's Point, many of whom made it a habit to nap on Sunday afternoon.

She'd now met Lord Winstead in a socially acceptable way, so it was suitable to walk out with him unescorted by a maid, wasn't it? She had only promised Barton not to walk alone. She wouldn't be alone and the fear of being accosted gave no concern, since she'd be with a protective male. In the country, surely the strictures governing a young lady's behavior weren't as strict as in town. An escorted woman, of age, on her own property shouldn't have to worry. Thoroughly justifying playing games with propriety, she rattled off more reasons: she had reached her majority, and was nigh onto the shelf, and if that wasn't enough, he was an eligible lord and a close neighbor.

Shy for a moment, she glanced up at him from under the brim of a fashionable bonnet. She chose to wear it, in hopes of pleasing him—hard to admit that, even to herself. The green silk walking dress she wore featured few of the furbelows of the day. She didn't want to appear to be flaunting her superior wealth or property in front of Lord Winstead, the former owner of her home.

"You look as fresh as spring in that shade of green, my dear." He said, bowing over her hand.

The endearment caught her by surprise. Did he mean that? Perhaps, but his tone hadn't been overly warm, but rather brotherly, in fact. Was she too suspicious? She twirled around, which allowed the pleated flounce near her feet to swirl out. "Do you like it?"

"The color is lovely on you."

Thinking better of coming across as silly, she stopped after one turn, straightened her dark green spencer jacket with a gentle tug, and tapped the pavement of the steps with the tip of her parasol. "Thank you. Shall we?"

"Certainly, let's begin our walk." Lord Winstead crooked his left elbow and extended it toward Rosanna, who placed her fingertips upon his forearm. "Have you explored all the paths yet?"

"Didn't you say there was a waterfall on the property somewhere? The day we got caught in the rain, remember? Waterfalls fascinate me."

He guided her a bit further along before answering. "Yes, I certainly do recall getting caught in the rain with you. How could I forget the web of glistening raindrops in the tree above our heads?"

She glanced over at him to ascertain whether he was teasing her about her poetic babblings. He looked serious. Gathering her addled wits, she responded, trying to defuse the sudden tension between them. "Of course, you remember. Silly me, who'd forget that? What a downpour that was. Can we get to the waterfall easily?" She hoped this flow of words covered up her nervousness. It wouldn't do for him to realize how he affected her.

He patted her fingers before covering them with his warm right hand. "It's this way. It's not all that easy to get to, and not because it's terribly far away. We will have to descend a set of rustic steps, ford a shallow stream on stepping-stones, and wend our way down a viney path. Do you have sturdy shoes on?"

Their progress interrupted, Rosanna looked down at feet clad in half-boots, having forgotten everything but the feel of his hand on hers, then up to meet his sparkly blue eyes. "I think these will suffice."

He gazed into her eyes. "Are you sure you are up to it?"

She nodded her chin in determination. "I've become something of a rambler since moving here and I'm longing to see it. You said it's not far."

Where the path entered the woods, the uneven surface of the descending trail soon caused her to cling to his arm with both hands. He appeared not to mind, in fact, she never recollected seeing him so relaxed.

He patted her hand. "More rocks and roots crop up on this path every year."

He seemed so happy without the brooding glower that used to hover on his brow, and there was an air of lightness in his demeanor so different from other times they'd met.

"Is it much farther?" She tried to keep any hint of complaint out of her voice.

"Not far now. Use this railing only for balance. Don't put your weight on it, though, it's none too sturdy." He gave the rail a shake to show her the truth of his warning. "But, I'll go first and make sure there are no cave-ins on the steps."

"Cave-ins? Are you positive this is safe?" She

sensed a waft of cool air sweeping down the hill behind them, and she shivered.

"Very safe. I've never gotten as much as a scrape here. It's simply a precaution since the steps follow the edge of a deep glen. Theoretically, the bank could give way, but we'll be fine. I assure you." He moved on down the rustic steps and she had no choice but to follow.

Not wanting Lord Winstead to think her a coward, she clarified things after they'd descended several steps. "I do love ravines, paths, grottos, and the like." That was just about as silly a remark as she could have made.

He made no response, so perhaps he didn't notice.

The railing came to an end, she arrived at the foot of the steps. Shafts of sunlight filtered from on high, lighting up stepping stones in a shallow stream. "Is this the lowest part of the glen?"

"Yes." Lord Winstead stood on a large, flat stepping stone facing her, holding out both of his hands. She hesitated, then decided there could be no harm in him merely wanting to help her across the rocks. She reached toward his hands. He grasped her fingers, then her hands, guiding her forward onto the stone, and to her surprise, into a sudden embrace. His lips descended upon hers.

Surprised at the response her traitorous body gave, she struggled to tamp down the flames of desire sparking inside. Her physical self had a mind of its own and wanted only to get closer to this man. Rosanna allowed a moment of this sublime pleasure, before pushing him away with a firmness that surprised her because all she craved was to be held in his arms forever.

30

Shocked at his own actions, Peter railed at himself, since pulling her into a hug had not been part of his plan for this Sunday outing. "Rosanna. Please forget I did that. My apologies. Shall I escort you home now?"

"Only if there is no waterfall for me to see." Rosanna looked stunned but straightened her jacket and brushed off her sleeves. "We've come all this way, through the perilous descent on those steps with the rickety railing. I, for one, am enamored of stepping stones as well, and don't want to miss them either."

"Of course. We can proceed."

Chin up, she edged past him and then picked her way across the shallow stream. Shafts of light guided her steps.

His heart sank like lead as he followed her from stone to stone. He read disapproval in the rigid set of her back. Would he never learn? Why take such liberties with a young, innocent lady? She deserved to despise him for taking her to this isolated place and practically molesting her. "The falls are that way." He pointed to the left. "The path on this side of the stream will lead us to the waterfall." His gut roiled over offending her, but since she wanted to keep going, he must attempt to be an efficient guide.

Silent, she managed to step over a few downed branches and some trailing vines that crept over the footpath. He hoped she could navigate the entire trail, because he must avoid touching her again.

A fallen tree blocked the way ahead. She stopped, stymied, the trunk too substantial for her to climb over unaided. He bent over and locked his hands together to make a step for her to use to get to the top of the trunk. He'd have to assist her down the other side as well.

"I'm steady now." She made quite a picture, sitting so ladylike on top of a downed tree in the shady, moist glen. He blocked her beauty out of his mind and clambered over the tree in a trice. In order to help her down so they could continue, he'd have to touch her, to reach out both his hands again—just as he'd done back by the stream when he'd pulled her into his arms.

"Please get me down. The bark is poking through my dress."

She did say the most delightful things, and he loved her unaffected personality. Did she realize how charming she was? Gathering the remnants of his courage, he wished he were at least a temporary eunuch. He had to place a hand on either side of her waist to lift her down. After he set her on her feet, he locked his hands behind his back.

She looked away for a moment then spoke. "Are we close to the falls? I'm a bit weary of this rough path."

What would she think if he picked her up in his arms and carried her to the secluded grotto? He should've thought through the pitfalls of this rough excursion. He'd never imagined she'd need so much assistance. Or that giving such assistance would become fraught with unruly physical attraction.

"We're quite close. It's only about twenty more feet. You'll be able to see it once we round this curve and pass that clump of hawthorn." He pushed the shrub aside for her to pass.

There it was, in all its dark glory, forty feet of glistening waterfall, tumbling into a shadowy pool. The water had carved out a grotto over the centuries, and the scene held a rare, sheltered allure. The heavy scent of plants and moisture gave the air the redolence of a jungle. Drops of the dark water escaped the rushing cascade and caught the filtered light, giving the whole spectacle a sparkling sheen.

Awed, Rosanna sank down onto a handy boulder, big enough for them both, so he sat down next to her to view the falls, careful to avoid any physical contact.

Peter wanted to remind her of the reason they ventured on such a temptation-strewn path. "Do you understand now why this is a renowned beauty spot?"

She spoke in a hushed, reverent voice. "This is marvelous. Thank you for bringing me here."

She thanked him? She was so kind and sweet. That would seem to indicate forgiveness for his precipitous embrace. Relieved that the awkward results of his impetuous act were subsiding, and his fair companion was able to forgive and forget, he passed his hand over his face in chagrin. God was good, to allow him to touch even the hem of her garment.

A sudden wash of relieved gratitude came over him. Peter noticed some moisture under his companion's eyes. "Miss Cabot, are you all right?" He whipped out a linen handkerchief and offered it to her. She took it and wiped her eyes.

"I'm fine, just overcome by the beauty of it all. To be honest, you overwhelm me as well." Tears swam in her warm brown gaze, and a flash of yearning showed itself for only a moment before it disappeared, leaving him unsure of what he'd seen.

31

Peter's eyes went smoky and his voice dropped. "*I* overwhelm you?"

Rosanna explained her tears. "You see, I haven't been hugged in so long. My parents are both dead, and my life contains little or no affection of that sort. Your warmth, well, it is more than I expected to find when I moved here. My reason for moving here was to live in a refuge of my own creation." Talking about her life to this attentive man gave her the sensation of being treasured.

"I understand. Think nothing of it. I'm glad my impulsive act had some merit after all." He glanced around, and changed the subject. "This spot has such peace and an aura of otherworldliness. It would affect many."

So kind of him, to try to put her at ease about her tears. Rosanna's chest throbbed with a mixture of pain and exhilaration. Her dim memories of loving Clarence didn't include this intense pull toward a man. Was this love, again? If life played a trick on her after all these years, would her resolve against love weaken under the gentle assault of this man's affection?

Awareness of their isolated location flashed into her mind. He'd compromised her with his embrace and kiss. Perhaps since no one knew, that would negate the consequences. But Lord Winstead knew. A trickle of unease ran down her spine. She hated the thought of him offering for her out of convention. She wasn't sure she wanted him to offer for any reason. Her long-held opposition to marriage still held some sway within her.

Having seen the waterfall, she gave a belated nod to propriety. "We should go now. I'll be missed at home. I really mustn't wander about without a maid again." She stood, brushed at her skirt, and tucked his handkerchief in the reticule hanging from her wrist. "I'll have it laundered."

Rosanna forged back the way they'd come, this time not holding his arm. She used her parasol to shove the hawthorn clump out of the way. While she navigated the uneven path, thoughts of Lord Winstead ran rampant. Being with him filled a deep unmet and previously unknown need. Hard to guess what would happen next.

According to convention a proposal might arrive later today. Tomorrow? After all, in the moral code of the *ton*, he'd compromised her.

The fact that she'd brought it on herself by willingly going off alone with him didn't matter. That kind of proposal didn't suit her dreams, however, and she fervently hoped societal mores wouldn't force him to the point.

She began a stream of nervous chatter. "The never-ending water of the falls recalls to me God's infinite love. Do you suppose this has been here since the creation?" She didn't expect an answer to her rhetorical question, but he surprised her.

"Not sure, but it reminds me of a hymn, 'Like a river glorious is God's perfect peace.'"

"I love that hymn, too. One of my favorites."

Oh, no. The fallen tree again. She steeled her nerves. Lord Winstead formed a hollow with his hands again. She stepped up, again steadied herself atop the trunk, and then, using her parasol for a brace, jumped down the other side on her own. *Why didn't I do that the first time?*

"See what a rambler I'm becoming? With all my walking the paths of Honor's Point, soon I'll think nothing of it." Moving along the path with alacrity, she hoped to diffuse the tension and normalize the situation by referring to the original purpose of their outing. A simple walk to see a waterfall. It had turned into something more, but with any grace, she could perhaps level things out between them to a comfortable distance. That's what she told herself she should want.

~*~

Peter scolded himself with each step. He'd gotten into something without an easy resolution. No denying that he cared for Rosanna. Such a charming young lady, and being with her gave unexpected delight. He scorned his own heart for caring when he would never again be in a position to offer for a lady as exalted as Rosanna.

"I've become a dab hand at stepping stones." Rosanna crossed the stream and then marched to the foot of the steps and began the ascent.

"Remember, don't lean on the rail." Keeping her safe for the remainder of their rustic ramble gave him something to focus on other than bewilderment about their putative future. Not even eligible to pursue a female of any rank, he'd nothing to offer a lady of her high caliber. For him to engender this awkward entanglement was beyond dreadful. Going on, as if a benign neighbor, all the while yearning for his true love, forever out of reach—untenable.

Love caught him by surprise. How funny it was, the very day he unburdened himself of his sins, his eyes opened to true love. Rosanna drew his heart out of hiding. He'd have to conceal his affection from her. She must never know. If she ever found out his scandalous behavior of not too long ago, she'd be repelled. The strikes against him were forgiven by God, but society didn't forgive as easily. He'd deliver her home and try to go on as though naught changed, when in fact, within him, nothing stayed the same.

They arrived at the manor's front door. He bowed over her hand and stood back. "This has been excellent exercise. Thank you for accompanying me, Miss Cabot." There, that sounded cool, yet neighborly.

Her eyes narrowed but she mustered a social smile. "It was all that I could have hoped for. The waterfall, that is."

"It is a marvel. I shall see you again someday."

Her fading smile smote his heart. "Yes, someday."

32

Working the soil was said to lead to serenity of mind. Each stab of the spade and toss of the heavy dirt brought up only shreds of that calm state. He'd been digging and hoeing in the garden behind the cottage for two hours. Peace eluded him thus far, though every weed vanquished gave a modicum of satisfaction.

Last night brought self-recriminations, and very little sleep. He woke with a drive to do something physical to release his anxiety. On the surface, things sat in an ambiguous state. If he left it to simmer down, it might be glossed over. His head told him to back away, but his heart would like nothing more than to be crystal clear in regard to his affections. But he could not very well pursue marriage with the woman who owned his former estate. That would appear mercenary.

He jabbed the spade into the dirt, straightened up, and reached in his pocket for a handkerchief. Not there. If memory served, the stray piece of linen resided in the possession of the young lady to whom his thoughts would not stop drifting. He wiped his forehead with the back of his hand. Hanging his head while leaning on the handle of the shovel, he became aware of sounds from the front of the house—a banging, knocking sound, and then the whinny of a horse.

Entering the rear door, he glanced in the mirror, and shoved his hair into order. He buttoned up his shirt and retied the neckcloth he'd loosened out in the sun. It would have to do.

"Yes?" He spoke as he opened the door. A refined gentleman stood on his doorstep, looking as though he'd stepped straight from the hands of a skillful London tailor. He wore gleaming boots, spotless breeches, a tasteful yet dramatic waistcoat, all surmounted by a dark coat tailored so well it looked like a second skin. Somewhat familiar to Peter, but he couldn't place him.

The man's face wore an easy, amiable expression. "Winstead?"

"I'm Winstead. Who might you be?" Peter felt a bit put out. He'd invited no guests and now this man knocked on his door and asked for him by name. He peered beyond the man's shoulder and observed a carriage.

The man gestured toward the carriage at which time the door swung open and a lady emerged, moving down the steps lowered in preparation for her descent. "I am Lord Russell. My wife and I have come to call on you."

Peter took a step back. Shock assailed his bones when he recognized the woman. None other than Melissa Southwood. He wanted the floor to open up and swallow him—to disappear—to die. His past with her was the source of his deepest shame.

The man stepped up into the main room of the cottage and then turned back, holding out his arm to assist his wife to enter as well. "Buck up, Winstead. We came to merely regain a footing of friendship with you, not to curse or rail at you."

Peter retained a measure of outward calm and the power of speech, but his mind spun. Fear and confusion swirled within. "This is quite a surprise."

"Winstead." Lord Russell took charge. "As I said, we are not here to take you to task. We are on a mission of sorts. As much as it is possible, we want to be at peace with all men." He seated his wife.

Melissa sat, turning her face up toward Peter. "'Tis good to see you, Peter."

She smiled at him, and the force of her beauty struck him anew. Her luscious, honey-colored hair peeked out from within the edges of a dainty bonnet. Her blue gown with matching pelisse reminded one of the sky on the prettiest of days. He hadn't truly loved her, but what an exquisite woman she was.

Peter attempted normalcy by uttering commonplaces. "Tell me, what brings you here? How was your journey?"

The three sat at the one table in the main room. Lord and Lady Russell occupied the bench and Peter the chair. He ate his rustic meals here, alone. Strange enough to entertain guests at the table, but for these two to appear, of a sudden, struck him. An unbidden, rueful smile crept onto his face.

Lord Russell sat back, well-satisfied with the visit so far. "You're smiling. That's good. We came to formally forgive you."

"You're here to forgive me?" Peter's mind whirled at this revelation. "I just yesterday confessed my sin before God and received a measure of peace. Then today, you arrive to grant me your forgiveness?"

Melissa smiled and looked at her husband again, as if for reassurance. "Yes, that's why we are here."

With calm he didn't really possess, Peter

responded. "If you'll allow, I prefer to tender my repentant apologies before accepting such a gracious blanket of mercy."

33

Russell responded with a patient overtone in his voice. "We won't force an apology out of you."

A bead of sweat ran down Peter's back. He wanted to get this over with. "It's not forced. This isn't particularly comfortable, you both here in the flesh. But I planned to pen a letter of apology. Now I'll deliver the words in person."

Melissa beamed at her husband. Probably secure and happy in her marriage, she exuded a more lighthearted spirit than during their brief arranged courtship. "Ooh. See, Mark? We did the right thing by coming here."

Peter cleared his throat. "Melissa, I committed a grievous sin upon you—an attempted crime. My sinful actions can rightly be called kidnapping and I give no excuse for my crime. I have repented before God, and I implore your forgiveness." There, he'd said the words. Peter let out a breath he didn't even realize he'd been holding.

"I forgive you, Peter." She smiled at him, and turned to look at her husband.

"And to you, Lord Russell…"

Russell interrupted, holding up one hand. "Please, call me Mark."

"Mark, then. To you, I ask forgiveness for attempting to steal a bride not meant for me, but for you. I would have robbed God if I had succeeded. Please forgive me." A further rush of relief coursed through him.

"It's yours, Winstead. Our hearts already granted forgiveness, but I agree, your words seal the peace agreement. You were right that an apology completes the circle, so to speak." Mark looked over at Melissa, who nodded.

A tinge of red crept across his cheeks as he continued. "Winstead, in turn, I am also regretful for assaulting you in the chapel. At the time, you surely must agree, your plot needed to be foiled?"

"I suffered no lasting injuries. Please blot that out of your mind. I deserved what you did, and more, for my actions." Peter rose. As beneficial as this meeting was, he had no wish to extend it.

Lord Russell rose too and assisted Melissa to her feet. "Thank you for allowing us an uninvited visit."

Melissa extended her gloved hand to Peter. "So glad we had this chance to put that episode of our lives to rest. God's peace is too valuable to be disrupted if it's at all possible to regain, isn't it?"

Peter bowed over her hand.

The group moved through the door and out into the sunshine again.

Lord Russell called out a parting question as he got into the carriage. "Back to the main road, then to the right? That's the way to Miss Cabot's, correct?"

Peter's stomach dropped to his feet. He managed to answer, though cold fear and a sickening premonition swept over him. "Yes."

"Thank you. You see, we are making double use of this trip. We're off to visit Melissa's old friend, Miss Cabot. Farewell!" Mark called as the vehicle began to roll away, "Blessings!"

~*~

Rosanna sighed, then softly stated her estimation of their social milieu. "I like the quiet and the seclusion here but having one caller as persistent as Halburt is too much."

Ellie held up a thread and a needle to the light. "A complete lack of callers is nicer at times. Of course, my relief at having attained refuge colors my opinion."

Rosanna mulled the truth that neither one of them wanted a social whirl at this time in their lives, and they were both weary of Halburt and his incessant calls. Miss Barton snoozed in a comfortable chair by the fireplace, while Rosanna sat with Ellie near the windows with the best light for needlework.

Ellie, the younger of the two, had borne half the brunt of his attentions. She pulled the thread through the needle. "Is he not aware of his pompous airs and preposterous flattery?"

"No, he is oblivious, Ellie. It's been clear since the very day I met him. He is still nattering on about me having a treasure hunt." Rosanna snipped a strand of yarn and looked up. "I've about decided to host a treasure hunt just to shut him up."

Ellie laughed, pausing her needle. Soon her fingers found their rhythm again. "This beaded reticule won't be useable if you keep making me laugh."

"My shawl will probably have holes from dropped stitches as well." Rosanna held up the knitted expanse and examined it, before flopping it down onto her lap. She stretched out her hands and wiggled her cramped fingers. "The day is fine. Shall we..." The sound of wheels on the gravel drive caused her to break off mid-sentence.

Ellie's gaze locked on Rosanna, seeking reassurance.

She kept her voice calm and steady for Ellie's sake. "Now who can that be? Not Halburt—he's been arriving on horseback. Not Mr. Clough, or Lord Winstead, for they arrive on foot. Perkins will announce whoever it is. Hmmm, we'll have to see."

As if on cue, Perkins tapped and opened the door without waiting for an answer. "Miss, Lord and Lady Russell have arrived. Are you at home?"

"Yes. I am most certainly at home to them. Please, show them in and order some cakes, sandwiches, and tea." Rosanna turned to Ellie. "My friend from academy days recently married. She wrote me saying they'd be in the neighborhood and would visit."

After a moment, Perkins showed the guests in, first sweeping open the door, then standing aside to allow them to enter the sunny drawing room. The handsome couple, glowing with newly wedded bliss, entered.

Rosanna immediately noticed the transformation in her friend. She remembered her as a pretty, but insecure merchant's daughter. But now, Melissa Southwood embodied an absolute paragon of confident female beauty from the top of her glossy blonde head to the tips of her fashionable slippers—stunning.

At school, Rosanna shared a room with Melissa, and proximity brought strong friendship. But life diverged on separate paths. Affection endured, however, and she threw herself into Melissa's arms and kissed her cheek, all the while laughing and hugging.

They stood apart and held each other's hands at arm's length.

"So good to see you, Melissa. Introduce me to your husband."

Melissa laughed again, broke away, and drew her spouse forward. "This is Lord Russell, we've been married two months."

"Charmed, Miss Cabot. We thank you for your hospitality."

"My pleasure. It's wonderful to see Melissa again, and so happy."

The group turned and Rosanna introduced them to Ellie. No flicker of recognition. Good. They didn't seem to recognize her. Ellie's time at the academy hadn't overlapped with Melissa's.

"Melissa, would you like to go above and freshen?"

"Thank you, but we lunched at an inn nearby, and I removed my travel dust there."

Rosanna took Melissa's hand and brought her to a comfortable settee. "You newlyweds sit together here."

Lord Russell joined his bride upon the plush upholstered seat.

"Perfect." Melissa proceeded to regale them with their travels. "We've had beautiful weather for our travels. And today, we visited Lord Peter Winstead, your neighbor. Such an important visit."

34

"Important?"

Lord Russell interjected. "Melissa, tell Miss Cabot about our wedding."

The couple exchanged smiles and Melissa complied. "We had two hundred guests. Held at St. George's, of course. The day's weather cooperated."

Rosanna noticed the abrupt change of subject. She had no idea of the reason behind it, but soon became wrapped up in the details of the wedding and forgot that Melissa had been about to mention something about their visit with Lord Winstead.

Tea arrived, and Melissa described the wedding day at length.

Setting her empty cup down, Rosanna turned toward the newlyweds. "Reuniting with you, Melissa, is so wonderful. I am reminded of our friendship and how we enjoyed our time together in school. In your letter, you mentioned stopping in for a visit, but it would be grand for you to stay for at least a few days. Company has been thin of late, hasn't it, Ellie?"

Ellie looked down at her teacup in her lap and murmured "Indeed."

"Can you put off your departure?"

Melissa gave her husband a yearning look. "Please? I'd love to stay a few days. Maybe until Wednesday?"

"We accept. We can send a message ahead informing Aunt Lucy of a slight delay. She'll understand." He patted his bride's hand and the two smiled into each other's eyes.

Rosanna reached for the bell. "I shall have a small dinner party tomorrow night."

Miss Barton piped up. "Dinner party? Tomorrow night?" Her voice sounded groggy, but she'd woken up in time to catch those important words. "Mr. Clough might be available."

"Yes, dear Miss Barton. I don't believe you've met Lord and Lady Russell? My friend Lady Russell was a schoolmate of mine. They will be staying for a few days."

Her companion came near and met the couple. "So pleased to meet you. Miss Cabot mentioned your name frequently." Formalities accomplished, Miss Barton turned to Rosanna. "I shall meet with Mrs. Good about accommodations, and tell Perkins to have their bags carried in." Miss Barton bustled out.

"Ladies, I think I will take a bit of a walk to stretch my legs, check on the horses, and get the lay of the land. I shall be back in time to dress for dinner." Lord Russell bowed to the three ladies, kissed his wife's hand, and left them to their visit.

Rosanna recalled her curiosity regarding the visit with Lord Winstead. "So, how was your visit to my neighbor, Lord Winstead? Such a coincidence that you are acquainted with him." She sat back with false nonchalance to listen to whatever Melissa would choose to share concerning the somewhat mysterious visit.

"Oh, yes. A coincidence indeed. We simply had to see him on a matter of spiritual importance." She sipped her tea and then closed her lips in a firm line.

At this, Rosanna, chastened at her own nosiness, stopped her probing. "We shall be eight for dinner tomorrow night. You and Lord Russell, our neighbor Lord Halburt, Ellie, me, Lord Winstead, Miss Barton and Mr. Clough. Unfortunately, Lady Brook is away— you'd love her. I'm off to see our Hannah. She's such a treasure of a cook. That reminds me, I must plan an amusement as well."

She hugged Melissa and moved to leave the room. She turned before going out the door. "You and Ellie can visit until Miss Barton returns to take you to your suite. I'm so glad you're staying. It will be so fun!"

~*~

Ensconced in her study, Rosanna tapped her forehead with her fingertips to get ideas rolling. She hadn't expected planning and then writing the clues for a treasure hunt would prove such a challenge. Renegade fantasies of Lord Winstead which kept popping into her head didn't help matters.

"*To step sixteen, left or right, where you turn, shall bide the night…*" Hmmm. Too obscure. How did one arrive at the correct level of mystery and challenge without crossing over into impossibility?

"*Lift the latch, dare not drop, reach too far, a wall will stop.*" The clues came easier once she began. Another problem loomed, however. She'd decided to hide the treasure in the bookshelves, but she hadn't selected the treasure.

Her eyes lit on a glass-fronted curio cabinet in the corner of the small room. A china dog collection crowded the shelves. Lady Winstead, the one who had probably collected them, must have had a serious predilection for dog figurines—there were fifty or more crammed in together.

A small figurine of a beagle adorned with a miniscule golden collar caught her eye. That was it— just the right touch of whimsy. She lifted it carefully from among its crowded fellows and cradled it in her hands for a moment. Idly stroking the glazed head of the little statue, she hummed a tuneless song as her mind went far away. Back to the glen and the moments after Lord Winstead hugged and kissed her. She puzzled over his attitude after the embrace. Yes, she'd gotten rather emotional, but that didn't really account for the subsequent chill emanating from him.

Shaking her head to dispel those fruitless thoughts, she sat down to finish the clues. A rap came upon the door as she finished the last one. "Come in." She called as she slid the stack of clues into the desk drawer.

Melissa slipped into the room and closed the door with a click of the latch. "Oh, I'm so glad to catch you alone."

"I'm pleased you sought me out. What with you a married lady now, and me with a companion and another guest in house, I wondered if we'd even have a chance for a *tête-à-tête*."

Melissa perched sideways on the window seat, drew up her legs and circled them with her arms, leaning her cheek on her knees, regarding Rosanna for a moment before speaking. "I would love to hear the story of this house."

"Story? What story?"

"Why you moved here, why you bought an estate,

why you aren't on the marriage mart. That story."

"You got my letter, didn't you? I explained therein how I was done with London and that Uncle George helped me buy this place."

"Oh, Rosanna. We used to be so close. Don't tell me there's nothing more to it. I know you better than that. You were never one to seclude yourself from society, even though you didn't want to marry after Clarence. There's more to the tale."

Perhaps it was providential that Melissa asked. As Lady Russell, she would be someone who could confidentially direct a desperate young lady to the refuge planned for Honor's Point. "You do know me too well. But you must be discreet with the information I shall share."

Melissa lowered her slippered feet to the floor and sat up straight, avid for the confidence. "I am the soul of discretion."

"This reminds me of academy days, when you and I shared our dreams and crossed pinkies. Solemnly swearing to keep all secrets. Funny—I can't remember now what any of them were."

Smiling, Melissa agreed. "Those days seem so far gone, don't they?"

Rosanna crossed the room, opened the door a crack, looked out, then closed it, and turned the lock. She returned to Melissa's orbit, and spoke in a hushed voice. "The story is, in a nutshell, I planned to establish a refuge for young ladies fleeing forced marriages of the distasteful variety. You certainly understand—the old men, the nasty first cousins, the rancid rakes."

Melissa's eyes grew wide. "No! You're bamming me. How on earth did you ever think you could keep it a secret?"

"You're smarter than me, Melissa. I never thought, until I arrived here, that I had no way of 'inviting' anyone to seek refuge without alerting the very people the young ladies would be running from."

"So that's the story. I shan't pry any more. Please do allow me to assist—perhaps with clothing for the fleeing young ladies? I've a trunk full of dresses along that I no longer want."

"How generous. Are you sure? A whole trunkful?"

"They hold bad memories. I only brought them along because my father's servants loaded the trunk without my knowledge."

"Well, then. That will be a boon for any young ladies who flee without luggage. I'll have a servant remove the trunk from your suite."

"Excellent. For now, I have a secret of my own to share."

"My dear. There's no obligation to unburden yourself."

"No, I want to tell. I myself was pressed toward an arranged marriage. No one too distasteful, but thank the Lord my Papa allowed me some latitude in the decision. Not that things didn't get hairy. The unfortunate man tried to force me to the altar. There—I shall say no more."

"You poor thing. I can only imagine how distressing that must have been."

"Distressing, yes, but now I am married to Lord Russell and all is right with the world."

35

At the breakfast table the next morning, Rosanna reviewed the treasure hunt clues, chortling now and then as she pictured her guests struggling to solve them. Were they too hard? She didn't think so. Besides, if made too easy, what was the fun in that?

Footsteps sounded behind her and she shoved the slips of paper into her lap and drew the folds of her morning dress over them. She turned to see who joined her, and gasped when Lord Halburt, hat in hand, approached her.

"Where's Perkins? How did you get in here?"

"Good morning to you, Miss Cabot." He smacked his gloves into his hat and placed it under his arm. "Nowhere in sight, your butler. All the better for me, no?"

Alarmed at his choice of words, her hand closed around a sharp fork, in case it was needed. She choked out a few polite words for this intrusive cad. "What brings you to Honor's Point so early? The party isn't for hours."

Halburt's face settled into its normal smugness. "I have some outstanding news. It will affect your numbers."

"My numbers? Have you found that you cannot attend after all?" That would qualify as 'outstanding' in her opinion.

"No, my fair one. My news is that Walter Scott's groom arrived this morning. The great man will be at Halburt Arms by mid-afternoon—earlier than expected. What say you to his joining your dinner party tonight?"

"Oh, my! Such a famous man, will he want to come to my humble party?"

"Miss Cabot, don't be silly. First of all, the man has to eat, second, I wouldn't miss your dinner party for the world, and third, he'll champ at the bit when I tell him of the legendary and mysterious treasure of Honor's Point. Mr. Scott is mad for legends."

"Does he travel alone? Is his wife along? What of my plans? The table will be uneven."

Preening, Halburt took his time answering. "I've been informed he is accompanied by his 17-year-old daughter, Sophia. So have no fear about your numbers being even."

With the menu planned, and the treasure hunt prepared, Rosanna had only to inform Mrs. Good of the two additional guests requiring two more place settings. "In that case, I shall be delighted. Such a maven for treasure should love the evening I have planned. Now, please show yourself out, as I am very busy."

"As am I. What with a noteworthy author and poet arriving as a houseguest. *Adieu*, Miss Cabot." He preened on his way out.

~*~

Though happy to leave society behind without an afterthought when she'd gotten the approval to move to her own estate, Rosanna brought her London wardrobe to Honor's Point.

She enjoyed choosing between two new evening dresses, neither of which she'd ever worn before. The first option, made of butter yellow silk, featured three scalloped flounces. The neckline lay off the shoulders and a filmy fichu lent modesty to the fashionably low neckline. Hand-painted fabric roses tinged with pink lay nestled around the flounces. The colors did wonderful things to her complexion.

She leaned toward choosing the other dress, however. Shimmery violet taffeta, its matching gauzy net overskirt fluttered around her when she moved — the effect suggestive of an elegant butterfly. Heavy embroidery of glistening magenta and silver threads stiffened the fashionable bodice, and she had a silvery-toned filet for her hair.

She held the gowns up before her one at a time and waited for her companion's opinion. "Miss Barton, which one? This, or this?"

"Neither will clash with my dress." Barton examined herself a bit before the mirror, already dressed for the evening, clad in a new peacock blue dress. The finest lightweight wool served well for her longstanding sensitivity to cold. "But I do think you'll have other chances to wear the yellow, so I say the purple."

"Violet, Miss Barton. That sounds better than purple."

"You are so clever with words." Her companion chuckled. "I'll see how Dot is coming along with Miss Moore's hair." She departed with a promise to send Dot to help Rosanna dress for the dinner party.

While waiting, Rosanna studied her face in the

mirror. Deeming her complexion a bit pale she pinched her cheeks and bit her lips. *That will have to do*. She did not want to dwell upon her appearance this evening. Once dressed, she made a habit of forgetting about her looks.

Dot entered after a tap on the door.

"Dot, the dresses are on the bed. Go look." Rosanna found it charming when Dot *oohed* and *aahed* over the gowns.

She clasped her hands under her chin. "Miss Cabot, these are so pretty, how will you decide?"

"I have chosen the violet. Yes, that one. Put the yellow away for another occasion."

"Yes, miss." Dot moved with efficiency, and soon had the dress put away.

"Now, Dot, what shall we do with my hair? Chignon, topknot, or a Grecian?"

"Miss, with this filet, a bun with wisps escaping. If that's what you called Grecian, then Grecian."

Rosanna enjoyed having her hair brushed and dressed by the young maid. Dot had a natural gift for the work, and she didn't make the mistake of chattering too much, like some youthful, nervous servant girls would.

Style complete, the maid held a brooch, first above the left temple, then the right. "Miss, may I suggest this pin for your hair? On the side of the filet?"

"The right' side is perfect, Dot. Now, please assist me with the gown." Rosanna stood up, and let her robe slip off her shoulders, revealing a silk chemise. Dot whisked it away and moved to retrieve the gown. With Dot's help, Rosanna soon wore all the requisite layers, fastened and arranged. Next, the maid held out an open jewel box.

"I shall not wear any more jewelry. The brooch and filet are enough. After all, this is a simple country dinner party."

Dot latched the jewel case and slipped it into the dressing table drawer. "Yes, miss."

Rosanna almost danced down the stairs. She met Ellie in the main hall. The diminutive redhead wore a deceptively simple, shimmery green evening gown. Nothing elaborate, but styled with skill and flattering to her coloring.

"You look darling, Ellie. 'Tis a regret no swains will be here for you tonight. Only Halburt."

"Oh, him." The corners of her mouth turned down. "I pray he doesn't actually have any intentions—toward either of us, for that matter. He does cast a wide net with his foolishness. I can only hope his flirtatious demeanor is a mere habit. His attentions carry a perfunctory air, don't they?" Ellie gave a shudder then rushed on, not waiting for an answer. "Swains. I believe I've had enough to last my life, and if I never attract another, that will suit me fine."

Rosanna hooked arms with Ellie. "Yes, I tend to agree. Let's go await the guests. We have about ten minutes. I must tell you some news. Where were you all day?"

"Squirrelled away writing, I'm afraid. So thankful Dot came to help me, or I might still be scribbling. Did you need me?"

Rosanna steered Ellie down the last flight of stairs and into the drawing room where a fire crackled in the hearth. "No, no. I only now realized I hadn't seen you at all today." Turning to face Ellie, Rosanna put a gentle hand on each shoulder. "You know I pulled together tonight's dinner party for my guests, the Russells. We'll have two additional guests, however. Walter Scott and his daughter."

Ellie's hand flew to her neck and fluttered there, while her eyes grew round. "Walter Scott? You can't mean the poet. The famous Scottish poet? He's really here? I thought all that was mere flummery on the part of Lord Halburt."

"I do mean that very man. Halburt has been corresponding with him about some antiquities, and the great man, on his way to London, accepted Halburt's invitation to break travel at Halburt Arms."

Ellie's hand went up to her throat. "Such a famous wordsmith. I'm meeting the author of *The Lady of the Lake*. Oh, my. I must sit down." She then sank back to rest against the settee and fanned her face.

"Yes, yes, do sit. Here's some cold water." Rosanna poured from a pitcher conveniently placed nearby on a tea tray. "Here you are." She proffered a glass to Ellie. "So glad tea's been brought in. Now if the guests want tea, it's already here."

Ellie sipped, set the glass down, and still rattled by the news, spoke in a hushed voice. "What do you have planned?"

"The clues for a treasure hunt are prepared. The treasure is hidden. I can only hope this satisfies Halburt and he quits pestering me. It's too bad Lady Brook is away. She'd be the perfect one to repress Halburt's impetuosity."

"What other gentleman would badger a neighbor for a complicated entertainment? He has been markedly odd about it, hasn't he? Lord Halburt is a spoiled man."

"He's sure to be in high alt, with his noted guest,

who   apparently   also   shares   Halburt's   love   of mysteries, old things, legends, and treasure."

36

Peter's stomach clenched as he waited. His tension mounted with each added guest, announced with pomp by Perkins.

Perkins swooped in followed by a group of three, presumably the last arrivals for the party of ten. "Lord Halburt, Mr. Walter Scott, Miss Scott." The butler swept his arm to the side, and then bent from the waist, bowed as he backed out of the room and shut the door on his way out, still bent over. The man must love his job.

Peter observed the arriving guests as Halburt brought the Scotts around to introduce them. His tension rose in waves as the trio neared.

"Lord Winstead—you did retain your title, correct? No matter, please meet the esteemed literary lion, Mr. Walter Scott, and his lovely eldest daughter, Miss Scott."

The Scotts glanced at each other, dumbfounded.

Even though his spine felt leaden at the snub, Peter responded to the embarrassed guests with courtesy. "The pleasure is mine. Wonderful to meet such an esteemed guest and you, too, Miss Scott." The young lady simpered and fluttered her lashes, before Halburt ushered them on to meet someone else.

As Halburt brushed past, trailing the Scotts, Peter

laid a staying hand on the man's forearm. "My title is intact. No act of Parliament has been writ against me, and I am no criminal. No further reference need be made by you regarding my familial misfortune. I'll thank you to guard your tongue in company." Peter released Halburt's arm with emphasis, then brushed his hands together and turned away. As he surveyed the room, he noted the world hadn't stopped turning, and indeed, no one other than the Scotts heard Halburt's verbal slap.

Small groups chatted, sipped punch, and waited for the call in to dinner.

Awkwardness gripped him, this party held a high potential for embarrassment. He stood near the fire, ostensibly conversing with Lord Russell, whose voice only skittered around the edge of his consciousness. Peter nodded, raised his eyebrows, and offered a semblance of a smile. He allowed himself a glance at Rosanna.

She stood with Lady Russell, Miss Scott and Miss Moore near a harpsichord on the other side of the room.

What if she learned of his misdeed? They may have told her. He sensed something disturbing would happen here tonight and if he got through this evening unscathed, he'd be surprised.

For starters, Rosanna's appearance in his line of sight distressed him in the region of his heart. And why did his blood course so strongly through his veins each time his gaze landed on her? Awareness of her pained him in its intensity.

She dazzled him. What possessed him to accept this invitation? Trapped in the same vicinity not only with her, the unattainable woman he'd compromised in the glen, but there were the Russells. They'd been kind, but he hadn't bargained on having to mingle with them here at Honor's Point. How much would they have told their dear friend, Rosanna? "Hmmm?" He dragged his attention back to Lord Russell.

"I said, have you known Halburt for very long?"

"For as long as I can remember. He grew up on a property adjoining this one." Peter kept his remarks brief.

Lord Russell's lips quirked in displeasure. "Has he always been so, um, impetuous? He won't stop nattering about some treasure hunt."

"Yes, I heard him. Bordering on nagging, what?" Peter sighed with relief when Perkins entered the room to announce dinner. This evening couldn't pass fast enough for him. He stood back while couples formed for the ritual of walking into the dining room according to rank.

Lord Halburt, though of equal title with Lord Russell, decided to seize precedence—barging forward to place Miss Cabot's hand on his arm. Next came the Russells.

Peter roused himself and bowed to Miss Moore, then held his arm out for her to rest her hand upon. Part of Peter's mind noticed her exquisite beauty, but his senses didn't reel when he looked at her. When he looked at Rosanna, however, his world tipped, emphasizing nothing would ever be the same.

Walter Scott and his daughter, Sophia, followed along, then came Miss Barton and Mr. Clough bringing up the rear.

The party of ten sat around a table laden with gleaming silver, fine china, and lit by tall candelabra. Mr. Clough anchored one end of the large table,

Rosanna the other. Soon, a prayer was offered and the serving of the first course began.

Seating arrangements could have been worse for Peter. As it was, he sat between Miss Barton and Miss Moore. He made small talk with his table companions. The gilded walls and painted ceiling of the lavish room were duly noted and complimented by the other guests. Peter rarely dined in this room when his family owned the house. His parents entertained guests here, almost never using it for family meals. If he could just get through this evening without any overt embarrassment, he'd never accept such an invitation again.

Across from him sat Melissa, now Lady Russell. Grateful for her forgiveness, he still wished she and her husband had left the vicinity after their call on him. Finding himself in this awkward situation served as another reminder of how little control over his life he had anymore. He'd thought losing his ancestral home, his fortune, his pride, and honor had brought him into the depths. But being here, near Miss Cabot, the woman he cared for, but would never to be in a position to make her his own, made his heart even more sore. The situation added up to almost more than his hard-won new equanimity could withstand.

He played with his soup, not really eating. His gaze kept drifting down to his right, to the end of the table where Miss Cabot presided. Why did she have to be so beautiful? His heart gave a painful squeeze just to view her pretty face. He noted her stunning violet gown of the latest fashion, but without the extreme low necklines that were *de rigueur*. Another thing to be thankful for. He couldn't have stood seeing more of her lovely flesh.

37

Rosanna fought distraction and played with her turtle soup. She brought the spoon to her lips, in a charade of eating. Her appetite fled the moment Lord Winstead walked into the drawing room. The excitement of seeing him again after their meaningful exchange in the glen took away all desire for food. The cook made several of Rosanna's favorite dishes, but the sight of him halfway down the table distracted her from the flavorful meal.

He glanced her way, off and on, but his gaze never rested long. She tried to catch his eye with an encouraging smile, but he didn't give her any eye contact. She began to perceive a coolness emanating from him. Their intimate interaction out in the midst of the glen began to take on the nature of a lost dream. Why did he abruptly act so cold? Being hurt by a man wasn't in her plans.

"Miss Cabot. You must tell our esteemed guest of the tales about this estate. Its reputed treasure and all."

"Lord Halburt, how you do go on. I've heard no more than what you've told me. However, Mr. Scott, the house itself is a treasure, and beautifully decorated by the prior mistress."

"I assure you, I agree, this being my first time in this part of England. My wee daughter and I are on our way to London for business and pleasure. Sure and begorrah, stopping here is a high note with the beautiful land hereabouts."

"Why, thank you. I hope you won't be disappointed that there's no treasure here."

"Young lady, relieve your doubts on that score. I can't say when I've enjoyed a bookish discussion the likes of what I've enjoyed with Miss Moore. We see eye to eye about the coming ascendancy of the novel as a literary form of great importance."

The sparkle in his eyes reassured Rosanna that the famed Scottish bard was sincerely enjoying his table partner. She breathed a sigh of relief that the seating arrangements were working out.

As the meal wore on, however, Rosanna became queasy. How could she misinterpret events to this degree? Winstead, very recently so sensitive and kind, but tonight giving her not a moment of attention. She wanted the evening to end. But the silly treasure hunt had to be gotten through first. She said the words expected of her, forcing an arch smile onto her stiff face. "Ladies, we shall adjourn."

The men stood and bowed the ladies out of the room.

Rosanna led the way. Gathered in the drawing room again, the ladies chattered to the accompaniment of Miss Barton's clicking needles.

"Rosanna, your menu surpassed anything I've enjoyed in London. I must get the recipe for that lemon pudding." Melissa waxed on. "As a newlywed, I find a great interest in the homemaking arts."

"May I obtain it too?" Sophia Scott asked in a sweet voice. "I've never had lemon pudding before."

"Thank you, ladies. I shall have my cook bring it to my study tomorrow and I'll make two fair copies, one for each of you." Rosanna's head ached at the base of her skull. Thinking of writing out a recipe didn't vanquish her other painful thoughts. *Would her head ever stop whirling with questions about Lord Winstead?* She dragged her mind back to the present.

The male contingent trailed into the room.

Halburt would begin to nag and pry if she didn't announce the treasure hunt within the first few minutes.

Lord Russell came directly to stand next to Melissa. Reverend Clough parked himself next to Miss Barton on the blue and white striped settee, and Lord Winstead strode over to the fireplace to lean a hand on the mantel. Halburt paraded along in Walter Scott's wake and then made a fuss settling the great man in a comfortable chair, offering footstool and shawl.

"I shall leave the orbit of a literary lion to pay court to a lamb of beauty." Halburt announced to no one in particular, and then sidled over to stand beside Rosanna's chair.

She cleared her throat. "Friends, we at Honor's Point prepared an amusement for this evening."

This announcement elicited murmurs of mild polite excitement.

"Lord Halburt has a penchant for treasure hunts, and I decided to pacify his urgings by planning one for this gathering."

"Oh, goody! This will be so fun." Halburt rubbed his hands together. "Playing as teams? Or on our own?"

"There are ten of us, and of course, I shall sit out, and that leaves nine. If it's agreeable, I'd like four teams of two, and you, Lord Halburt, will be on a one-man team."

"That's suits me. I'm quite good at this." Halburt surveyed the group with a smug face. "I've done this before."

Hard for her to believe the lengths the man would go to for his own amusement. Did he not perceive at all how selfish and pompous he sounded? She glanced at Ellie and caught a distinct flicker of merriment sparkling in her green eyes.

Lowering her gaze so as not to laugh, Rosanna willed her shoulders not to shake and made a show of checking her list, collecting herself before speaking. "Lord Winstead, you and Miss Scott make up team one. Miss Barton and Mr. Clough, team two. Lord and Lady Russell, team three, Miss Moore and Mr. Scott, team four. During the treasure hunt, I shall be roaming about, perhaps offering cryptic assistance, perhaps sniggering behind your backs."

Melissa Russell's giggle of anticipatory glee emerged from her perfect pink lips. "Miss Cabot, you wouldn't do that to us—your friends?"

"Yes, I would. The kitchens are off limits, as are the bedrooms. There are no clues or treasure in those rooms. Once you've found a clue, each of which exist four copies, take your copy and leave the rest for those who come after. I've made the clues difficult, but within reason. I shall now read aloud the first clue." Rosanna held a small piece of paper cupped in one delicate hand. "Listen:

Find the picture, 'What is It?'
Tho' they grumbled when It was found,
Your clue is also on the ground."

"Off you all go!"

The guests streamed out of the room.

Rosanna swept her shawl off the chair and handed

it to Dot, who emerged from a corner and stood behind the chair. "Dot, we'll give them a few minutes' start, then you will accompany me about the house. I'll be hinting both toward and away from clues by wherever we traverse."

"Ooh. Miss, that's so clever." The maid's wispy hair moved in sync with her nodding head. "I've got your shawl, anything else?"

Rosanna allowed Dot to position the shawl across her shoulders. The fashionable thin silk and muslin dresses were feminine, but not warm for the wearer, thus bringing shawls into great popularity and necessity, especially welcome in the evenings. "Since we need to give them time to start, I do believe I'd like my vinaigrette. Let's go together to retrieve it from my rooms, before we begin moving about."

The maid lagged behind.

As Rosanna rounded the corner, and turned right at the top of the stairs, she let out a slight gasp and stepped back, knocking into Dot. "Oof. Oh my." She'd spotted Halburt backing out of the Lilac Room—Ellie's room.

His evening jacket was the only bright blue one among the company and even in the dim light of the upper hall, it was clearly he who pulled the door shut then scuttled to the far end of the corridor toward the servants' stairs. The man was a self-important popinjay, but was it possible he was serious about pursuing Ellie? Perhaps that explained his presence in her bedroom, in a room clearly stated as off limits for the hunt. He didn't seem the type to hand-deliver love-notes, poems, or nosegays, but it could be possible.

38

Dot's voice held a whiny reproach. "Miss, what's the matter? Why did we stop?"

"Nothing, nothing. I merely had a thought." Rosanna delayed several seconds, letting Halburt get out of sight. Servants' gossip was never beneficial. She peeked around the corner, not detecting the blue-clad man's presence in the hall any longer. "Wait here, Dot."

She proceeded to the end of the hall, wanting to be sure of Halburt's departure. Yes, the door to the back stairs stood open a crack. A house rule ordered that door to be always closed at night. She reached out and latched it. She didn't want anyone else to wander down the dark stairs, and possibly fall down the steps. No one would, if they followed the rules of the game. And if Halburt fell, he'd have his recompense for being a snoop and a boor. Reversing her steps, she paused at the head of the main stairs. "The stair door was open, Dot. Let's go to my rooms."

Dot followed, huffing to keep up with Rosanna's quick steps. To the left of the main stairs lay Rosanna's suite. Pensive, she sank onto the bench at her dressing table for a moment, trying to make sense of what she observed. Twiddling her fingers over her comb, brush, and hand mirror, she came to a decision. The question of Halburt's presence in the Lilac Room would have to be set aside for the moment, for the sake of the other guests, but she would not forget. She'd speak with Ellie about Halburt's intrusion, later.

"Dot, get the vinaigrette, we must hasten to do our part. Since clue number one leads to the long gallery, we shall go there." She rose and with a brisk step, swept out, navigated the halls to the narrow room lined with windows on one side.

Dot, having scurried to keep up, panted out an observation. "No one's here yet."

Rosanna checked the niche which held the slips of paper. "And no clues taken, thus far. Hmm. Perhaps I made them too hard. At least, the first one. I shall play the pianoforte. That will draw them to this room."

Dot scurried to assist with opening the instrument and swept the seat with a feather duster kept nearby for that purpose.

Rosanna seated herself, flexed her fingers and began to play a Mozart piano sonata.

The poignancy of the music eased her emotional state. My, how she wished this evening was over. Being near Winstead with his strained and cold behavior gave her an almost physical pain. Her befuddled heart squeezed with the agony of uncertaintly. No mistake about the warmth he'd shown her in the glen, though his current behavior told a different tale.

Thoughts interrupted, she looked up and stopped playing as Winstead entered the gallery. She wasn't surprised, for he'd be one of the few treasure hunters who would recall the series of Biblical paintings hung at the far end of the gallery, one of which portrayed the Israelites in the desert, complaining. The remaining guests would have to straggle in as they ruled out other rooms, or perhaps would hear the music and realize it as a clue.

"Oh, hello. Where's your partner? Sophia, correct?" Her calm voice belied the way her heart pounded.

His gaze flicked over to where the maid stood by the wall. "She tore her hem, so we separated, while she went with the housekeeper to repair it. I shan't be long. Just here to get my clue before the others." He moved down the narrow room and reached down into the pertinent alcove. Straightening, he read the next clue.

Attraction clenched Rosanna's stomach as she watched him run raking fingers through his springy, attractive hair.

He strode back to where she sat with one hand still on the keys.

"Please resume your delightful music. When I heard it, my mind flew back to the long gallery and the clue made sense. My mother used to play here by the hour. She's also the one who explained the meaning of the Hebrew word *manna* to me." He edged toward the door as if he couldn't get away fast enough.

"Fascinating. You are the first, however, so don't tarry if you want to stay ahead of the rest. Halburt is rabid about this hunt." Though hurt by his seeming disregard, she met his eyes, holding her gaze steady, willing him to look at her. Coolness, no, coldness shrouded his expression, and his eyes didn't meet hers.

"Thank you for the advice, I shall be off." He gave a minimal bow—little more than a nod, and shot out the door at a fast clip.

Rosanna's head dipped in discouragement, but her hands sought out the keys as she moved into a mournful nocturne. Before she concluded the piece, the other seven treasure hunters appeared all at once.

Stymied by the clue, they'd finally followed the sound of the music and now, gathered around, expectant, waiting for hints and help.

Miss Barton, Mr. Clough, Melissa, and Lord Russell all acted lighthearted and as if they were having a jolly time, hunting around the manor house.

Ellie and Mr. Scott stood off to the side, chatting about literature.

Rosanna could pick up a few words, such as editor, printer, books.

"Don't say you're all stumped?"

Halburt, however, had a pout on his face that threatened to become a full sulk.

"Miss Cabot, do tell us how you thought we'd decipher your impenetrable clue." He placed his hands on his hips and put one foot ahead, pointed forward.

She fully expected him to begin to dramatically gesticulate and expound, so she forestalled him with a hint. She swept her left arm in the direction of the painting. "My dear friends, please take a stroll to the other end of the gallery. There you'll see a scene that fits the clue."

Halburt dashed ahead of the others, giving Mr. Clough a slight shove. He reached the alcove, grabbed up a slip of paper and without even stopping to read it, ran out into the hall.

Rosanna laughed behind her hand, since the light in that passage shone much too dim for reading. Her amusement at Halburt's' expense short-lived, as a swath of mortified chagrin again sank her spirits as she remembered Winstead's rejecting attitude.

The rest of the guests stood around the alcove, sharing ideas, laughing, and having a pleasant time with the process.

"I say, didn't I read somewhere that manna tastes like coriander?" Mr. Clough offered. "Whatever that is."

"It's a spice. I'm hoping 'tis a mild one since they had to eat those flakes for years on end." Miss Barton tapped Mr. Clough's arm with her gloved finger for emphasis.

Rosanna kept a smile on her face While she watched them—a good façade to hide her heartache, though her entertaining evening had turned sour.

The way Winstead acted now didn't make sense combined with his actions in the glen. She remembered every golden moment, and she'd done nothing to give him a sudden disgust of her. Or had she? Rumors said that some men preferred young ladies not to show any amorous responses. He'd been so close, so kind. The episode receded as if she'd imagined the whole thing, but she hadn't.

Something else was wrong.

39

Pressing her fingers into her temples, Rosanna returned to the sitting room where she gave the first clue an hour ago and waited for the group to reconvene. She'd done her best to both help and misdirect the treasure hunters.

The final clue would lead the guests to return here—to square one.

Sitting motionless, thoughts of Winstead rushed in again. Her head pounded. She sent Dot on an errand. "Dot, please scamper down to the kitchen for some willow bark tea. My head is sore. Do hurry." She massaged her temples. Moments after Dot scooted out of the room, Rosanna heard steps and steeled herself to face all the guests and the denouement of the hunt. But the footsteps belonged to one guest, again out ahead of the pack.

Lord Winstead entered the room, leaving the door open. "Miss Cabot. The search for treasure proved to be an excellent diversion. Pardon me while I find the prize." With those words he turned away and scanned the bookshelves to the right of the fireplace. He stepped over with confidence, let his long fingers play over the surface of the books, then drew out two thick volumes. After placing the books on the table nearby, he reached into the gap.

"Eureka!" He held out the canine figurine with the

golden collar. "What's this, a beagle?"

Before she could answer, the others entered in a cluster.

Still floating on a cloud of happy excitement, Miss Barton enthused, "That's a darling treasure!"

Her partner beamed down at her through his wire-rimmed glasses, then turned his attention to their hostess. "Miss Cabot, I can't remember when I've been so diverted. You have a marvelous way with words and your hints were great fun." Mr. Clough rocked back on his heels and smiled about at the other guests.

Walter Scott added his plaudits. "Your clues were quite poetic. I find myself inspired to replicate this fine entertainment when I'm next home at Abbotsford."

The group fell silent, as if waiting for pearls from the renowned wordsmith. He went on, "Such figurines shall be collected for centuries, if I don't miss my guess." Mr. Scott contributed from his fund of knowledge. "The market for antiquities continues to expand."

"May I hold it?" Miss Barton reached out toward Lord Winstead, who handed the china beagle over to her.

Lord Halburt frowned at Rosanna as he spoke "Not the treasure I expected. But, Miss Cabot, I will credit you. You gave us a challenge. Some of your clues perplexed me to no end." He chatted with the other guests, giving special attention to Sophia Scott, while alternating glances at the clock on the mantel and at the door.

Melissa gave her opinion, too. "The clues were excellent. Each time I deciphered one, I kicked myself for not seeing sooner what you were driving at."

"Indeed, once solved, they were crystal clear."

Lord Russell patted his wife's hand. "Easy for us to say, now, isn't that right, darling?"

Dot bustled into the room and froze in her tracks. She looked down at the single cup and saucer in her hands, then up at the roomful of guests.

"Bring that here, Dot. It's fine." Rosanna accepted the cup and set it down on a nearby table. Drat. She couldn't drink the concoction and her head pounded worse than ever.

Relief came in the form of Lord Winstead speaking up, almost as if he perceived her discomfort. "This has been a lovely evening like no other, but the hour is late and the travelers," he nodded toward the Russells, "must be off early tomorrow, if I'm not mistaken. So, I shall be saying my 'goodbyes'." He bowed to all the guests, then to Rosanna, lifted her hand to his lips, and bowed over it without an actual kiss.

His warm hand sent an electric throb up that side of her body and a tingle shot down her legs. *How scandalous of me. I must get control.* When he let go, he backed away, eyes averted. She stood up to receive parting comments from the other three gentlemen.

"I thank you, Miss Cabot, for a most diverting evening. The dinner, delicious, the company, delightful. I shall see you Friday as we discussed." Mr. Clough raised his eyebrows, glanced smiling at Miss Barton and then bowed, once toward each lady present, before exiting the room.

Perkins appeared in the doorway, chin up, standing stiff and ready to hand the men their hats, and show them the door.

Carrying on as if he were on stage, handsome Lord Halburt orated his parting words. "You've surely made the Scotts' evening memorable. I'll bring them over tomorrow so they can see the house in daylight."

"Certainly, I'm sure." Rosanna was flummoxed, and at a loss for words at the temerity of Halburt. "You forestalled me. I was about to invite the Scotts to join me for tea tomorrow at their convenience."

She reached out and clasped Miss Scott's hand, and then offered her hand to the courtly Mr. Scott, who beamed and bowed over it. After bowing he addressed her. "Ah, lass, to see this delightful, noble home in the light of day would be charming, but 'twill have to be upon another trip. My daughter and I are leaving at first light. Thank you for your hospitality." He offered his arm to his daughter and moved regally out into the hall.

Halburt, taken by surprise at the abrupt turn of events, scurried along behind the illustrious man of letters.

The door closed behind him, and a collective sigh of relief could be heard.

Ellie let out a giggle and then her fingers shot up to cover her mouth. Guilt and amusement warred on her face.

Lord Russell took his wife's hand and tucked it in the crook of his elbow. "We have a long journey tomorrow, so we shall depart from this charming party."

With all the goodnights said, Ellie and Miss Barton sat back in a group of chairs near the fire.

Rosanna joined them there. Even though she sensed a contemplative mood, she took a sip of her now-tepid medicinal tea and broke the silence. She glanced at Barton, then gazed at Ellie, as though she'd have the answer. "What could Lord Halburt have been doing coming out of a bedroom upstairs?"

40

Ellie sat up straight. "A bedroom? You specifically made bedrooms off limits."

Miss Barton gave a derisive sniff, folded her arms across her chest, and raised her chin. "That man, such an interloper. I've never seen the like. As handsome-looking as can be, but so off-putting."

While watching Ellie for any revealing reaction, Rosanna added fuel to the fire. "He didn't see me, but I observed him leaving the Lilac Room." Nothing but shock on Ellie's face told Rosanna the young lady had no knowledge of Halburt's visit to her room. She hadn't really believed Ellie to be complicit, but had wanted to make sure.

"That man is so pushy. To intrude into a private area of a home is beyond rude." Ellie rubbed her arms as though a chill passed over her. "Did you say the Lilac Room? That's my room. I'd like to know why he went into my room. Did he go into any others?"

A chill of fear raced up Rosanna's spine. "Not that I saw. He scooted away down the back stair after he closed the door to your room." The man's behavior wore the shape of a sinister puzzle—one with missing pieces. First, he'd almost insisted she plan a treasure hunt. After all, if he liked them so much, why didn't he host one at his own house?

Miss Barton pounded her fist on the arm of her

chair, and spoke with decisiveness. "Rosanna, please forego inviting that man here again if at all possible."

"Miss Barton, he won't be invited by me, but he has shown himself not above arriving here at his good pleasure." Rosanna clasped her hands in her lap, and shivered. "I will instruct Perkins to say I'm not at home to Lord Halburt for the forseeable future. At least until I can solve the riddle of the man's presence in the Lilac Room—Ellie's bedroom."

"Fine, I concur with that. If he materializes anywhere near me, I shall give him a proper set-down." Miss Barton made this pronouncement then clamped her lips shut, as if she'd said more than she'd intended.

~*~

Rosanna swam up out of a deep sleep, groaned, pushed back the bed curtains and listened. Something woke her. Intense in an instant, she focused, taking small breaths, listening for the sound to occur again. It had been a loud clunk. Hard to know where it came from, but if she heard it again, maybe she could identify the source.

A scream rent the air of the silent house.

Rosanna shot out of bed, grabbed a wrapper, and ran out into the hall.

Miss Barton emerged from her room next door, shoving her arms into her robe. The older woman wore a tilting nightcap giving her a raffish air.

The two huddled together.

Miss Barton whispered. "Where did that come from?"

"That had to be Ellie. The only woman in this part of the house is Ellie, and it came from the direction of the guest wing. Let's go." Without waiting for an answer, Rosanna grabbed Miss Barton's forearm and pulled her down the hall and across the landing, toward the Lilac Room.

Rosanna tapped on the door, and then swept into the room. Miss Barton entered in her wake and both women stopped short at the sight that met them.

Ellie huddled in a lump as far away in the corner of the large four-poster bed as possible. The window stood wide open and the drapes were blowing around as a gusty wind gained entrance and continued to rampage through the room.

Miss Barton hustled over to shut and latch the window.

Rosanna surveyed the scene as she moved toward the bed. The room, uncomfortably cold, had the look of a disaster. A hassock tipped over, a rug rumpled, and several drawers hanging askew.

"Ellie, was that you screaming?" Rosanna hastened to ascertain the facts. "A clunking noise woke me. Then came a scream."

Covers clutched to her chin and gulping for both air and composure, Ellie spoke in a rush of words. "Yes, I screamed. I heard the squeak of a drawer, then a footstep. Half asleep—so confused." She held a clenched fist in front of her mouth and her shoulders convulsed.

"There, there, now." Miss Barton patted Ellie's arm, then wrapped a shawl around her shaking shoulders. She helped her to rise, then guided her over to Rosanna. "Sit down dearie, while I stoke the fire."

Rosanna poured reassurance into her voice and

hoped Ellie would soon stop shaking. "Sit here. You're fine, whoever it was is gone."

"So frightened, a man, all in black—oh, Rosanna, I was terrified. He stood right there." Pointing to the center of the rug, Ellie gripped the arm of the settee, perhaps to still her shaking. "I screamed, then he climbed out over the sill and was gone. What was he searching for?"

"Is anything missing?" Rosanna's eyes scanned the disarrayed room.

"I can't tell for sure, but my manuscript is still here, Praise God. Miss Barton, would you please hand me that?" She indicated a stack of paper on the desk, and when Barton placed it in her hands, Ellie hugged it to her chest.

Rosanna lifted the sash and gave a quick look around before locking the window again. "It appears whoever came in used a ladder, which would explain the clunking sound. There's no convenient tree or drain spout anywhere near this window. I shall have Bramstock investigate the grounds in the morning. I'll also direct Perkins to check the locks on all doors and windows every night before retiring. For now, my friend, you come sleep in my room. I have a trundle bed in my dressing room and a wonderful down comforter."

Rosanna led Ellie, with Miss Barton bringing up the rear. They traversed the hall, jumpy and scared of their own shadows as the fearsome events had shaken them. Rosanna tried to reassure. "Ladies, this has me scared of my own shadow."

It took some time to settle in. Rosanna tossed and turned, the heavy responsibility of the estate weighing on her. She hadn't been prepared to manage an estate, but her determination brought her this far. Who could she consult about this? Her options were few. She neither expected to face such danger, nor the urge to fling herself into Lord Winstead's arms.

41

Rosanna's eyes flew open and she threw off the covers. She needed to instruct the servants to be extra quiet this morning. Sounds of doors opening and closing, and people clomping upstairs to do their duties might wake Ellie. Poor Ellie must have peace and rest after last night's shock.

Rosanna padded over to her wardrobe, thankful that she had a few morning gowns that could be donned unaided. One of her own design, it went on over the head and then tied to fit under the bosom. Stuffing her feet into shoes, she tiptoed out of her room, and down the stairs to warn the staff to avoid her bedroom. Arriving in the hall, she spied the butler sorting mail. "Ah, there you are, Perkins. Tell the staff not to tend to my room this morning, Miss Moore slept on my trundle bed last night and must not be disturbed."

The butler's reedy voice came out a bit rusty this early. "Very good, Miss. Anything else?"

"I'm going to my study and I'd like some coffee there. I'll need a message delivered to the rectory in approximately ten minutes." *There, that sets things in motion. Now to the next step.*

"Very good, miss."

"And Perkins? Lord and Lady Russell plan to depart after breakfast. Please alert me when they arrive in the dining room. I shall join them."

Perkins scurried off to enact her instructions. She entered her study and the soothing colors of the room had their effect. Her mind cleared as she pulled a piece of paper toward herself and dipped a pen to load it with ink.

Wednesday

Dear Mr. Clough,

Though we planned to meet for a talk on Friday, I find myself needing counsel post haste. If workable for you, I'd like to speak with you later this morning. Would 11:00 at Honor's Point be convenient? Please send a reply with my messenger.

Cordially, Miss Rosanna Cabot

"There." Taking a deep breath, she placed the note in an envelope and sealed it with wax. She'd brought her seal, a rose, when she'd moved in, but had found in the desk, a seal with the letters "HP" intertwined. Today, she used the Honor's Point seal. Her commitment to making a life here caused her to want to make a statement any way possible. Circumstances would not force her away. Not intruders, nor friends turning cold, nor her own sore heart.

She rang the bell again, waiting for Perkins to come get the message. The staff here were so reliable, so good. Such a blessing that none of them seemed to resent her presence here. *Lord, thank You that I can still be grateful for Your provision. I need—*

The door opened, Perkins leaned through the doorway, a smile on his face. Another blessing. She worked well with the butler. Perkins seemed to approve of her. But Peter Winstead, on the other hand, what were his feelings? Shoving that intruding thought aside, she smiled at the servant, raising her eyebrows in inquiry.

"Miss Cabot, Lord and Lady Russell just entered the dining room." Perkins's loud, yet reedy voice certainly took some getting used to.

"Thank you. Here's a message for Reverend Clough. Tell whoever you send to wait for a reply. And please cancel the coffee, I'll go to the dining room." She stood, smoothed her dress, and gave a moment's thought to whether it sufficed for appearing in company. It would need to. After all, Melissa was here to visit her, not to judge her wardrobe. And the newlyweds only had eyes for each other.

The couple, heads together, whispered and laughed and broke away from each other only when Rosanna cleared her throat. "Good morning. I trust you rested well? No disturbances in the night?" With nonchalance, Rosanna moved along the sideboard, selecting her usual choices, eggs, bacon, and coffee.

The new bride gave a glowing glance to her husband. "We slept like children. Country air is so good for that."

Melissa's contentment made Rosanna happy for her friend. Witnessing the couple so blissful gave her hope. Someday, maybe she'd have someone to look at that way. She sat at the end of the table, murmuring thanks to the footman who pulled the chair out for her. Sipping coffee, she glanced out the window and caught a fleeting glimpse of someone, she couldn't make out who, carrying a ladder across the lawn. She sputtered a bit and her cup clanked down into its saucer.

The Russells looked at her, concern on their faces.

Melissa half rose, asking, "Are you fine? Did you choke?"

"I'm fine. A worker walked past out in the yard

and it startled me, that's all." Oh, it would be nice to unburden her fears to her friends. But no, she would not heap her problems onto the happy newlyweds. They'd be leaving in less than an hour, if departure went as planned. No need to share her burdensome woes since she fully expected to speak to Mr. Clough later in the morning. Instead, Rosanna began a strand of conversation regarding the Russell's plans for the next leg of their trip. Talk went on around this and some peripheral matters, until the time came for them to take their leave.

Rising, Lord Russell gave a parting compliment. He assisted Lady Russell to her feet. She beamed up at him, obvious pride shining in her eyes. "Miss Cabot, I'm so glad we were able to visit you here at Honor's Point. It's a lovely estate. And meeting Walter Scott was priceless. He's truly noble as well. I predict he'll be knighted by the Prince Regent who is a great admirer of the poet's work."

"Thank you. I'm beginning to settle in completely here, and it was an honor to have you two as overnight guests. It was wonderful to see you again after all this time." Rosanna reached out to grasp hands, but Melissa moved in for a ladylike hug.

"So glad you are doing so well. And such nice neighbors, too—Lord Halburt, Lady Brook, and Lord Winstead." Melissa's brow arched, and her husband took her hand, interrupting her flow of words.

"My dear, we must be off."

~*~

Turning away after a final wave, Rosanna stepped

back through the heavy, brass-trimmed front door.

The butler closed it behind her.

"Perkins, I'll be in my study." She strode down the hall, to her study, relishing having a room of her own in which to take care of correspondence and business matters. Seating herself at the delicate, yet efficient writing desk, she pulled an account book out of its slot. Open, the book took up almost the whole surface of the desk. She bent her head to the task, but her mind refused to focus on the columns of numbers, and instead ran ahead to her meeting with Mr. Clough. She closed the book, and rose, going to stand by the window. The sight of the lawn made her blink. How could she have let this slip her mind? She dashed out into the hall, calling, "Perkins! Perkins, where are you?"

The elderly retainer emerged from the library, a feather duster in one hand and a leather-bound tome in the other. "Yes, miss?" He stood at attention, clearly surprised at her mode of calling.

"Sorry for raising my voice, but I recalled something. Something important, and I need to see Bramstock immediately. Before Mr. Clough arrives." She clasped her hands beneath her bosom, attempting to regain a composed appearance. It would never do for Perkins think her a flighty miss.

"I will call Bramstock, miss." Perkins bowed and set the book and duster on a side table, folded his cuffs down, straightened his cravat, and marched toward the back of the house to locate the steward.

Rosanna rubbed her forehead as she returned to her study, barely gaining the room when a tap came on the door.

Bramstock entered, looking curious, but like a man

with no time to waste.

"Thank you, Bramstock. It's simple. I mean a simple question. I saw, I mean, there was a ladder. I saw a tall ladder this morning. Outside. One of the gardeners, I believe, carried it across the lawn. Where did it come from? Is there a project going on or a repair on the house, perhaps?" She schooled her face to reflect mild interest and kicked herself for sounding like such a flibbertigibbet.

Impatient, the steward wasted no words. "Miss Cabot, I am aware of no projects that require a tall ladder."

Rosanna debated whether to ask the steward to investigate and decided against it. It would seem odd to show so much interest in a ladder being used, and by whom. She'd have to find out another way, discreetly, if possible. It wouldn't do to spread the news about evidence of a strange man climbing into Ellie's room. "That is all. I thought you might know, but it's of no real importance." She smiled before turning away, and he exited, closing the door.

She needed to organize a list of her thoughts for Mr. Clough's visit. Where to start? The intruder. Lord Winstead's coldness. Those two topics would suffice. It amazed her how life could go from uneventful, peaceful days one after another, to this constant niggling unease at the back of her mind.

The hour of eleven came and Dot entered saying the minister had arrived.

Rosanna immediately went to the drawing room and found Mr. Clough standing by the window. She closed the door before greeting the clergyman. "Good morning!" Rosanna held out her hand and led the minister to the settee. She sat down and patted the seat next to her. "Thank you for coming here on such short notice. I need a fair amount of wisdom and advice from you, I'm afraid. Life is becoming complicated and I need your wise counsel."

The dark-haired, older man swept the tails of his coat out of the way as he seated himself. "Happy to be of service. Let us begin with a word of prayer."

Rosanna murmured assent and bowed her head.

"Our Father in Heaven, please guide our words, and by Your Spirit bring Your wisdom to bear on the life of Miss Cabot."

"Thank you." Her voice shook, and unshed tears threatened to fall. The paternal loving kindness in the man's voice about undid her. She clenched her hands, digging her nails into her palms. She didn't want to turn into a watering pot now of all times.

"So, Miss Cabot, you are in need of advice, and I am in need of tea. I took the liberty of telling Perkins to send a tray." He raised his craggy brows and gave a crooked grin. She caught a flash of the boy he once had been—a reminder of the minister's humanity. She could only hope he epitomized a fount of wisdom.

"That's fine. Now, before the tray arrives, I shall tell you one of my concerns. Nobody knows of this save my companion, Miss Barton, and my friend, Miss Moore. Last night, a prowler intruded into Miss Moore's bedroom. The Lilac Room. Through the window, I might add. A sound woke her, she screamed...a figure dressed in black, the room's contents askew..." She stopped to take a breath.

"There now. You just breathe for a minute, I hear the tea trolley." He held up a finger.

Dot backed into the room, pulling a wheeled tray. She brought it into position and bobbed a curtsey.

"Dot, thank you. Right there, that's perfect. Now, I have a request, please go outside and try to ascertain who used a ladder on the grounds yesterday. Just say you need a ladder and heard one was near the house yesterday, and you thought it might still be handy. See what is said. Don't actually bring me the ladder, though. Do you understand?" Rosanna looked intently into the young maid's face.

"Yes, miss." The girl bobbed again, off to do the mistress's bidding, closing the door behind her.

"Now, take some deep breaths." Mr. Clough eyed the tray, but didn't overturn custom by pouring his own. He smiled in avuncular fashion. "There, you just sit still and gather your thoughts. When you have your composure, begin again."

He was like a veritable shepherd and she was the lost lamb. So solicitous. She picked up the thread of her tale. "Nothing was taken. There are no trees or downspouts near that window. That was the point of entry. Of all things, I caught a glimpse of a ladder being toted across the lawn this morning but couldn't tell where it had come from."

"This is serious. I am glad you came to me for advice. My first inclination is to post a guard. Second, lock the windows of both the first and second floors. Third you must consider calling in the magistrate." His brows were low, as the man concentrated on her information. "Hmmm. A spot of tea?"

"Oh, my, yes. Sorry to keep you waiting." She went about the process of brewing the tea. "It will be only a few minutes, now." She folded her hands in her lap and forced herself not to wring them. "I have already instituted a new rule that all doors and windows are to be checked each evening prior to the staff retiring. I assigned that job to Perkins."

"If nothing was missing, do you have any idea what the prowler was after?"

"No, that's the puzzling thing. It was my houseguest Miss Moore's room. Another piece of unsettling information is that during the treasure hunt, I spied Lord Halburt coming out of that room before scurrying down the back stairs. He, however, didn't see me. I'd clearly stated the bedrooms and kitchen area were not included in the treasure hunt."

"I shall have to think about this. About what would be the next step, the best approach to this delicate problem. Thank the Lord the intruder departed the way he came and didn't hurt anyone."

"Here's your tea. Sugar, correct?" Rosanna held out the cup and saucer, happy her hand was steady. Glad the man wasn't an alarmist, she agreed with his calming plan to think things through before raising any hue and cry. While the man took a few sips, she collected her thoughts about her next problem—Lord Winstead.

42

"There's more. I have a confession to make." Rosanna spoke in a soft tone, not wanting to be overheard. Her cheeks warmed. "I've inadvertently gotten myself into a compromising situation. No one knows but me, and the other party."

Mr. Clough shifted in his chair and twitched his mustache. "If no one knows, and you didn't intentionally harm another, why do you need to confess?"

Her face hot, she hung her head and lowered her gaze to her lap. "I've been less than honest. I'd promised Miss Barton not to walk out alone anymore, and I willfully and deceitfully broke that promise."

"Ah, Miss Barton. One doesn't want to disappoint that dear lady, now does one? Surely you can go to her? She seems such a compassionate woman."

That sounded serious. Rosanna made a mental note to make a few additional observations the next time Miss Barton and Mr. Clough were together. She peeked up at the man through her eyelashes. "Yes, I know she is a good listener. I just need to get up my courage to face her. I've never liked disappointing her. However, that sin merely led me to a much more serious problem. While on that last unaccompanied excursion, I purposely met up with Lord Winstead to view a waterfall he told me about."

He gave Rosanna an encouraging smile, one touched with ruefulness. "Now we are getting to the crux of the matter. It's more than simply taking a walk against Miss Barton's wishes?"

"Yes, that's right. In addition to that—much more. We, shall I say, exchanged expressions of affection. I fear my heart was rearranged that day." She fell silent, thoughts far away in the glen, she gazed towards the window and relived the amazing and sudden thawing of her long-held ambivalence to men and romance.

He set down his teacup with a clatter. "Excellent. I am more than pleased that you two found each other. You'll be a perfect match."

Attention snapping back to the present, she held up a hand, palm facing out. "Stop. He doesn't want me."

"Absurd, of course he does."

"No. Please listen. I don't understand why, but by the time we returned to the house, to reality, he'd turned formal and cold. I will admit I wasn't sure myself if we'd go forward together. My emotions were deeply engaged, however, and I had every reason to believe his were as well. I am not mistaken on that point. My imagination did not trick me. The next thing I expected was for him to call on me privately and offer for me."

The minister's eyebrows raised and he radiated doubt. "And since he didn't?"

Rosanna's heart sank as she realized how her words must sound. Like a disappointed miss, yearning for a proposal. "Please understand, I am not sure I would have accepted, not sure at all. I just don't comprehend his sudden coolness—the change in him. Oh, there's more."

"Let's have it all. Don't leave anything out." Clough patted her hand and sat back to listen, his hands on the arms of his chair.

"Fine. The rest is more of the same. Last night, at the dinner party? He did not seek me out to continue on our path to love and affection," her voice took on a cynical tone, "he continued with his coolness and didn't further our connection in the least." By this point, she didn't care what her listener thought, she just needed to speak her fears.

"I understand the situation. If I could snap my fingers and give a solution, I would. But as it is, we do have recourse. We can turn to our perfect Advocate. Let us pray." He bowed his head and folded his hands, and Rosanna did likewise. After a moment or two, Mr. Clough began to speak in a low voice. "Lord God, King of the Universe, You have blessed us with life and we thank Thee most heartily. We do implore Your wisdom in the matters just discussed. Please provide insight and enlighten our minds on how to proceed…"

A few more petitions followed, and they said "Amen" together. Mr. Clough patted Rosanna's hand. "The course of love never does run completely smooth. I believe there's hope." He steepled his hands in front of his chest, preparing to expound further.

Ellie burst into the room, out of breath.

43

"Rosanna, I..." Ellie came to a stop, her green morning dress swishing into position as she stopped moving and regained a dignified, feminine posture, then dropped a light curtsey. "Oh, Mr. Clough. So nice to see you." Smiling, and clearly ready to burst, she had come into the room with such momentum, it took a minute for the dust to settle.

Rosanna noticed the heavy satchel in the young lady's hand.

The unusual manner in which Ellie arrived on the scene dispersed the seriousness from the air.

"Miss Moore, your delightful arrival has mimicked the uplifting of the spirits the Lord gave as we lifted our burdens to him." Mr. Clough scrabbled in his pockets. "I need to write down a sermon idea."

Rosanna calmly handed him a pencil and piece of paper. "Will this do?"

"Ah, yes." He placed the paper on his knee and bent over it.

Rosanna gestured toward the satchel. "Ellie, what have you got there?"

Ellie's eyebrows raised, and her nervous gaze slanted to the minister.

Rosanna urged her to speak. "It's all right, sit down, tell us." She indicated the chair next to hers. "Mr. Clough is exceedingly confidential."

"I thought to search my room a bit. It seemed the intruder was after something. Since my waking up forestalled him, I decided to poke around. I found this." She lifted the bag from her lap and held it out to Rosanna.

Rosanna took the bag . Surprised at its weight, she set it on the tea table. "Where was it hidden? What is it?"

"It was concealed behind a fire screen. There's a second, unused, fireplace in my room. It has a secret compartment. You will soon see what it is. Go ahead, open it." Ellie closed her mouth with an emphatic nod.

Rosanna leaned forward and unclasped the satchel, and then opened it wide. She lifted out a large wooden box with an inlaid design on top. Mr. Clough swept the bag away and helped her place the box on her lap. She laid both hands on the smooth top of the box, and stroked the floral inlay, as if she had a premonition of the importance of the contents. She took her sweet time, drawing out the anticipation. She let her fingers play over the clasp, lifting the latch, but not opening the lid.

"Rosanna, please, you are keeping us in suspense too long." Mr. Clough spoke from the edge of his seat, gaze glued to the lid.

Rosanna lifted it, ever so slow. She opened the box halfway, looked in, then allowed the lid to fall open, exposing a glittering pile of jewelry. "Oh, my! A real treasure, nothing like last night's prize." Her gentle fingers probed and lifted items from the pile. "There's a piece of paper underneath all this."

Ellie's eyes were wide with excitement. "I didn't notice that."

"Ellie, put a clean tea towel on that plate and I'll

move some of these out of the way. I don't want to risk dislodging anything onto the floor and having it lost or damaged."

Ellie whisked a towel into place, and then Rosanna lifted a large cluster of tangled jewelry, using two hands and moved it to the cloth-covered plate. "Now I can get at the paper." She pried it out by an edge and opened a note folded three times. A quick glance showed it to be a letter. She placed the rest of the jewelry back into the chest, closed the lid and set the box on the table. Smoothing the parchment on her lap, she began to read the short missive. Looking up at the others, she assessed the discretion and wisdom of sharing the contents of the mysterious letter. Coming to a decision, she began to read aloud.

Dear '?' I salute you this way since I have no way of knowing who will eventually find this message. My tale is a sad one, for I married, at my parents' insistence, a man whom time revealed to be a wastrel. My husband ran his estate, Honor's Point, into the ground, gambling and frivoling our wealth away. I am ailing with not long to live and I foresee him losing all, hence this letter. I had my personal jewels copied and hid these, the genuine ones. I had to secure them thusly since my husband would have sold all to finance his revels. The gems in this chest are my sole property. The box contains only one piece of Winstead family jewelry, the betrothal ring given to me before my marriage. My beloved and only child, Peter, is to receive the contents of this chest as a bequest. So dear '?', it is up to you to ensure that they are delivered to him, the rightful heir to my treasure.

Lady Adele Winstead

Ellie, quick on the uptake, put the pieces together. "Oh, Lady Winstead. That's Lord Winstead's mother—

the one who decorated the bedrooms with floral themes."

Mr. Clough's voice held a tone of fond remembrance. "Yes, I knew Lady Winstead very well. A fine person who, shall we say, endured a trying marriage. I can easily imagine her doing this. She was a wise and loving woman."

"If only her parents let her choose her spouse. Oh, well. That's water under the bridge, or over the dam, or however that saying goes." Rosanna believed on an intellectual level that God's providence covered that too, but it did seem so unfair.

A tap on the door preceded Perkins, who entered and announced in his reedy voice, "Lady Brook, come to call." He bowed and swept the drawing room door wide open to admit her.

Heart pounding, Rosanna slid the box under the settee, and then stood up, both arms extended. "Lady Brook, welcome. Please be seated. I trust your travels are over for a time now? We sorely missed your presence, especially last night."

She sat down on an uncomfortable-looking Egyptian-style chair nearby. "Oh, leave it to me to miss such goings on. I already heard tell of a spectacular dinner party, which included a literary giant and a treasure hunt. Seems I've some catching up to do."

After exchanging greetings with the others, Lady Brook once again turned to Rosanna, and pinned her down with her intense gaze, faded blue though it was. "Are you well, my dear? Your color looks quite heightened."

44

"I'm fit as a fiddle, or, fine as sixpence, I think they say." Rosanna averted her eyes as she spoke, making a diversionary commotion of slipping shawls, hair needing to be patted, and rearrangement of her skirts.

She pinned what she hoped passed as a carefree smile on her face. This wasn't the time for any more revelations, dear as this lady was. She'd had quite enough for one day. After her lengthy unburdening to the pastor, and the discovery of the jewels and the letter, she desired to grab her bonnet and head for one of the paths. Walking helped her think. But no, she must curtail her freedoms. She set her mind to having as normal a visit as possible with one of her favorite neighbors.

Mr. Clough and Ellie were also present to help shoulder the social niceties.

She reached behind for a convenient bell pull, and gave it a tug. Only a minute went by before Perkins stepped in.

"Perkins, please inform my companion, dear Miss Barton, that her presence is desired here, also more hot water." Rosanna tilted her head and glanced at Mr. Clough. She watched him for any reaction to the mention of Miss Barton, but he continued to keep busy chatting with Ellie and Lady Brook.

Miss Barton soon entered the room, eager energy

to her stride. Clearly delighted to join the group, she gave a simpering smile to the minister.

Dot returned with more hot water, and Rosanna set another pot of tea to brew.

"No more for me, thank you." Mr. Clough got to his feet. "Oh, Miss Barton, I was just leaving, may I be blessed by your company for a small portion of my walk home? Perhaps to the foot of the drive?"

She looked at Rosanna for permission, who smiled to herself, since the shoe was now on the other foot. "Mr. Clough, that's a fine idea. Miss Barton, you go ahead, I shall see you when you return." Rosanna wanted to laugh but managed to hold it in. She began a description of last night's party for Lady Brook's sake.

Lady Brook, Ellie, and Rosanna sipped tea and exchanged a few more pleasantries, after which the neighbor took her leave.

Rosanna extended a hand to Ellie and gave a reassuring clasp. Rosanna's mind already leapt ahead to what needed to be done."Ah, finally. A pleasant visit, but strained, on the heels of your discovery of the jewels." She rose and moved toward an escritoire in a corner. "Of course, I'll need to inform Lord Winstead of this…this treasure. I will write a message and have it delivered."

"That's the thing to do. I shall leave you to your pen." Ellie left the room, closing the door behind her.

After thinking for a few minutes, Rosanna bent to her task.

Dear Lord Winstead,

Something has come to light here at Honor's Point. Something of great import to you. I request your presence tomorrow at ten o'clock.

Regards, Miss Cabot

Next, she sealed the note, and rang for Perkins. "Perkins, deliver this to Lord Winstead. It must go into his hands alone, so instruct the messenger, please." Handing over the envelope, optimism swept over her and she began to imagine how it would play out. Would he be warm? Or would his coldness continue?

~*~

Rosanna's slumber that night proved poor. Between playing scenarios over and over in her imagination, vivid dreams, and the presence of the jewel box under her bed, her night of sleep left much to be desired.

The sound of opening drapes woke her. It was Dot bringing coffee which she set on the bedside table before slipping into the dressing room.

Easing herself up to a sitting position, Rosanna took a sip or two, then laid back. Replaying the dreams in complete form proved impossible, since waking up scattered them, but she could grasp snippets, one of which involved Lord Winstead on a ladder outside her room, knocking on the window and holding out the figurine from the treasure hunt. Dreams bordered on the bizarre so often, but some said they held nuggets of the future. *Not in this case* she told herself, suppressing her desires. She drank the rest of her coffee and then swung her legs over the side of the bed.

She stretched her arms, and tipped her head from side to side, attempting to remove the kinks from her neck. Enough dawdling. "Dot, please come here," she called out. "I'd like your assistance in selecting a gown this morning." In truth, she'd be quite able to choose her own dress, but as a kindness to the maid, who showed great interest in the wardrobe, she included her in the process. "But first, tell me if you learned anything about a ladder on the premises."

"Miss, I did not. Nobody knew anything."

Frustrating. The more time passed, the less likely to find a clue. "Thank you for trying, Dot. A blue day dress, I think. Bring me a few to choose from. I'll be meeting with Lord Winstead at ten o-clock, so something dressier than my normal morning wear." Some of the styles for at-home mornings looked like glorified boudoir robes, and she didn't want to give that impression.

Dot pulled several muslin day dresses from the armoire. "Here, miss. I thought the delphinium, the sapphire, or the azure print." The girl looked pleased with herself as she used the color names Rosanna taught her.

"Good. Those are excellent options." Rosanna tapped her chin, then decided. "The delphinium today, Dot. With my paisley shawl and Mother's pearls. The small ones."

Hair dressed, wearing a gown of white calico sprigged in delphinium blue, and banded with matching blue silk ribbons at waist and sleeve, Rosanna prepared to face her day. She prayed for peace of mind all the way to the dining room. She slipped into the room where she found a selection of her favorite breakfast foods in covered dishes on the sideboard. Pointing to eggs, bacon, and toast, she allowed a footman to fill her plate and place it on the table. He assisted her with her chair then retreated to his post against the far wall.

After breakfast, Miss Barton joined Rosanna in the

morning room. She dismissed the maid and footman, then related the discovery of the jewels and the accompanying letter, ending her tale with "...and I expect him here at ten."

Miss Barton, hands pressed together, fingers touching her chin, gave her reaction to the tale. "This is fantastic—like something out of a fairy tale."

"Indeed." Rosanna entertained a mental picture of Winstead upon a white horse, come to rescue a damsel.

An aura of excitement pervaded the room. The significance of the coming meeting with Lord Winstead hung in the air like a tangible object. Sketchy details known, but the notion of a lost fortune titillated the imagination. Not every day brought a task of such import. Rosanna had never been involved in restoring a fortune. The imminent meeting involved a story with almost biblical themes.

She mused that the only logical explanation for Peter's sudden coldness was his loss of status. He must think she wouldn't deign to consider his suit. While Barton chattered on, excited about the coming significant event, Rosanna's heart was squeezed by a combination of fear and desire. The banked fires of attraction might be relit today.

45

"Good morning. Won't you join me for tea?" She held up a cup. By ten, Rosanna's nerves were stretched thin. The anticipation of this meeting had taken a toll on her serenity. Between restoring his fortune and their awkward interpersonal standing, she struggled to present a calm exterior. She glanced at the door, left open for propriety's sake.

A footman lounged on a hallway bench, but far enough away that he couldn't hear their words.

"No, thank you. No tea for me." Lord Winstead appeared distant and impatient—as if he'd like to be anywhere else

"Please sit down. I have something of great importance to deliver to you today. Not a chiding, or a charity subscription request, nor a question about the history of the estate." She didn't want to draw things out too long, but it seemed appropriate to give some preface, some build-up. After all, the poor man had no idea at all what was about to be handed to him.

"Deliver? Has some mail been misdirected?" His tone was annoyed—did he think she'd bring him up here at a set time to hand him a letter that could have been sent to him with a messenger? He sat on the edge of his seat, ready to bolt.

"Not mail. Please sit back. This may come as a shock to you." She rose, went over to a shelf next to the fireplace and retrieved the heavy jewel box. She held it out to him and he raised his hands, somewhat hesitantly, to take the box from her.

"This belongs to you. It was found in the Lilac Room."

"Miss Cabot, I distinctly remember the terms of the property sale. All the contents of the property were included. So, if this box was found here, it surely belongs to you. It's a beautiful box, with this inlaid marquetry flower cluster. You must know that it is yours."

He made as if to lift the box off his lap, but she forestalled him with an outstretched hand.

"I assure you, this is an exceptional item. Its existence was unknown, and never would have been included with the estate and contents. This was inside. Read it first, then you'll understand." She handed him the folded piece of paper and moved over to the window. With her back to the room, she afforded him privacy. Her heart ached for the man. So proud, so honest.

After a few minutes, he spoke, and she whirled around, hands clasped at her waist.

"I see. Thank you. I shall treasure this letter, it's the only one I have from Mother." His voice sounded constrained, as if he were choking back a sob.

"You need to be alone. I'll leave you for a time." Rosanna slipped out of the room and shut the door with a gentle click.

~*~

Shaken to his core by this unexpected turn of events, Peter didn't even look inside the box. He dropped his head into his hands and let the tears flow.

The pain of losing his mother stung afresh. As he read the letter, he heard her voice in his mind. "… dear and only son…" She'd called him that many times. He'd used to respond, "Yes, dear and only mother?"

The shock of his circumstances being overturned overwhelmed him as well. He'd just gotten himself resigned to his new life in poverty, faced the world again in his reduced circumstances, and now came this upheaval.

Good news though it was, it still shocked him to the soles of his feet. He'd been brought so low, and now, top of the trees again. How would he keep his newfound spiritual focus? He'd only started to understand his riches in Christ. "Lord," he prayed, under his breath. "Keep me on Your paths. Thank You for restoring my spiritual fortune, and a measure of earthly means. Guide me in righteousness." Striding over to the door, he wrenched it open. Spying a footman in the hall, he gave an order, "Summon Miss Cabot."

Serious turmoil rocked his heart. What to say to her in the midst of such uncertainty? He paced, brain working overtime. He rehearsed different approaches, discarding them each in turn. Forget it. He would not plan his words. He would trust God to guide his speech. *Here she is, oh, what a darling.*

Rosanna entered the room again, compassion on her face. How sweet. Even after his coldness toward her, she still treated him well.

He held up the letter, kissed it, then secreted it in an inner pocket of his coat, and laid a hand over it. "Thank you for delivering this treasure to me."

"You are quite welcome." She twisted a dusky curl by her cheek. "Have you looked inside the box yet?"

46

"Let's do that now, together." Peter took Rosanna's hand and led her over to the settee. He placed the box on a small table and sat down next to her. "Based on the letter and knowing my mother, this is quite full of exquisite jewelry. Am I correct?"

Rosanna, looking flummoxed, answered. "Yes, that's right. You didn't even look at it yet?"

Not able to stop himself, he reached over and slipped his hand over hers. "No. You see, I have thoroughly accepted the loss of my financial and societal status. I've come to terms with my life as it is. Or, was. God's given me peace, not peace as the world gives, but His peace."

Gathering his wits, he went on. "I'd like us to look at it together, if you don't mind." He reached out to clasp the jewel box. Drawing it onto his knees, he released the catch and opened the lid. Sparkling gems and the burnished gleam of precious metals met his eyes. In possession of a small fortune again, it truly struck him how content he'd become with his new life. Other than the lack of peace caused by loving Rosanna and knowing her to be above his touch. The drive he'd felt to make her his own, knowing he couldn't, had been agony. Treating her coldly when he'd wanted only to caress and embrace her had been unbearable.

No more, though. He now could let his natural desires and intentions toward her flower into matrimony. Possessing her as wife became his goal.

Now turning his attention to the tangle of jewelry, he spied a blue sparkle. With care, he extracted a golden chain from which suspended a tear-shaped blue sapphire. He took her hand in his, turned her palm up, and let the chain and pendant descend into her hand. Then he closed her fingers over it. "As your 'reward' for restoring my fortune to me, I humbly implore you to accept this gift as a token. It shall be a memento of this incredible event."

He looked directly into her eyes, willing her to read the message in his own. She returned his gaze for a moment, silent, then refocused on the necklace, appearing to have accepted the gift. She held it in one palm, stroking it with the tip of a finger.

She blinked, and looked up at him again, cheeks aflame. "I was hurt by your cold attitude toward me, after our interlude in the glen."

A drop of sweat formed and began to trickle down his back. "Ah, that. Yes, well, I am very sorry, my dear. I felt I could do nothing else. I had no means to offer you anything, and it seemed best to create some distance between us."

So innocent and sweet.

His heart warmed even further toward her. Many women would be raging at him right about now, demanding an offer. He set the box on the table again and closed the lid. "My dear. Please forgive me." He began. Letting his heart guide his words, he allowed his newly-freed emotions into his voice. "You enrapture me, my love. I've never felt such waves of love and passion as that day in the glen." He hoped the word 'passion' didn't scare her. "Tell me I haven't spoiled things between us with my coldness."

She gazed into his eyes. "I forgive you. I felt as if my heart would burst into flames. I wanted only to be in your arms forever."

Close on the settee now, he edged away, then placed his hands on her shoulders, turning her to face him. He leaned forward and took her into his arms in a gentle embrace. After a moment or two, with a ragged sigh, he pushed himself back, and rose.

Rosanna whispered. "Don't leave."

He rushed to answer. "I'm not leaving, dearest, I just thought it best to move around a bit. Here, I will sit in this chair, right next to you."

47

"From whom do I need to obtain permission to court you, Miss Cabot?" His hand felt hard and warm, so warm, as it covered hers.

She stalled for time. Not desiring this bliss to end, yet she needed more time to decide if she would go forward. "Court me? For marriage?"

He took the necklace out of her hand and clasped it around her neck. "For a life together in wedded bliss. Since I can claim the semblance of a fortune once again, I can rightfully court you. And I will, Miss Cabot, until you are mine."

At these words, a thrill coursed through her body. This sensation must be passion. "That sounds delightful, but please call me Rosanna."

His eyes caressed her, and he reached out to gently capture her hand. "Rosanna, please call me Peter. I couldn't pursue you without any fortune. It would have looked havey-cavey if I sought marriage with you. The *ton* would have accused me of being the basest fortune hunter. That's no longer a concern."

She clutched her chest. "Oh, Peter. To think how I fled here to escape those hounds who sought to force me into a dynastic marriage. My uncle, dear man, thought nothing of selecting one titled candidate after another to cast my way. You would not believe the pressure I was under. He was my guardian only until I gained my majority. So, you needn't ask him for permission."

Paleness overtook Peter's face. His skin had turned an ashen shade and he drew back his hand.

She wanted to tell him now. He must know everything about her. "I moved here to get away from arranged marriage and fortune hunters. I finally got my uncle to assist me to buy my own estate and I left London and its marriage mart behind forever. Before meeting you, I never wanted to marry after my first love was brutally killed four years ago."

Odd, his face had a shuttered look. Puzzled at his expression, she sought to reassure him. "But when you held me that day in the glen, my heart melted, and my world shifted. I believe getting away from pressures of the marriage mart allowed me to heal from my loss and to love again."

"I planned to use Honor's Point to offer a formal place of refuge to other women under that same duress. Alas, that hasn't worked out. But, you see, God used that plan to bring us together." She noticed Peter's mood had gone quiet, and she gave a tenuous, questioning smile.

Peter scooped up the box and held it against his chest. Something about his stance made it look like a shield. "We've been alone too long, Miss Cabot, I must go now."

Miss Cabot? She held out a beseeching hand. "When shall I see you again?"

"Soon." Then he was gone.

.₋*₋.

Lord, how can this be? How can I be given love and moments later, a stumbling block? Peter blindly staggered along the path to his home. He wanted to hide. Slamming through the door, he shoved the jewel box onto the scarred table and threw himself across the bed in the alcove.

He couldn't marry her with such a black secret. That was no way to begin a life together. But, if she found out, she wouldn't want anything to do with him. He rolled over onto his back and put one hand behind his head and one over his eyes. *Think. What are your options?*

Lie. Say nothing. Ask Mr. Clough explain to it to her. None of these choices sufficed to salve his honor. Only one solution stared him in the face. He'd have to make a final confession. To Rosanna. Baring the awful truth about what he did to Melissa.

48

He'd like to put off this necessary meeting with Rosanna. Avoiding such a revelatory scene appealed to him on some level. However, if he went on any longer with what amounted to deceit, the delay could forever taint and spoil their extraordinary love.

That might happen anyway, but it would be better to tell her soon, if there were to be any chance at happiness. But why must it be this way? His own sin caused this debacle. Even though he'd done the right thing and confessed to God and man, the consequences of his misdeed lived on and affected him. He'd go immediately—this afternoon.

~*~

One last glance in the mirror. Preparing to make such a momentous call, he tried to appear at his best, even donning an embroidered waistcoat and a few fobs. Dressing well gave one confidence, correct? Then why did he feel lower than dirt?

He forced himself to set out for Honor's Point after a failed attempt at eating a light lunch. He couldn't eat a thing at this moment to save his life.

He reached Rosanna's front door much quicker than he really wanted. It needed to be done. Cooling his heels while Perkins extended his invitation, he firmed his resolve to do the right thing.

"Miss Cabot, Lord Winstead's here to see if you would care to walk out with him." The butler's loud, reedy voice carried from three rooms away. Perkins came back down the hall. "Miss Cabot and her maid will be with you shortly."

And soon, they were on the garden path. Rosanna at Peter's side. Dot about twenty paces behind.

"Shall we sit on that bench under the pergola?" By now, Peter regained his composure and steeled himself for his distasteful task.

"Yes, that's one of my favorite places. Dot, would you please sit over on the seat by the oak? Yes, that one. Thank you."

Treating the maid so kindly showed her to be a true lady of character and virtue. Peter cherished the hope of enjoying Rosanna's fine disposition the rest of his life and that revealing his peccadillo would not derail true love.

"I brought you out on this walk for a specific reason, my dear. If, after I tell you my story, I can still call you 'my dear', I shall be a happy man."

"What is it?" Rosanna's voice held a teasing giggle, and it made his insides groan to know how he was about to disappoint her.

"I have a confession to make. It has to do with your friend, Melissa, Lady Russell." He paused, assessing her reaction, and giving her time to digest this information.

"Melissa? Something to do with her?" Confusion swept away Rosanna's lighthearted expression of a moment ago.

"Yes, I was acquainted with her in London, you

see." Hard words to say and his heart pounded.

"Oh. Did you and she… Where you an item at one time?"

If only that were the extent of the problem, it could be explained easily. "Sort of." *Get it out, man.* "I had her wealthy father's permission to court her. After two months, she wasn't sure."

Rosanna's eyes flickered with doubt and her delicate brows were lifted in inquiry. "And you agreed to end the courtship?"

"Not exactly that simple. She wanted more time to decide. She'd agreed to her father arranging a marriage to an aristocrat, but she retained the final say. I, desiring to cling to my estates, put myself in the running. The marriage settlements would have saved Honor's Point. Her father selected me out of a host of down-at-the-heels aristocrats." Self-deprecation seemed all too appropriate.

Rosanna's voice and her mood flattened. "Oh? Oh."

Finish breaking her heart, you bounder. "Creditors were nipping at my heels and I was floating on the River Tick. So, I did something heinous. Something wrong, sinful, and disgusting. I abducted her and took her to a prearranged site for a forced wedding ceremony."

Surprised, she forgot for a moment, in her stress, that her newlywed friend Melissa wed Lord Russell. "Don't say you were married."

"No. It didn't come off. I am grateful that my sinful plan was prevented by none other than Lord Russell who came on the scene, and rescued Melissa from my wicked clutches."

Rosanna recoiled away from him as full

understanding dawned. She stood up, outrage written across her gentle features. "You cad!"

"Rosanna, I have repented, confessed, and been forgiven by God. I have entered into a new life of following His ways. Telling the ugly tale is so very difficult. Please…"

She interrupted his outpouring. "No more excuses for what you did, please. I cannot believe this. The thing that is most repellant to me, forcing a marriage for financial gain, is not something I can gloss over."

49

"Let's return to the house, Dot." Rosanna controlled her ire and pasted a social smile on her face as she swept by the maid.

Dot stood up and followed in her mistress's wake.

Rosanna hoped the maid didn't realize anything amiss. Refusing to even glance back, she told Dot to go around to the kitchen entrance and prepare a tray with a tisane. Rosanna rushed through the front door, startling Perkins. With steely self-control and yet in a soft voice, she tried to hide her stress. "I am not at home to Lord Winstead until further notice."

At times like this, Rosanna sorely missed her mother, dead these long, three years. But, thankful to have a companion at all, she tried to have a grateful heart. On her way up the stairs, she spoke over her shoulder, "And Perkins, please locate Miss Barton and send her to my room, I find I am in need of her."

~*~

Entering the bedroom, Miss Barton's face held a coy expression. "I thought you went on a walk with Lord Winstead?"

In response, Rosanna threw her bonnet onto her

bed and kicked off her shoes. "You can stop that smirking, Miss Barton. He is *persona non-grata* in my life from this moment on."

The two women fell silent upon the arrival of the maid with the tray. As soon as Dot left the room, Rosanna sloshed the tisane into a cup. She sat back down on the edge of the bed, holding the warm cup in her hands and taking sips in mechanical fashion.

Needing relief, but gracious enough not to spread his misdeeds, she gave vent to a censored tirade. "To think I thought him a friend. I'll admit, he breached my defenses. Yes, I'd considered what it would be like to be married to him, especially after his fortunes were restored and he became so attentive. He has put himself beyond the pale." She crossed her legs at the ankles, and her arms across her chest, began to rock back and forth and then to cry.

Barton sat next to her on the bed and pulled Rosanna over to rest her head on her ample bosom. "Let me have that cup before you spill. Dearie, what happened? There, there, you cry it out. Nothing can be that bad." She patted Rosanna's shoulder and kept up a stream of soothing words and sounds, as she did when she'd been a nursemaid, years ago. She lowered Rosanna onto the bed, covered her with a down coverlet, and sat in a nearby rocker while the young lady cried herself to sleep.

Rosanna emerged for supper. Subdued, and clad in a dark gray dress trimmed in black, she gave minimal responses to Ellie and Miss Barton at the table.

"I shall be writing a letter tonight, to Mr. Clough." Miss Barton paused to gauge reaction. "I intend to invite him here for lunch tomorrow, if there are no other plans?"

~*~

The night hours crept by, and Rosanna decided to take a sleeping powder. Her upset, combined with the afternoon nap made sleep elusive. She slipped on a robe, located the medicine and took it, stirred into a glass of water. On her way back to bed, she stopped by the window. The night, lit by a half moon, made the whole world appear dark blue. The wind blew scraps of clouds across the moon's face, and stars twinkled from afar. The black trees mocked her, something so green and alive, appearing black due to absence of light.

Her head pounded as she went over the facts for the hundredth time. How could he turn out to be a bad man? Such a special man—able to touch her heart with his mere presence. She crawled into her bed and sank into a dream-filled sleep.

In the dream, there stood a boulder. She sat on top of it, unable to get down either side. Peter stood nearby and turned away, ignoring her plight. He disappeared from view, and the boulder began to roll toward the waterfall. The dream played over and over again, her sleeping mind trying to come to terms with her loss.

She awoke at ten, rolled over, and opened one eye to spy a cup on her bedside table. Propped up on her elbow, she grasped the lukewarm cup and stared down into congealed hot cocoa. Sighing, she set down the cup and eased her aching body out of bed, stretched, then rang the bell to call Dot for assistance.

A tap on the door preceded Dot's entry. "Mornin', Miss Cabot. Miss Barton sez to remind you the minister's comin' fer lunch today." The girl moved over to the clothespress and began to shuffle down the row of gowns. "This one'll be a picture."

"Fine, Dot, whatever dress you pick is fine." Rosanna summoned up a façade of normalcy, and submitted to being dressed and coifed. The white muslin with lavender and green sprigs made her eyes sparkle most days, but today, it brought no more enjoyment than if it were a gray shroud.

She descended to the dining room, where she selected toast and coffee. Murmuring her thanks to the footman who assisted her, she forced herself to take a nibble or two. After the second cup of coffee, her normal vigor began to assert itself. She pushed away from the table and told the footman to send a messenger to her study.

Reaching the haven of her favorite room, she reached behind her neck, and unclasped the necklace Peter bestowed upon her. Hard to believe he gave it to her just yesterday. It couldn't be helped. There was no accepting of valuable gifts as an unmarried lady. Certainly, not from a bounder like him. *He is no longer my intended*. This came unbidden, as she lectured herself to stay cold toward him.

She rummaged in her reticule until she found the square of linen she'd gotten from him that day in the glen. She'd laundered it but hadn't returned it yet. That would have to go back, too. She opened the cloth, placed the necklace on it, and folded it again, before slipping the packet into an envelope. It crossed her mind to enclose a note, but no—anger and hurt read poorly on paper. She'd surely write something to regret. Wordless missive sealed, she held it between the palms of her hands for a moment, placed a light kiss on it, and put it on a table by the door. When the servant came, she indicated it and gave instructions for delivery. If only the ache in her heart could disappear as swiftly.

50

"Miss Barton. Imagine my delight when I received your note inviting me to lunch." Mr. Clough chortled. After bowing over her hand, he went to the fireplace and leaned against the mantel.

Miss Barton admired his stance, but after a few seconds, she interrupted his reverie. "Quick, listen. I need your help. Well, it's actually Miss Cabot that needs help. Your wise counsel."

"Calm down, start over. What happened to Miss Cabot?" The minister hastened over to the cluster of chairs where Miss Barton sat, and joined her.

"There's been an upset. I don't know what about. But you know he, that's Lord Winstead, was given the jewels yesterday morning."

"Yes, I was here when they were found by Miss Moore. What happened since?"

"Miss Cabot summoned Lord Winstead here. She gave him the jewels. The next day, yesterday, he paid a call on her, as you know."

Mr. Clough leaned forward, worried. "Is there more?"

"Yes, After his visit, they parted on excellent terms, but he came back in the afternoon and took her out on a walk. They spoke, seated on a bench under the pergola, and my stars, something went very wrong." She paused for breath.

"You are saying they had a disagreement?"

"I can only guess. She spoke so cryptic. Knowing her, if he did something, she'd never spread any word of gossip. She was mortal upset, crying, throwing herself on her bed, kicking things."

The man's hand crept over to hers and covered it. "Oh, my dear. How upsetting for you, Miss Barton."

"Yes, but do talk to her. Mayhap she'll tell you. Can you help her? You are so wonderful with people's problems."

~*~

Rosanna walked in and at a glance took in the look of hero-worship on Miss Barton's face and the location of the minister's hand just before he pulled it back. Perhaps those two had a future.

Mr. Clough stood, flustered, and bowed to Rosanna. "My dear Miss Cabot, how kind of you, and dear Miss Barton, to include me in your luncheon plans today."

"Oh, my. You are welcome any time. It was just a little idea my dear Miss Barton had. She said to me 'Let's invite Mr. Clough over for lunch tomorrow?'" Rosanna teased mildly but kept her facial expression placid. It wouldn't do to make the man nervous or self-conscious around 'Dear Miss Barton'.

The night's travails wrote sorrow on her visage and she hoped the tear tracks she'd attempted to obscure were covered well enough—so glad she had access to a pot of powder and cold compresses.

"Excuse me for a minute or two. I must give the cook a few instructions about our lunch. I've ordered something special for our dear Mr. Clough." Miss Barton rose from her chair, smoothed the back of her skirt, and minced out of the room.

Not ever having seen her companion walk quite that way, Rosanna sat dumbstruck until the minister's voice pierced her consciousness.

"...you feeling?" He waited with raised brows.

"Feeling? Me? Fine. Feeling fine. Yesterday was quite tumultuous, what with the fortune in jewels to deal with." She hoped nonchalance would serve to deflect any probing questions. She started to wonder if this luncheon was a set piece of Miss Barton's doing.

"I suspect that Lord Winstead's coolness toward you is a thing of the past? Surely 'twas his lack of means, deficiency of fortune, that forbore him from pursuing you? That explains it perfectly." He looked satisfied with his analysis, but as if he held something back.

Rosanna, tired of exerting control, blurted out an answer. *After all, if I can't trust and speak openly to Mr. Clough...?* "That *was* it. But another shameful difficulty has arisen and curtailed any courtship, present or future."

"Don't say. Surely...?" The minister's voice trailed off as his gift of gab departed and he grasped for the delicate words needed in this indelicate situation.

"I wonder. Are you aware what a bounder and cad our Lord Winstead really is? He is practically a kidnapper." This came out in a harsh whisper. She didn't want to be overheard.

"Now, now. He's a sinner like the rest of us. Do you really think God ranks sins of this sort? Yes, there are some called 'abominations', but this is not one of those."

"Fine. But it's just about the worst thing a man of my class can do to a woman like me. You have no way of knowing this, but I have a personal and especial antipathy toward men who would force unwanted arranged marriages upon young ladies. That's what drove me from London. Drove me here, to this refuge. And who do I find on my doorstep? One of the type of dastards I fled. Oh, to love again, and have that love crushed like a tender flower underfoot." Breathing hard, on the verge of tears, waves of disappointment crashed on the shoals of her heart, pounding like a ship forced onto the rocks by a storm.

51

Mr. Clough's brows rose, and he sputtered. "Miss Cabot, what about forgiveness? If you are unwilling to forgive, will your own sins be forgiven?" Tenacious, he drove home his point, "All have sinned—all."

"Mr. Clough, do you mean to tell me…" Shocked, she gasped for a breath, then went on. "That I should accept an unrepentant kidnapper as a suitor? Never."

"Hoping this isn't a breach of confidentiality, Miss Cabot, but I feel constrained to tell you that Lord Winstead is repentant. He has humbly confessed this matter to me, and has formally repented, in person, to the Russells' themselves." He delivered this information as if a *coup de grace*.

"Oh!" She gasped again, and raised her hands to cover her mouth, pressing as though to keep from crying out. This didn't fit in with her anger. The anger she'd thought so right, so righteous. Her mind whirled and she slumped in the chair, losing touch with reality and escaping from the horrid truth.

~*~

"Wake up, wake up." Miss Barton waved the vinaigrette under Rosanna's nose and she sat up, shaking her head.

"What happened?" The memory of Mr. Clough's revelations and reproof came sweeping back into her overtaxed mind.

"You must have fainted, dearie." Miss Barton chafed Roseanna's wrists for a few moments then thrust a cup of tea into her hands. "Drink this."

She sipped and noticed a tea tray had appeared on the table in front of the chairs. Miss Barton must have brought it when she came back from wherever she'd minced off to prior to Rosanna's explosive conversation with Mr. Clough.

"Ladies, it is imperative that I bring God's word into this situation. Miss Barton, without revealing matters entrusted to me in the confessional, let me just say there's been a misunderstanding between our two young people. Surely, you've both heard the verse, 'If we confess our sins, God is faithful and just to forgive us our sins, and to cleanse us from all unrighteousness?'"

"Oh, such a perfect reference." Miss Barton gushed.

"We have words from the common parlance of poesy, 'To err is human; To forgive, divine.' Have we not?" He glanced back and forth between the two women, sparing Rosanna from being pinned down with his words.

"I cannot say at this time that I will be able to forgive him. But I shall take your words into consideration, Mr. Clough."

"That's all I ask of you. A partial, facile forgiveness when one isn't made ready by the Spirit is not to be desired, either. Let's close this little conference with prayer, shall we?" He bowed his head, and the two ladies did the same. After a silent moment, he began.

"Lord, You have taught us to love our neighbor. To treat others as we would have them treat us. Please enable us, by Your Spirit, to do Your will, to show Your perfect mercy and grace to our fellowman. Amen."

"I beg you to excuse me from lunching together. You two go and enjoy it. I am sure that Hannah has outdone herself for Mr. Clough. I will be thinking and praying. Thank you so much." Rosanna went out into the hall, where she found Perkins. "Please find Dot. She'll be accompanying me on a walk."

No more walking alone.

Cooling her heels in the hall, waiting for the maid, Rosanna realized she'd been neglecting her other guest. When Dot appeared, she sent her on a mission. "Dot, go find Miss Moore, see if she'll walk with me."

Before long, Ellie and Dot returned.

"Such a grand idea, Rosanna. I'd love a walk."

They handed shawls to Dot, who would be trailing behind them, put their own bonnets on, and exited the front door. Choosing one of the paths leading explicitly away from Lord Winstead's corner of the estate, Roseanna led the way to a hilltop known for its expansive view. She and Ellie sat down on their shawls and Dot sat a way off.

Ellie hadn't been on this path before and she enthused about the vista. "The views alone make Honor's Point an exceptional property. I love it here. So peaceful, so quiet, so safe." She glanced over at Dot, as if evaluating whether the maid could hear what they were saying.

"Don't worry, Ellie, Dot's mind is elsewhere. I've never known one so 'head in the clouds'. 'Tis amazing she's so good with hair and wardrobe."

"That's an excellent quality. I'm so glad that there hasn't been even a whiff of exposure or hint of my presence causing any interest. Living such a quiet life is a blessing." Ellie twisted a piece of grass between her fingers.

"It's safe here, in a way," Rosanna said. "My heart isn't protected here, though. I may as well tell you, Lord Winstead has breached my heart's defenses, but the slings and arrows of life have trampled upon our budding love. I fear love's labor is lost." Rosanna sighed.

Ellie's eyes grew round, and she clutched the front of her bodice. "This happened right under my nose? I should have suspected, I suppose, but whatever transpired is a mystery to me."

"Thank you for not taking the news askance. Speaking to you of my trampled heart relieves my feelings somewhat. Though I do not care to go into detail. I'm afraid going into specifics would bring tears again. Perhaps someday I'll tell you the entire sorry tale. For now, however, it's good to be on a walk with such an excellent friend."

"I hear our neighbor Lord Halburt made a sudden trip to London today, after his guests left. It's a relief not to suffer his frequent flowery accolades. He makes my skin crawl." Ellie didn't mince words.

"I agree. A little bit of him goes a long way." Rosanna began to giggle, and her infectious laugh soon had Ellie chortling.

"He is good for a laugh." Ellie said when she could speak again.

"On that note, let's head back. My appetite has returned."

52

Rosanna struggled to pardon Peter's sin. If she were to proffer forgiveness, how would she tender it? Write a note? Offer to meet in person? Did she truly forgive him? Such questions troubled her sleep and she dreamed of the glen, the boulder, and the waterfall each night.

At dawn a few days later, she swung out of bed, rang the bell, and went right to the wardrobe to select a favorite gown. Summer meant sprigged muslin during the day. A variety of trimmings and an array of colors made for a wide selection. She pulled out a pale, creamy yellow dress trimmed in green.

By this time, Dot had arrived with coffee, opened the drapes, and stood ready with a hairbrush in hand.

The maid set down the brush and helped Roseanna fasten the gown. "Dot, a simple ribboned queue today, please. Yes, that's it." Rosanna stood up, twirled once in front of her cheval mirror, and almost danced out the door and down to breakfast.

"You look wonderful this morning, dearie. Are your spirits finally restored?" Miss Barton selected a piece of bacon and raised her eyebrows, waiting for a response.

"All's right with the world, again, my friend." She selected eggs, strawberries, and ham, and the footman carried it to the table while she poured herself a cup of coffee.

"You certainly have a happy air of peace and joy this morning. That's a relief. I've been so concerned—after all that transpired."

"You're so kind. Has Mr. Clough been a consolation to you in your distress?" Rosanna put the coffee cup in front of her lips to hide her grin.

"You scapegrace. Don't taunt me, just because I may have a gentleman friend after all these years." Miss Barton broke her bacon into pieces and dropped them one by one on her plate.

The door opened and Lord Halburt crossed the threshold. He entered as if making an entrance onto a theater stage. He made a flourishing bow, straightened, and in a smooth motion, flapped his gloves toward protesting Perkins who had entered the room on the tails of the unwelcome Halburt.

Miss Barton whispered behind her hand. "Did he rehearse that?"

Perkins's irritation at the lord's rude intrusion was palpable.

Rosanna didn't want to make a scene. "Good morning, Lord Halburt, this is quite a surprise. I'd heard you were in London. Perkins, it's all right, you may go."

The man's gestures suited the stage, and accompanied each phrase. "Ah, yes. London's a fine city, but the air is so bad for one's health this time of year. Alas, business required me to journey forth from this fair region."

"I see. Breakfast?" Rosanna couldn't think of another response to his folderol.

"Nay. I've broken my fast at home. No, Miss Cabot, I'm here to request your charming presence on a stroll about your grounds. In sight of the house. That way we can be unchaperoned, correct?" He looked at Miss Barton for approval.

"Miss Cabot has my permission. Yes, that's fine. She's reached her majority, you know?"

Miss Barton must be extracting revenge by answering so fast. Rosanna heard a snicker, hidden within a fake cough. Struggling with reluctance, politeness won out, she rose from the table, and like a lamb led to the slaughter, retrieved her bonnet and shawl from the hall.

Perkins held the door open.

Rosanna reluctantly took Lord Halburt's arm to descend the front steps.

The man began to hum. "Fine day. Hmm."

She must put a stop to this before she smacked the fop. "Lord Halburt?"

He stopped.

She'd won his attention. Scrambling for something to say to the man, to keep him from any more humming, and get him talking, probably for about twenty minutes. Anything rather than the humming. She settled on a commonplace. "Your business in London — it must have been important to pry you away from home."

Distracted, he answered uncharacteristically briefly. "Indeed. Deuced important." As they passed a stone bench, he swung Rosanna around, and with a move that would do a *danseur* proud, landed her on the seat and himself on one knee in front of her.

53

Rosanna tried to stand, but his knees on the hem of her dress forestalled her rising. "Get up, you oaf."

"Now, dear young lady, don't be embarrassed. I'm here for the most honorable of purposes. To join our estates in holy matrimony."

She lightly pushed his shoulders to encourage him to rise. In sight of the house as the bench was, she hoped no one witnessed this debacle. "Halburt, I'll explain something to you. Estates can't get married. Get off my dress."

He didn't obey. "Oh, er, I mean join our *lives* in holy…"

"Stop right there. I get your meaning, and no."

"No? I haven't proposed yet. Listen. Make me the happiest of men. You are a treasure, Miss Cabot. Since you are over twenty-one years old, I don't need to ask permission to pay my addresses. Thus, I pay them directly to you and ask you to be my wedded wife." He then produced a further cascade of words extolling the estates' mutual proximity.

Rosanna put up with the flow as long as it took to form the proper set down. Her face flamed. She gave him a mighty shove and stood up. Before he could get up off the ground, she placed one half-booted foot upon his chest. "Now don't say another word until I've said my piece, or I'll grind my sole into your cravat, and it will never be the same." That would pin the fop down for the time she needed to set him straight. "You have not studied your prey, Lord Halburt. A basic knowledge of me or anyone intimate with me would have informed you that I abhor marriages formed for financial gain, status, or property enhancement."

He sputtered and flopped like a fish on the bank of a river.

Roseanna added, "I avoided it for four London seasons and, in fact, moved to Honor's Point to live away from society and for a refuge from such arrangements. You are hereby informed of my philosophy. Now, I shall let you up if you promise not to pester me with your importunities again."

"I shan't. Now let me up, you little vixen."

She removed her foot.

He rose to his feet. Anger flashed in his eyes and infused his posture as he brushed off his breeches and straightened his coat.

Concerned that she'd stepped across a line, she held out a hand. "Let's cry friends. Link arms with me and you may deliver me to my front door. We shall bid each other a friendly *adieu*, and never refer to this unfortunate incident again."

His face an alarming shade of purplish red, he submitted to her face-saving plan. He linked arms with hers, pretending to be laughing and talking, but the tense rigidity of his arm told her that he only performed for the sake of his reputation. If anyone observed them, they'd surely think the prior scene some sort of joke, because after all, they walked back arm in arm.

After Halburt delivered her to the front door, bowed, and stalked off, Rosanna gave Perkins another directive. "I remain not at home to Lord Halburt until further notice."

The chastened butler raised his eyebrows but said nothing.

~*~

Spurts of girlish laughter brightened Rosanna's mood. She and Ellie rested their feet on hassocks in the sitting area of Rosanna's room—its coziness inspired late-night confidences.

Ellie's voice rose to a high pitch as she expressed her disbelief at Halburt's misplaced ardor. "No. He didn't say that."

"Yes. He did. He proposed that our estates marry each other. I am not bamming you. Those were his words. Good thing he thought eyes might be on us or he would have flown up into the boughs for sure, so great was his rage."

"Did he behave angrily?"

"His eyes flashed with fury. He was in high dudgeon."

Due to nervous, suppressed laughter, Ellie's voice came out a twitter. "Let's hope he's not the vengeful sort." She tossed her head, sending ribbons of her silky red hair cascading over her shoulders before stating her estimation of the male species. "Men. Some of them think they are God's gift, don't they? As if their offers of their precious titled persons outweigh all other considerations."

"I suppose. They're not all like that, though." Rosanna sank into a reverie. The frivolity engendered by the day's contretemps hadn't erased her concern over the status of her relationship with Peter.

Ellie wrinkled her nose in distaste. "Well, in my opinion, men are, for the most part, shabsters. I can only think of a few admirable ones."

Poor girl, what she must have been through to be so jaded regarding the male gender. Maybe she'd talk about it more someday. Rosanna patted Ellie's arm. "You've found a refuge, so try to let it go. Whatever happened, you made it here and you're safe, thanks be to God. Late though it is, I must write a letter before I retire, so we bring to an end this little *tete a tete*."

Ellie departed, leaving Rosanna to her task.

The momentousness of the letter she needed to write crashed down. Hesitation held her for long minutes. A daydream intruded on her mind. She imagined Peter, alone in his cottage. Surely a sad, ashamed, and sorrowful man. Did he pine for her? Or was he already resigned to losing her? This thought banished her hesitation and she went to her desk. She hoped his love for her stayed true and pure. She realized the price he'd paid by confessing. That had to be torture for him. Dating the letter with tomorrow's date, she began,

Dearest friend,

Please forgive me. Yes, me. I have sinned against you. 'Tis hard for me, but I must admit my lack of love. You humbly confessed to me. Because of my life experiences and bitterness towards those who attempted to pressure me into loveless marriage, I denigrated your repentance. I loved once before. When he was killed something in me closed off, and I was left to fend off unwanted and unrighteous suitors. I am grateful, so grateful the Lord brought me to Honor's Point. Looking back, I see His hand of providence guiding me to you and healing my heart through you. I forgive you fully and completely. Please, meet me at the falls, at one o'clock, this afternoon.

Fondly yours, Rosanna

54

Perkins spoke up while assisting Rosanna at the breakfast buffet the following morning. "Miss Cabot, the footmen both have the lungrot. Cook's dosing them. Harrumph. Sorry, I meant to say, they are ailing."

"That's too bad. Tell Hannah to send to Lady Brook if she needs medicines. Her tinctures have a superb reputation." As Perkins pushed her chair in, Rosanna made a mental note to check on ailing servants later. For now, hunger took over. She'd slept late, and the clock just chimed ten. Having regained her taste for food, lost since Peter's revelation, she dug into the plate of ham and eggs. Peace of mind did wonders for the appetite.

While she nibbled her food, and sipped her coffee, Perkins's reedy, yet loud voice was audible through the closed door. The sounds of a disputatious interaction were recognizable, but unable to make out the words through the thick door, she disregarded the matter, until Perkins returned to continue footman duty.

"Did someone call, Perkins? I thought I heard arguing." She indicated that she had finished by placing her napkin on the table and made to get up.

Perkins rushed over and pulled the chair out for her before answering. "Sorry for the disturbance, Miss.

I followed your instructions, Miss, and told Lord Halburt ye wasn't home. He walked into the front hall liked he owned the place." The butler sniffed his disapproval. "I don't intend to criticize my betters."

"No offense taken. Rather, you did the right thing. Thank you, Perkins. Did you see the envelope I left on the hall table? I want that delivered right away to Lord Winstead…"

Another commotion erupted as Hannah, the cook, entered the dining room. Face red, she lifted the corners of her apron and made a humble curtsey. "Miss, the boys, the footmen? They be mortal sick, and me cures, they don't be helping." She wrung her hands with a miserable look on her face.

"That's terrible. I shall go see Lady Brook directly and bring her back here. Perkins, have the stables prepare a carriage and find Dot, she'll come along. While they get the horses hitched and ready, I will look in on the patients."

The cook continued to wring her hands. "Oh miss. That's not necessary, you bein' the mistress and all."

"Not to worry, Hannah. You go back to your kitchen and don't have a care. My mother trained me to have concern for all creatures, whether noble, gentry, or laborer, and I shall take a look at those two. Where are they?" After receiving directions, she hiked up several flights of stairs with Perkins at her heels.

The young men weren't too sick to be mortified by the appearance of the young mistress.

She soon caught the drift that modesty precluded any real evaluation of their cases and retreated just as fast as she had come.

~*~

"Lady Brook, I implore your assistance." Rosanna arrived at Brook House to find the neighbor toiling in her stillroom, preparing yet more supplies for her vast medicine closet. "Two of my footmen are ill. It appears to be inflammation of the lungs and exceeds what our household can cure. Since the local medical man is down with a broken leg, you are our only recourse."

"Dear Miss Cabot, rest easy. I shall finish this tincture and be ready to go with you within a few minutes."

Rosanna watched in admiration as the older lady handily corked two bottles, took off her apron, and patted her hair. "I'm ready. Is your carriage out front?"

"Yes, and thank you for coming to our rescue."

"Oh, la." She fluttered her hands in a dismissive gesture. "I live for helping the sick. This is a treat for me. Let me find my wrap."

Rosanna followed Lady Brook out into the hall where Dot waited under the eye of Frimley, the butler. He handed Lady Brook her shawl and bonnet.

"Just open the door, Frimley. The groom will help us into the coach."

The groom hoisted her sizeable medicine bag after her. Rosanna and Lady Brook faced forward, and Dot sat in the less desirable position with her back to the horses.

Rosanna's spoke with feeling, and patted Lady Brook's hand. "I'm so glad you are my neighbor. Tis such a comfort, knowing you are near with all your cures."

The lady had a faraway look in her eyes. "Thank you, my dear. I live to bring my healing knowledge to others. Since Lord Brook died, it gives my life some purpose."

"It's a blessing to those around you." The coach gave a jostle, and Rosanna fell silent, her thoughts ran ahead to her assignation with Peter. How would it be? Would they be able to regain their rapport?

The coachman traversed the circular drive, stopping at the front door of Honor's Point. A groom ran out to hold the horses, and Perkins emerged from the house to assist the ladies from the carriage.

Once in the hall, Rosanna directed Perkins to lead Lady Brook to the sick footmen. She disappeared up the stairs.

Rosanna looked at the hall clock, surprised at the hour, then turned to Dot. "I will go out walking as soon as I take a bite to eat. You may accompany me. Meet me here after you do the same."

The maid scurried off in the direction of the kitchens.

55

"Dot, I want you to wait here." She'd stopped at the top of the rickety stairs. Intending to make peace with Lord Winstead, Rosanna didn't desire any witnesses to the emotional scene to come.

"Yes, miss." Dot sank down on a patch of grass and began to pluck dandelions for a chain. The girl appeared to be satisfied with her lot.

With good conscience, Rosanna traversed the last leg of her journey to the falls. Her feet had wings, and she no longer had any doubts about Peter. He'd be there, waiting for her, they would reconcile, and emerge from the grotto, betrothed.

Recalling Peter's instructions, she descended without putting weight on the railing, yet used it as a balancing aid. Reaching the bottom of the stairs, she took a deep breath and began crossing the stepping stones. That done, she proceeded down the viney path.

At the large downed tree, she used her parasol to brace her scramble atop the horizontal tree. Resting for the briefest pause upon the massive trunk, she positioned the parasol a second time to steady her descent. Anticipation gave energy to her tentative pace, picking her way through vines, divots, and finding the dry spots to enable her to move ahead.

Pushing aside the hawthorn bush and thrilling with the hope of an encounter of reconciliation with her love, Peter, she caught her breath when an unexpected person loomed out from behind the bush.

"Halburt? What on earth…?"

"Nothing to alarm about, Miss Cabot. I got your note to meet you here."

"My note? I sent you no note." She held the parasol with a tight grip.

"Oh, that note on the hall table wasn't for me? Saying to meet you here in this secluded glen? Oh, my, what a mistake. But we're here. Alone." His hands reached out and grasped her by the shoulders.

Squirming, she attempted to stomp on his feet, but he, guard up, danced out of her way, and her struggles to break free didn't succeed.

"You'll be thoroughly compromised soon. Then the house, and the treasure it holds, will be mine by rights." His grip on her shoulders became more painful.

"Ow! You're hurting me. Let me go." She squirmed, then stilled, hoping to lull him into relaxing his vigilance. "My house holds no treasure. Why you obsess over that idea I'd like to know."

"The lost treasure of Honor's Point has been the subject of talk in the neighborhood for a long time. One of the Winsteads' maids caught wind of something years ago and told one of my servants. I've never forgotten the story."

She sneered. "Servants' gossip?"

"So you say. The lure of the treasure has led me to do many things…."

"You! You were the intruder. I should have known, what with your fascination and insistence that I hold a treasure hunt. I saw you in the guest wing the night of the party. It's clear why you were there even though that was off limits."

"I don't deny it. But you'll never convince anyone that it was me. Especially not after we're married." He emphasized these words with a shake of her shoulders.

Rosanna wrenched out of his grasp but didn't catch him off guard. He spread his arms to block her escape, then looped both arms around her, one at her back, one behind her knees and swept her off her feet.

The beast is strong, I'll give him that much. "You'll not find it easy to manipulate me into any compromised entanglement for it will be your word against mine." Rosanna wriggled and tried to strike Lord Halburt's face, but he captured her free hand with his strong right arm.

"I'll consider letting you go and keeping silent about your loose conduct on two conditions. One, turn over the real treasure to me, and two, give me a kiss."

"That, I'll never do."

"So you say." He bent his head to capture his kiss, and Rosanna screamed in his ear. He loosened his hold, half dropped her, half set her down, staggered a few steps away, and clutched his ear.

He reached toward her again, hands clenched into a claw-like position. "You vixen! You'll pay for that!"

"Look, behind you!" Rosanna shrieked, hoping to avoid being clawed by the enraged nobleman.

56

"I'll not fall for that" Halburt snarled as he grabbed her arm in a vise-like grip.

Rosanna's heart sank, for she knew that she was truly alone with the enraged neighbor. She'd gone to extremes to avoid entanglements, yet fell into the clutches of a mercenary, mad, suitor.

Appeasement seemed the best course at the moment—she wouldn't put it past him to resort to further violence against her. "Oh, I thought I heard someone."

"Have you heard of Gretna Green? For that is where we are headed."

"I've only heard of consenting couples running to the border, not abductors and unwilling brides."

"Oh, you'll be willing after a night or two or three of ruin...I mean pleasure, at the inns along the way."

She quailed at his words, foreseeing that he meant each one and was deranged by his lust for wealth. "Never."

"Come along quiet-like now. That's a girl."

He gave the command as if to a horse, or a favorite dog. She complied, however, stumbling along the path as he dragged her with his fingers digging into the flesh of her arm.

~*~

Reaching the top of the steps, Rosanna searched the tall grass for Dot. Nowhere in sight. The girl, so reliable—where was she?

"Oh, I see you are looking for that little chit of a maid? She's been taken out of commission."

"What? You haven't…"

Halburt's eyes glittered. "Settle down, she's only been removed from play, like a pawn in a game of chess, not killed. What do you think me, a murderer?"

Mad, you're mad. "Not necessarily. I just want my lady's maid. You know how a lady wants her maid with her when she's to be wed?"

"You've got my loving care, you don't need your servant along. We'll go this way."

Rosanna's heart sank. Fear, apprehension, and dread mingled in a fog of dismay which her mind refused to grasp. The truth was too hard to bear, and she retreated into a stupor of distant echoes—reality fading into sorrow. She staggered along as he dragged her through the woods, taking a trail she'd never seen before.

The distinctive sound of jangling harnesses snapped her to alertness. She wrenched her arm, hoping to free it, but his grip still clamped like iron. The path emerged onto an overgrown track, barely wide enough to accommodate the axle width of a massive black closed carriage.

"Up you go, Miss Cabot."

He shoved her up the steps and she fell onto the floorboards of the conveyance. As she scrambled to rise, Halburt lurched in, slammed shut the door, and hovered over her. The coach began to move.

"If you choose to sit, I'll allow it. But, be warned,

the doors are locked, and the outriders are all armed and instructed to incapacitate anyone who attempts to flee this vehicle."

She cringed on the floor, preferring not to sit up as if the situation was normal. "So, your minions would shoot a woman? A woman who is of high standing, not a doxy, or criminal?"

"Their concern is only for the reward promised upon the successful completion of this journey, not upon the caliber of person they may be required to injure."

"I'll be missed, you know. Someone will come after me." She lifted her head to ascertain how her words affected him.

He crossed his legs, folded his arms, and lifted his chin. She sensed him seeking the best angle of his jaw for her to admire. "The way I see it, Miss Cabot, is thus." He flung out one arm, in an exhorting gesture. "Your household staff expects that you have gone on a long walk, nay, assignation. No alarm shall be raised for several hours, then a search will be made, taking up further hours and by that time, we will be well out of reach of any pursuit."

"I don't agree, you scoundrel. You'll see."

"Get up off the floor. Relax. You may as well accept your fate. There are worse things than being married to me—a lord of the realm. In good standing, mind you—no lost fortune, no scandal. No one will ever need to find out the secrets of the beginnings of our union."

Contemplating such a future caused black despair to roost in Rosanna's heart, but she wasn't done hoping. She hitched up onto the seat facing her tormentor, and brushed her hands down her arms, as if trying to remove the soiling of his actions. Failing this, she lifted her prayers to the Lord. *Please deliver me and protect me, Amen.*

"Miss Cabot," Halburt said with a sneer, "Feel free to rest your lovely head back upon the squabs. We will not arrive at our lodging for several, nay many, hours. I'd hate for you to disembark at our love-nest at less than your best."

Choosing to remain silent, Rosanna's mind worked furiously at calculating the truth of Halburt's words. Would anyone miss her? What had he done with Dot? How long before anyone at home—the word 'home' stung her heart with longing—would notice her missing? If not missed for a few hours, even a rider on a fast horse couldn't catch up to them before Lord Halburt forced her to her fate at an inn.

A thunderous jolt rocked the coach and Halburt, never taking his eyes off Rosanna, slid open the window and called out to the coachman, "What was that?"

"Just a dip. A rut—but we are upright and steady now, sir."

"All right, be quick and get us across the River Esk and into Northampton by cock's crow, and all will be well for you."

Rosanna caught the words cock's crow and a droplet of hope dampened her despair. Only a bud, not a flowering, but it helped. That meant he'd run the coach all day and night, changing horses along the way, and only then stopping at an inn sometime the next morning. Perhaps her ruin could be postponed, and rescue would arrive in time.

Halburt obsessively checked the door locks, and patted his waistcoat where he'd secreted the key over and over. He repeatedly smoothed his hair, brushed his coat and breeches, and examined his shiny boots.

Pretending to sleep, Rosanna chose to say nothing more. Soon, actual sleep took over and the blissful relief of slumber gave a respite from her ordeal.

~*~

On the road home to his cottage, Peter sagged in the saddle. Having used one of his mother's lesser jewels as temporary currency with the stable in town, he now owned a respectable mount—something he'd sorely missed during his recent impoverished days.

As much as he was pleased to have a horse again, dismal, hopeless fears surrounded him. Aching for the chance to win Rosanna, he saw no way around her antipathy.

A soft wailing reached his consciousness. Was someone hurt? The sound came from somewhere ahead—it had to be around the next bend. He spurred the horse, then reined in when a curious bundle staggering down the road appeared before his eyes.

A small woman, taking shuffling steps, was wrapped in what looked like a carpet runner, tied round with rope. A gag between her teeth kept her cries muted, and the bindings made her steps laughably short.

"Whoa." He patted the jittery mount, then swung down. "Who are you? What misfortune's overtaken you?"

The small female tottered up to him, and he saw that she was familiar. It was Dot, Rosanna's maid. He moved behind her and untied the cloth gag.

She shrieked. "Help!"

"Hush, girl. I am help. Calm down, I'll have you freed from this ghastly rug in a moment or two."

He walked around her, unwinding the rope, stopping now and then to untie a fiendish knot. "Who did this to you?"

"I don't know who they was. But they grabbed me by the top of the steps to the waterfall. They dragged me through the woods, bound me and threw me into the luggage boot of a carriage."

"How did you get away?"

"The Lord God gave me a way out. I was peeking out of the lid, which I pushed up with me head, guessing whether to jump out or not. Right then, the carriage hit a large rut and during the racket and banging of the vehicle, I rolled on out."

"Are you hurt?"

"No, the Lord preserved me. Not only did I land well, but the carpet padded me, and I rolled right off into the ditch. The men must've had their eyes on a rough patch of road ahead." She hugged her arms and gave a tremble.

"Here, I will put you upon my horse and get you back to your mistress." He swung into the saddle, then hoisted her on behind himself. He wheeled the horse around in the direction of the manor house. "Hang on."

Her voice shook, and she trembled against his back. "Sir?"

"Yes, Dot? What is it? Speak up. Don't be afraid. You're safe now."

"It's about getting me back to me mistress."

"What about that?"

"Umm, I don't know if she got back to the house."

"Got back?"

"Yes, sir. She was down in the glen. She told me to wait up top."

"What was she doing?"

"I dunno. Seemed like she might have been meeting someone."

Peter spurred the horse, disregarding the squeals coming from Dot, and her chokehold around his neck. A full gallop brought him to the house. A groom ran up, Peter threw him the reins. "Dot, you'll be fine. Go around to Mrs. Good. She'll know what to do for you."

He leapt up the steps and wrenched open the door to face a surprised butler. "Perkins. Is Miss Cabot here?"

"No, she went on a walk with her maid. Oh, that reminds me, we had a bit of a commotion and I neglected to have a message taken over to you." Perkins shuffled to the hall table and rummaged for a few moments. "Hmm. It looks as though it's gone. Now, who would have taken it, with the footmen down with lungrot?"

"Never mind that. Get Miss Barton and Miss Moore. Now."

Affronted, Perkins nevertheless collected himself. "They are both in here." He went to the door of the morning room and opened it. "Lord Winstead," he intoned on his best dignity.

"Thank you, Perkins, that will be all for now, but stay at hand."

Both ladies rose and turned toward him.

Ellie's hand rose to her throat and her already pale skin went ashen.

Miss Barton gripped the back of her chair with one hand and clutched the bib of her apron with the other.

"What's wrong, Lord Winstead?"

"I believe Miss Cabot is…well…in trouble."

"Trouble?" Ellie's voice came out a whisper and she looked greatly alarmed.

"I came upon Dot, gagged and bound, on the road. When I loosened her bonds, she told me she'd been thrown into the baggage compartment of a coach and only by God's intervention was able to heave herself out at an opportune moment."

"What is the meaning of this?" Miss Barton's voice quivered, and tears pooled in her eyes.

"I don't know. But Dot said she thought Miss Cabot was meeting someone in the glen. I plan to go there immediately, on foot, since that will be quickest. But I'd like you two to get a carriage to the fork of the north road. Bring my horse, too. Do you understand? She might need you."

His heart throbbed with urgency as he ran to the head of the trail. The path's uneven surface kept him focused and without a trip or a stumble he arrived at the top of the steps. Taking them two at a time, he breathed a prayer. *Oh, God. Have mercy, Help.*

57

Wanting to leap straight over the stream, he instead made swift, but careful progress across the very stones his love trod only a short time ago.

Down the path, he ran and vaulted the downed tree, forged ahead past the hawthorn, and stopped in his tracks upon realizing the site held not his darling. She was not there. But, what was that? Scuff marks in the dirt. He didn't remember anything like that—oh yes, that was a drag mark. And—what is that? Paper. He snatched at a folded white object caught in the undergrowth.

The faint scent of flowers wafted from the fine linen stationery. Unfolding it with speed, he was shocked to see it was a note to himself. His hand rose to push his hair out of the way, so he could read in the dim light.

Dearest friend, he read, and his heart skipped a beat. Eyes scanned the remaining words, landing on the pertinent ones: *meet me at the falls, at one o'clock, this afternoon.*

Though he wanted to drink in the mercy she held out to him in the rest of the letter, he had no time for emotions. He took care to fold the letter and put it inside his shirt, and then dashed toward the stream, crossing it in a trice, and bounded up the steps.

~*~

"I'm jolted to pieces. And what about breakfast? You're not much of a courtier if you think this trip will do anything to soften me toward you." Rosanna used deceit with the cur, believing it justified.

"Glad you are having reasonable thoughts about me. I knew you'd come to your senses."

Seething, Rosanna held her tongue and turned her face away, making a show of looking out the window, but simply avoiding more interaction with her abductor. She put her hand inside her sadly crushed bonnet, pressed out the dents, donned it, and then tied the strings with determined motions. *I must stay alert.* At an inn, there might be a way to escape.

When the carriage rolled to a halt, it stood directly in front the door of a rustic inn.

Halburt unlocked the carriage door, assisted Rosanna down, and ushered her straight into the inn, using an iron grip. Once in the musty hall, she wrenched her arm away. "You've bruised my arm enough this trip. I need breakfast, since I am near to perishing from lack of food and water."

"Step through there. The innkeeper's wife will bring in a repast for us. I warn you, be silent about our arrangements, or it's back into the carriage without food at this time." He lifted his brows toward her. He then half lowered lids which gave him a ridiculous air—a failed attempt to mix dominance and appeal. That such a wicked fool sought to triumph over her caused her heart to lurch between determination and fear.

She glanced around the room, to see if any guests looked like sympathetic sorts who would believe her unbelievable tale. But no promising folk lurked nearby, merely a few dirty, rough-hewn men who'd as soon laugh in her face than help her by the looks of them. No, for now, she'd bide her time, eat to retain her strength, and search for a weakness in her abductor's plan.

The innkeeper's wife came in with a tray. Short and stout, she appeared clean, but had a downtrodden demeanor, and a meek voice.

No help in that quarter, Rosanna sensed not to try. Not yet. She'd eat the porridge, drink the coffee, and watch for a chance.

Halburt held up his cup and winked at her over the rim. "Never cared for coffee, myself." He spoke as if they were the best of friends, simply sharing a light meal. "I much prefer the tradition of chocolate for breakfast. So, unfortunate they don't have that here. I've settled for tea."

Rosanna's stomach clenched, and she bit her tongue. She gave a noncommittal smile then glanced down at her bowl as though it were fascinating.

He nodded to his servants who entered, having finished seeing to the horses and carriage. Halburt clattered his cup into its saucer. "I wonder—perhaps there's a congenial parson in this town. Wouldn't be any need for another long leg to our journey."

Bile rose in her throat and she bent over, retching.

Halburt snapped his fingers toward the group of men. "Pass the girl a bucket." He shoved it against her side. "Here. You mustn't be a public disgrace."

Rosanna, still bent over, clutched the bucket like a lifeline and took some test breaths to see if the wave of nausea passed. "I need to visit the necessary. I don't want to disgrace you, Lord Halburt."

"Shhh. Don't say my name. Slack, you there, follow her out back to the necessary. Don't lose her, or it'll be your hide."

She took her cue and scampered out of the dining room holding her head low over the bucket and making excessive sound effects all the way.

Unfortunately, when she came out of the structure, the servant inappropriately named Slack, of all things, stood right where she'd left him with a martial stance of hands on hips, feet apart, relaxed not one iota.

"Look over there!" Rosanna pointed to a spot behind his head and got ready to knock him into the mud.

But he refused to comply. He didn't vary his gaze off her.

"Fine. Humph." Rosanna flounced past him and shoved the bucket into his hands, then re-entered the inn, Slack on her heels. The backyard was fenced anyway, and she probably wouldn't have escaped, but for this bounder to be dogging her steps added insult to grave injury and she was now even more unhappy with Halburt, if that were possible.

"So, you're back. My minions will be watching er...protecting you while I locate the local clergy and investigate his level of cooperation with the lords of the land." Halburt rose and shook a velvet purse toward Rosanna, clanking the coins. He stalked away.

Rosanna diddled with her spoon, pretending to eat, while assessing the guards. One, with steely eyes, sat near the door with arms crossed, staring holes into her. Another sat at the table within arm's reach of her. Another one lurked behind her, but she didn't need to turn to look—since he breathed audibly.

"Could someone call the mistress of this inn? I

need more food."

The one by the door pounded his elbow against the wall, and bawled, "Good woman! More food for the lady." He subsided into his stare, silent again.

The innkeeper's wife re-entered the room, with another tray. "All's I gots is these scones. They's from yesterday, but all tells that they're mighty good."

The guards crowded around the woman, forgetting their duties in order to grab for the scones.

Rosanna took this chance to slip out of the room, running for the front door only a few steps down the hall. She ran across the small innyard, peeked around the corner of the stable, glimpsed Halburt in his bright blue coat walking in her direction and dove into the nearest convenient haystack.

She didn't know what to do next, but at least she was out of his clutches. Rosanna, deathly afraid of being caught again, pulled hay over her head and shoved herself as far into the stack as she could. When Halburt passed her on his way back to the inn, his cuff brushed the tip of her nose. Good thing she wasn't prone to sneezing.

A coach appeared, coming from the opposite direction from that which she arrived. As the coach turned into the yard, a distant uproar from inside the inn met her ears—surely Halburt throwing a wild tantrum by now. Those sounds were soon surpassed by the jangling of the harness, the clip-clop of the newly arriving horses, and the shouting of the ostlers.

"Egads, ye bumpkins, clear the way for a gentleman."

More sounds, steps being lowered, door creaking open, then the cultured voice of an older man greeting the innkeeper.

"George Cabot, Esquire. Here to take morning tea. I've been on the south road for three hours, my good man, and must rest myself."

Uncle George! Here? *Thank you, Lord.* Rosanna stood , hay cascading from her dusty, bedraggled person. Brushing herself off, she ran over, peeked around the carriage, and perceived that it really was her uncle.

"Hello, Uncle George. It's me, your niece, come to join you on your journey, just as we planned." She positioned herself facing him and fixed his eyes with hers. She raised an index finger and pressed it vertically across her lips, raised her eyebrows, then whispered, "Don't say anything. Not my name. You must save me—I've been abducted."

She linked her arm through his, and he patted her hand. He reached inside his dove gray coat and left his hand in there as they entered the inn. "Drake, Handsworth, follow me." Two burly outriders fell in behind, and before long, Rosanna was back in the dining room.

"Lord Halburt, meet my uncle. He doesn't look like it, but he's an angel. God sent him to save me from the devil that is you. Tell your servants to leave the room."

"Now." Uncle George's voice held command, and Halburt's henchmen, who looked puny next to Uncle's men, scuttled out without a backward glance. "Drake, you and Handsworth stand outside this room and guard the door. Don't let anyone in here."

Halburt took a stance in one of the corners, trying to appear composed.

But Rosanna could tell he was shaking by the fob trembling on a chain suspended across his waistcoat.

Uncle George cut to the chase. "Rosanna. What is the meaning of this?"

"This cur is my neighbor, Lord Halburt, who stole me from my home woods. He intends to carry me off to Gretna Green, force marriage upon me, and has sorely mistreated me." She held up an index finger, indicating one more point of important. "Also, he openly stated to me that he intends to ruin me."

"I think I understand." Uncle George's face blanched, but he forged ahead. "Has he harmed you?"

"Other than pinioning my arm in a painful vise-like grip, dragging me through thick woods, casting me down on the floor of his carriage and locking me in? No, unless you count forcing me to sleep in a moving closed carriage all through the night. Not to mention unsavory threats, including his plans to force himself upon me this very day."

"Say no more, young lady." The older man turned to face Rosanna's tormenter. "I don't give much veracity to your words, Halburt, but where were you taking my niece?"

"We were on a journey to marry over the anvil. I expect to be there by nightfall tomorrow since we shall cross the River Esk tonight."

"That's an odd plan, since you are nowhere near the River Esk. It's much farther than a day's drive from here."

"No matter. Perhaps we'd have a private ceremony today."

"Nothing of the kind. My beloved niece will be leaving here in my care. Now listen carefully. Here are my instructions. Leave this place, speaking to no one, take your minions with you and begone."

Sulking, Halburt sidled past Uncle George,

cringing like a dog expecting to be struck. He had his hand on the door knob yet turned back to drip poison. "Be sure of this, she is lying. You might want to think twice about taking her away from me, since her reputation is now in tatters."

"You'll say nothing. If one breath of scandal touches her, you'll find yourself dragged through the mud and you'll rue the day you tried this folly. I assure you of that. Now take your hand off the doorknob."

Halburt let his hand slip off and Rosanna saw his chin tremble. What would Uncle George do next?

"Drake!" He called out. "Come in here."

One of the outriders entered. "Yes, sir?"

"Escort this man to his coach. Make sure he keeps his mouth shut. If he tries to talk, you have my orders to muzzle him any way you think best."

Lord Halburt squawked as he was muscled out of the inn.

Rosanna ran to the window in time to see him trundled into his coach and Uncle's servant smack the rump of one of the horses to send it off at a spanking pace.

She turned back to Uncle George. His face stern, she quaked, expecting to face a scolding, but then he opened his arms and she rushed into them, sobbing in relief.

"There, there, Rosa." He patted her back with his large hands, and then held her a little way from him. "Let's wipe those tears."

His capacious linen hanky helped her to cease crying, and he sat on the fireside bench with her, waiting while she took some deep breaths.

"Now, now. Don't hang your head. You just rest it here on my shoulder. We'll not tarry here. Do you have any luggage? For you are worse for wear, my dear girl."

"No. I have no luggage. He grabbed me in the woods on my own property."

"Fine. Calm down. Just ascertaining your needs. You've always been a good girl. There's a much finer inn on the other side of this town. We shall go there, and you will rest and repair from your ordeal. My travel can wait since I was on my way home from dealing with a problem on one of my northern holdings."

"Oh, Uncle George, thank the Lord you were on this road at the exact time I needed you. Such mercy. I was sore pressed and had no idea what to do next. That haystack was so itchy and dirty, too."

"Now that's easily dealt with. Just muster up the courage to walk out of here and we shall travel to the other inn."

58

Soaking chin deep in a hip bath, which the inn servants had labored to fill from cans of hot water carried up a steep flight of stairs, Rosanna was only able to relax after glancing at the locked door numerous times. She closed her eyes and tried to pray. Heart's cries were all that she could produce—words having for once escaped her.

Traumatized nerves on edge, she forced her shoulders down, and reviewed her plight. She was here, far from home, with no extra clothing. And since her dress needed to be washed, dried and ironed by the inn's maid, she'd need to sit wrapped in a blanket until the dress was returned. Not to mention the look of disappointment in Uncle George's eyes—after the crisis was over, he'd quizzed her on how she happened to be so unsafe at Honor's Point that a man could abduct her. More quizzing and disapproval to come from Uncle George.

Uncle George would tackle her about the unwise choice of her living arrangements. He'd probably prodce a handy list of possible suitors, assuring her she'd be better off with one of them.

Once she was home in her own domain, she'd be better able to withstand his arguments, if he persisted in them. But the people at home—surely agog with worry by now. She groaned and levered out of the tub, dripping. Making quick work of drying off, she wrapped up in the blanket. *Lord, thank You, it's a warm spring day.* Extracting one arm from the blanket, she pulled a piece of paper from the writing desk. A fine inn, to provide a desk, paper and ink to guests. Another thing to thank Uncle George for—removing her to such a superior hostelry.

The mail coach due in an hour, her letter would arrive at Woodvale and then to Honor's Point by tomorrow. Well before she'd return.

Dear Loved Ones,

Alas, I was forcefully taken from the woods. But God provided a rescuer. Just as I was in the direst of straits, my Uncle George happened by (by God's providential mercy alone) and he wrested me from the clutches of disaster. My person is intact, and I have no injuries other than an odd bruise or two. Try to reassure anyone who is worried. Please tell our dear neighbors, Lady Brook and Lord Winstead (but not Halburt) that I am fine, and not to worry—I'll be home soon whence I shall explain all.

Fond Regards, Rosanna Cabot

She sanded the letter, folded it, and readied it for the mail.

A tap came upon the door—it was the maid, with Rosanna's freshly laundered dress. "Here tis, mum."

"Thank you, and can you stay to help me fasten it?"

Rosanna went behind the convenient folding screen provided for dressing privacy and got her underthings and now faded muslin dress on. The inn's soap was surely harsher than the fine soap used at Honor's Point. Oh well, she'd never want to wear the dress again after this misadventure. All that was needed was assistance with fastenings.

"There ye are, miss. Anything else?"

"Tell my uncle, Mr. Cabot, that I can receive him now in the sitting alcove." Rosanna waved her hand to indicate a corner with a sunny bow window. "Please have some tea brought in as well. Thank you." She latched the door behind the servant and moved over to the window, and her mood lowered, not at all matching the bright late spring day. Her forehead pressed the glass, while her hands wrung against each other. How would this contretemps be played out? If only her uncle's compassion ran as strong as his gallantry. She had enough to face at home, and didn't relish a scolding. A knock came upon the door. She jumped, then asked "Who is it?"

"It's your Uncle George."

She unlatched the door and let him in.

"Ah, there you are. Feeling more the thing?" He plunked down a parcel on an empty chair by the door.

Uncle's jaunty air bade well, and Rosanna managed a smile and responded. "There are few ills a hot bath can't help." She slid onto the window seat and sat silent as Uncle George pulled up one of the side chairs.

He brushed down his gray sleeves in a nervous tic and then leaned his wrists on the edge of the table and clasped his hands. "Tea is on its way?"

"Oh, yes—any minute now." She leaned back, and her words came true. A tap on the door, a maid backed into the room and *voila*, a fully laden tea cart appeared. Rosanna indicated the letter on the desk. "Please take that letter and see that it gets on the mail coach. Thank you, that will be all."

Uncle George held up a staying hand. "Wait." The maid obeyed, eyes intent for further instructions. "Tell the innkeeper I'll need a horseman to ride with a message. The mail coach could take days. Come back for it when all is arranged."

The maid bobbed a curtsey and departed to do his bidding.

"Thank you, Uncle George. A much better idea." Rosanna poured tea for her uncle and for herself. She loaded a plate of cucumber sandwiches, cheeses, and tarts for him, and selected a scone for herself. After taking her first sip, she held her cup aloft and said, "Tea—another great curative."

"Indeed." He partook heartily, and then pushed his plate away. "Can't say when I've had an adventure on the road such as today's. My life has grown staid. But, coming to your aid in timely fashion will be a long-remembered *coup* for me and shall go down in the annals of time."

"You do know how to turn a phrase, Uncle. I am so grateful…." Sniffles and teardrops embarrassed Rosanna, but she pressed her eyelids and soon overcame them. "I must get back to Honor's Point. Can you escort me there?"

"I can, but are you certain that's the best?"

"You doubt me again?"

"Hear me out, Rosanna. I have several reasons for suggesting that you visit my home in London. We've missed you, dear. The girls would love to see their cousin. They do admire you. But most importantly, if we can quickly establish your presence there, and through mild subterfuge, indicate your visit started a week ago, no one will credit any such gossip about this escapade which might leak out into society's ears."

"You think Halburt will dare?"

"I do. He gives the impression of being a pompous

fool. He's certain to feel quite aggrieved. He will want to strike back at you."

"And he won't resist the urge, because he is of weak character?"

"Yes. His pride and arrogance will probably master him and open his mouth. I meant my threats, however, and will carry them out. He will be sorry when I get though with him, if he does what I predict."

"But is protecting my reputation that important, since I don't plan to rejoin society? Or live in London again?"

"Rosanna." Uncle's voice was larded with tried patience. "You don't know the future. You may yet marry. You may have children. Those children may want to go to London to move in advantageous circles in which to acquire spouses, and so on."

"I suppose you have a point. I will take you up on that suggestion, however, not because I am cowed by the tabbies. I miss the girls, too, and I just don't feel ready to return to the site of my near-doom. It's too fresh."

"I own I am pleasantly surprised you agreed to my wishes so readily, but I will accept your assent without question and am happy with it. I shall say no more about your future...right now. For the journey, I purchased for you a cloak from the proprietor's wife. It should fit you—she's about your size." He handed her a gray homespun bundle.

"Thank you for your thoughtfulness. Now, I must add a line to my letter, explaining the change in our plans. "

"Excellent. I'll have another one of those tarts, while you rewrite your note. And then, I'll add one of my own."

~*~

The wood pile mounted by the hour next to Peter's cottage. No matter how many logs he split with the maul and hammer, no matter how many swings of the axe, his leaden heart stayed heavy.

Two frantic days and nights of searching the roads for any word of Rosanna, had not produced her. Putting the scant clues together, he surmised Dot had been taken out of commission by someone who met Rosanna in his place and abducted her. At a loss, the search party dragged home, misery their only find. The frustration and bitter sorrow was about killing him. *Lord, please protect her. Please.*

"Sir! There's been a letter!" Dot ran into the clearing, out of breath.

"A letter?" Peter threw down the axe and ran to the frail maid. Grabbing her shoulders, he tried not to yell. "From Miss Cabot? Tell me, who?"

"Yes, sir, from Miss Cabot. The ladies up at the manor are awaiting you." She panted, then bent over with hands on her knees.

He ran into his cottage, yanked his coat off a hook inside the door, slammed it shut, and splashed some water on his face from a bucket on the stoop. He shot past Dot, and plunged into the woods.

Reaching Honor's Point, he slowed his steps only at the massive door. Crashing the knocker against the heavy door, he gasped, breathing hard from the run. When Perkins opened the door, he brushed past. "Where is Miss Barton?"

"Right in here, sir." Perkins grabbed the doorknob

to the drawing room and hastily ushered Peter inside.

Within, Ellie and Miss Barton rose from their satin chairs, faces tight with anxiety.

"The letter? May I see it?"

"Of course, please sit down first." Miss Barton indicated the plush settee next to her. "Here it is." She handed over the letter.

His eyes raced through the words. *Dear Loved Ones...Alas...forcefully taken...direst straits...Uncle George...wrested me from the clutches of disaster...intact...no injuries...Please tell...dear...Lord Winstead...but not Halburt...home soon...Rosanna P.S. I am going to London to visit Uncle George's family for a week, first.*

"Praise God! She's safe. What a trial. It sounds as though she's come through fairly unscathed." He dropped his head into his hands, dry sobbing.

Perkins opened the door a crack and stuck his head through. "Ladies, Lord Winstead? Another letter has just arrived. This one by special messenger." He entered, arm extended, holding the missive. He handed the envelope to Miss Barton, bowed and reversed his tracks, closing the door again with a thunk.

Peter worked toward a semblance of composure, but he felt wrung out, like a rag twisted one too many times. Drained and silent, he waited while Miss Barton broke the seal, drew out the folded paper, then unfolded it.

Head moving as she scanned line by line, and eyebrows rising, the letter crumpled as Barton's hands fell to her lap. "I am so surprised." She placed her fingertips across her lips and stared at the fire.

"Please read the letter out loud, Miss Barton." Ellie

laid her small hand upon the companion's wrist. "Or should I?"

Wordless, Barton passed the crinkled page to Ellie.

Relief and the aftermath of sick worry warred within Peter. He waited for another shoe to drop.

Ellie touched the bottom of the page with her forefinger. "This letter is from George Cabot, Esquire. That is Rosanna's uncle who lives in London. She's mentioned him fondly to me and that he was instrumental in her moving here. He was her legal guardian since her parents died."

Peter interrupted, his voice weak with emotion. "Please read the letter, Miss Moore?"

"Of course."

Dear Miss Barton,

My niece Rosanna Cabot asked me to write. She has consented to go on to London with me for a family visit at this time, rather than coming directly home after the recent 'contretemps' you are surely aware of.

My niece says she wrote of the providential circumstances that led us to join forces in such an unusual event. Let me assure you that she is well, albeit shaken up, and willingly agreed to spend a visit at my London townhouse, where her aunt, and cousins, Phoebe and Myrtle, will be delighted to see her.

She will communicate soon as to when, if ever, she returns to her estate, Honor's Point. That vicinity holds bad connotations now, so we shall have to see.

Yours,

Cabot

Peter rocketed to his feet, the settee shoved back by the force of his movements. He laid a hand on the arm of the settee, as if he were calming it. "Ladies, I must leave you now. The trip to London should be accomplished in two days on the road. Then I shall see clearly, face to face, if she's truly in London of her own volition."

"Lord Winstead," Ellie stiffened, "You have her word, from Rosanna herself, that her uncle is a benevolent man. Rosanna spoke nothing but good of him. You really don't have to worry."

Hand extended to calm him, Miss Barton chimed in. "If she's in London with her uncle George Cabot, a staunch man of good character with whom I have been acquainted for decades, she's in good hands."

Peter patted his jacket, to feel the folded missive resting within. "Unless I see her myself, I won't be able to be rest assured of her well-being. Don't forget, the love note from Rosanna that Halburt intercepted was for me, and therefore you understand why I am leaving."

"Far be it from us to stop you, then." Miss Barton spoke for both. Ellie nodded agreement, face serious.

"Miss Barton, please jot down Cabot's address."

She complied, and he bowed, one arm in front of his waist, and one behind his back, then stalked out of the room, head high.

59

Myrtle Cabot, seventeen and the older of Uncle George's two girls, agog with the story of her father rescuing Rosanna from a crazed swain, pleaded for the particulars. "Cousin Rosanna, please tell us all."

"Yes, Rosanna, tell us how you raced to Gretna Green with a suitor." Phoebe, sixteen, leaned forward, avid for the tale.

"Girls, I wouldn't put it that way. Yes, your dear father saved me. I was not a willing participant on a dash to marry over the anvil." Rosanna sighed and pulled the lap robe higher. "You mustn't romanticize a wicked trick played on me by a neighbor." She'd downplayed the horrors for the sake of her cousins' tender innocence. To share the true details would serve no purpose.

Myrtle pressed her fingers together and posed with them against her throat, eyes dreamy. "I think I'd love it if some young lord swept me up into a carriage, all caused by his passion for me."

Uncle George entered the cozy morning room and strode over to group clustered near the fire. "Late spring can surprise us with some chilly days. How are you?" On his way to his special armchair, he patted Rosanna's shoulder.

Sitting close to the fire, huddled against a chill that came from within, she gave a pained smile. "I am better than yesterday, and not as good as tomorrow."

"Excellent attitude." He addressed his daughters, "Girls, go see your mama, she's got some swatches for you to look over."

"They do love new clothes," Rosanna said as the girls vanished.

"Good, they don't need to hear what I am about to tell you. I must say I'm very glad they aren't 'out' yet and can't gossip about your misadventure. Except to each other."

"They are so sweet. I'm sure they mean no harm with their interest."

"I've been doing some checking on Lord Halburt."

"Oh, him. I'm sick of that man. Must we talk about him?"

"Not too much, but you must be aware of the seriousness of some information I have obtained."

"Obtained? How?"

"I hired an investigator to nose around town discreetly. Wanted to assess the caliber of his reputation in London, if any, and perhaps receive some fodder to use against him."

"I don't want revenge. Only never to see him again, if possible."

"Not revenge, dear—protection. Only material to use if he were ever to act maliciously toward you. One can never be too careful with an unbalanced man. For all we know, he may think himself the aggrieved one."

Rosanna gave an audible sigh. "Will this nightmare never end?"

"Don't despair, you'll get over it. It's only been a few days since the sad event occurred...why, your bruises haven't even faded completely yet."

"You're right, it will take some time. Also, I must

remember my faith in God who will not forsake me or forget me."

"That's the spirit. Now, I'll be brief, but what I found out involves not only Halburt, but his deceased father, the previous Lord Halburt. It seems he had a longstanding enmity against Lord Winstead, the deceased father of the current Lord Winstead, former owner of your estate, Honor's Point."

"Yes, Uncle George," Rosanna said with asperity, "I know who you meant. I'm healing from a trauma, but I haven't lost my mind or memory."

"Don't be testy with me."

"I'm sorry, my patience is short today. What form did this enmity take?"

"It appears the elder Halburt was enamored of a certain lady. That lady, chose another man, the elder Lord Winstead. That was an ancient piece of gossip my sleuth unearthed. The other information, however, is much more shocking, but hard to prove."

"Do we really need to comb over old scandal?"

"Maybe not, but hear me out and I think you'll understand the importance of my information. It seems the two men would go up to London together, at Lord H's invitation. He lured Lord W into excessive gaming. The rest took care of itself when Lord W became addicted to the tables and lost his fortune."

Rosanna's hands flew to her cheeks. "Oh, my! How terrible."

"There's a rumor that he, that's the elder Lord H, repeatedly pressed Lord W to sell him Honor's Point, a property Lord H long coveted."

She chafed her hands, cold again. "That I certainly believe, based on the covetousness of his heir with his perpetual nosiness about my house and its contents.

How sickening."

"Let me put on another log." Uncle George grabbed the tongs and poked a birch log onto the embers in the grate. "I have a plan. I'll only enact it if you agree. I'll contact the current Lord H. and invite him here to meet with you. I'll have a magistrate and guards hidden behind that screen," he gestured to the corner, "and they'll throw Halburt into the Tower."

"A lord of the realm? Uncle, please be realistic. What he did was heinous but won't be deemed worthy of the Tower by the authorities or anyone outside our humble, non-titled family."

Uncle George's lower lip jutted before he agreed, with reluctance. "I suppose you are correct. I'll have to go back to the drawing board on that. I just don't want to see him get away without punishment."

"God above knows Lord Halburt's every sin, and will deal justly with him whether in this life or the next."

"You're too kind, dear. I shall leave you now and go wrack my brain for a while. I'll come up with something." He departed, leaving Rosanna alone with her thoughts and a roaring fire.

~*~

Her eyes flew open sometime later, welcome sleep having visited her after Uncle George left. A noise intruded on her slumber. A creaking door, and then stealthy footsteps. Alarmed, she tried to rise, but was entangled in the blanket.

"No need to get up," whispered Lord Halburt, entering the room on his tiptoes.

"What are you doing here? Please leave before I have you thrown out."

"Alas, the entire household is down the block aiding a fire-fighting effort. I think my diversion a success—don't you?"

"You started a fire? You cad."

"Tut, tut. You thought you could get away from me so easily? That I would give up my prize?"

"I am not your prize. My heart belongs to someone else."

"You think that matters to me? Hah!" He snarled and produced a large bag and length of rope from behind his back. "Step into this politely, and you won't get hurt."

She moved toward him. "And if I don't?" Rosanna's eyes scanned for something to use as a weapon.

"Very excellent question. If I don't emerge from the house in...," he referred to a watch extracted from a waistcoat pocket, "two minutes, this room will be set on fire, and I will carry you out over my shoulder. It will appear as though I am rescuing you from another fire. Such a flammable neighborhood. So sad to see the damage to your uncle's house. Especially as he is nobly fighting a fire down the block. So ironic, no?"

She put some warmth in her voice and batted her lashes. "Before I get in your vile sack, please come close. I want to tell you something."

"What is it?"

She flung off the clinging blanket, approached him and cupped her hands to his ear, then screamed at the top of her lungs, "Help!"

He bent over in pain, yowling. He straightened and staggered toward her, fingers clawed. "Why, you vixen. Wait until I get my hands on you!"

Rosanna pointed to a spot over Halburt's shoulder. "Look, behind you!"

"You are a pretty little liar," growled Halburt, advancing upon her. But a hand clamped down on his shoulder before he got halfway across the room.

Lord Winstead stepped into sight moving out in front of his enemy. "Ah, but she's telling the truth. You'll cease your schemes regarding Miss Cabot this instant." Lord Winstead held out a staying hand to Rosanna. "Stay clear, my love."

She scampered to the far corner. "Halburt stole the note I wrote you, Lord Winstead, asking you to meet me at the falls. Maybe he has it on him."

He touched his chest. "Darling, I have the note, right here."

"The note," mocked Halburt, sneering. "You'll make a fine pair once I get through with blackening your names."

"Halburt, you are the one whose tattered reputation stands in peril. Please leave now. I shall present things clearly to you, come morning light. Be gone!"

"We shall see." Halburt left in a huff, cradling his ear.

She emerged from the dark corner. "He was about to abduct me again."

"Thank God I came right away. The minute we got your uncle's letter, I left for London. I arrived here just as he entered the house. Through the front door—he's full of brass."

"He started a diversionary fire down the block, then tried to force me into a large bag. He had it all planned."

"Those minutes must have felt like hours, darling. Come to me."

He enfolded her in his arms, and her world righted itself.

He stroked her hair. "There, now."

Recalling herself, she moved away, retrieved her robe from a bedpost, and turned to Peter with a rueful smile. "As irregular as is our situation," she made a gentle circular wave of the hand, "I think we should descend to the morning room."

"Of course."

He guided her down the stairs. A complete absence of servants indicated the fire down the block required more hands.

Once ensconced in an arm chair, with a coverlet over her lap and a shawl around her shoulders, Rosanna shared the latest news. "My uncle told me today that he has evidence that the Halburt family was after the Honor's Point property and its treasure for decades."

"So he was after the treasure? He didn't see the real treasure under his nose, my love." He pulled her to her feet again, enfolded her in a gentle embrace, and nuzzled his face into her neck.

She pushed away but stayed in his arms. "No, listen, you don't understand his villainy. His father had an intentional hand in your father's ruin."

"I am not surprised. But those losses brought you into my life." She sagged against him and he put his face against her hair. After a few seconds, he released her from his arms. Her shawl slipped, chilled again, and bereft, she looked up at him, questioning.

"The heat of the moment, rescuing my beloved, does not give me the right to caress you." He draped the shawl around her shoulders.

"I'm grateful you arrived when you did. With Halburt about to both abduct me and set this house on fire." She shivered and clutched the shawl tighter, missing his warmth. "Your presence vanquished him."

"You vanquished my heart with your love." Peter pulled the precious note from within his jacket. "When I found this, snagged on a bush in the glen, my heart was joyous and stricken at the same time, since I knew you'd met with foul play."

She gasped.

He replaced the coverlet over her, and then spoke. "Back to the contents of the note. Thank you for forgiving me, darling. It seems this time, however, I am the one rescuing the damsel in distress." He smiled ruefully, and Rosanna perceived the irony of this situation following along the lines of Melissa being rescued by Mark.

"Let's put that in the past, where it belongs. You've repented to God, to the Russells, and to me. No reasonable person could expect more." She waited for the words of love that she hoped would flow now.

"I must fetch your uncle back to the house. No one else needs to know we have been alone together here. Less chance of anyone giving credence to any gossip and lies Halburt may choose to spread about these unfortunate incidents."

"Before you go, I hope you can assure me that Dot hasn't crossed paths with Halburt." Belated concern about Dot having been accosted by Lord Halburt clouded her joy.

"She was taken by force, bound and gagged and thrown into the baggage compartment of Halburt's carriage. But she bravely vaulted out and valiantly headed for Honor's Point, all while rolled and bound in a piece of carpet. I was on horseback when I came across her shuffling along the road. I brought her home, her tale alerted everyone your peril, and a search for you began."

Rosanna's hand flew to her mouth. "Oh! I recall a loud thunk when the carriage hit a rut—that may have been her jumping out."

Formal again, he bowed over her hand, brushing it with the lightest of kisses. "I must leave you for now, dear."

Even though relieved about Dot's safety, Rosanna's heart stung with frustration. She'd thought surely by this time, all would be settled between them.

60

The next evening, Miss Barton and Ellie arrived at Uncle George's house in London, much to Rosanna's delight.

"We have plenty of guest rooms, so you must stay here." She spoke a few words to the butler. "The staff will take you to your rooms, and I will order a light meal to be served here in the drawing room."

When Miss Barton and Ellie returned from removing travel dust, Rosanna poured tea into thin porcelain cups and handed out delicate plates of food. She then quickly related all that happened, knowing the ladies would want to hear it all from her lips.

Miss Barton rose. "I am not feeling very well. I must retire for the night. This has been a lot to take in."

Rosanna got up. "I'll take you upstairs."

"No, I'll have a servant show me up. You stay here. Young people need to have time to talk. But for me, I want to retire."

"I knew Lord Halburt to be an unpleasant person, but this last attempt exceeds all. So glad you screamed into his ear. He deserves much worse, though—the madman." Ellie hopped to her feet and clamped her hands on her hips. Irate after hearing the sorry tale of Rosanna's travails, her blue eyes sparked with anger.

Rosanna, at her ease on a lavender brocade sofa, leaned on her elbow and twiddled a strand of hair with her fingers. "Sit down, Ellie. I might as well admit something. You know that I wrote a note to Lord Winstead—the one Halburt intercepted. That note was an attempt to clear away an impediment standing between us which had stopped me from accepting Lord Winstead's suit."

Ellie sat down on the other end of a sofa, angled toward Rosanna. "I knew love was in the air between you two, but I was not aware that he'd come to the point."

"Yes, he asked for my hand. I kept that under my hat. Since all impediments appear to be vanquished, I expected a renewed proposal by now." She glanced at the clock. "It's quite late."

"From what you described of the second attack here in London, dear, I am not surprised Lord Winstead forbore asking for your hand immediately. After all, the romantic atmosphere has been, shall we say, compromised by Lord Halburt's infamy."

"You're right. that's probably the explanation. But I long for those words. Since I've forgiven him, and of course, his fortune's been restored—which was important to him, I desire only to be with him and righteously betrothed."

"I understand."

Rosanna held out her left hand, extending her fingers and gazed as if admiring a ring. She mused, "I wonder what the Winstead betrothal ring looks like? Surely his father wouldn't have sold that."

"You're miles away, so dreamy." Ellie captured Rosanna's hand and patted it. "Tell me exactly how it was left with that cad, Halburt."

"He stalked off, acting the injured party. Lord Winstead told him he'd speak with him about matters.

Today, in fact."

"I'd like to be a mouse in the corner for that comeuppance," said Ellie.

"Not me, I've had my fill of violence and drama. And I'm tired of London and of waiting for Winstead. Let's go home tomorrow. Back to Honor's Point."

"I'd love that. London makes me nervous. Though I'm an obscure person and draped myself with thick veils on the way here, I'm deathly afraid of someone recognizing me."

Rosanna let out a sigh and rose. "You poor thing—all the more reason to leave. I'll tell Miss Barton, Uncle George, and the girls. We don't have much luggage—I have virtually none—so it shouldn't be a problem to depart after breakfast."

"Thank you, that suits me very well. Good night, then, the sooner we retire for the night, the sooner tomorrow will come and we can go home."

"Thank you for all the support and encouragement, Ellie. It's wonderful to have a friend like you. Good night."

~*~

Lord Winstead's patience waned dangerously by the next morning. It had taken an extra day to run the sneaky villain to ground and the man's petulant self-absorption knew no bounds.

Upon arrival at Halburt's set of rooms, Peter shouldered past the butler. He confronted Halburt as he sat at breakfast. Interrupting the man's repast didn't bother Peter at all. He selected a grape from a silver platter on the table and tossed it in his hand.

Fear in his eyes, Halburt blustered, "What have you got to say to me? Why should I listen to you? You're no relation to Miss Cabot, so I don't have to answer to you." His lower lip jutted out.

His sulky demeanor, and arrogant attitude aggravated Peter's already-frayed restraint. "Let's not quibble at this time about familial ties, Halburt. You threatened a lady. One whose peace is important to me. I am here to ensure your silence."

Halburt pushed away from the table. "My silence? About what?"

Winstead scoffed at the man's bluff. "You know very well. You intimated that you would spread distasteful rumors about Miss Cabot. I can't have that. I won't."

"That's all well and good for you to say, but you don't have any control of the matter." Raising his defiant chin, he tossed his linen napkin onto the table and spat out his next words. "I shall tell whomever I please about Miss Cabot."

"You'll do nothing of the kind." Peter insisted. "I see I have to apprise you of a couple of consequences for you, since you lack understanding. You not only assaulted Miss Cabot's person, you burgled her home, and stole her mail. Do you think a known thief will continue to be welcomed into society? Let alone the suspicion of your involvement in arson?"

"But nobody knows about that. Miss Cabot doesn't go in London society, so she can't tell anyone." Halburt smirked, as if that would settle it.

"You are closely acquainted with the Woodvale magistrate, Squire Bredon? We're close friends. He particularly despises burglary and assault on women. Also, Miss Cabot may not grace London society any longer, but nothing stops me from dropping in at White's or Almack's. I do love to speak the truth." Peter raised his brows and gave Halburt a look of significance.

"What are you saying?" Halburt blustered.

"Here's the crux. You'll no longer reside at Halburt Arms. You will move to one of your lesser estates. If anyone inquires, you'll tell people your home estate's climate is bad for your health. That will be the truth." Peter put the grape in his mouth, then smacked one fist into the other hand.

Face paper white, Lord Halburt sniffed and sputtered. "I'll consider it."

"No. You won't. I've considered it all night and you are moving away. Good day." He got up to leave, but before he reached the door, Lord Halburt spoke.

He wrung his hands. "All right. I've wanted to move for a while, anyway. Do you promise to keep quiet about me?"

"I'll keep silent, if you leave by week's end. That will mean leaving London immediately for Halburt Arms to put your estate's affairs in order. Shake my hand like a gentleman." Peter gave a firm squeeze and grasped hard. He glared at Halburt for a moment. "See that you leave soon, very soon. You're being watched."

~*~

When Peter came into view, walking up the drive at Honor's Point, Rosanna vaulted off the bedroom's window seat and ran down the stairs. She grabbed a bonnet, fan, and shawl off the stand in the hall and slipped out the front door, leaving Perkins standing with his mouth agape.

Settling the bonnet on her head and tying the ribbons, she put the shawl around her shoulders and stood, fidgeting with one of its tassels, waiting for Peter to reach her. He stopped at the foot of the steps and placed one booted foot on the lowest step. "Good morning, Miss Cabot. May I escort you on a walk around the grounds? I have something to tell you."

"I'd love to." With an irrepressible bubble of joy spiraling up from her chest, she forced herself to come down the steps at a sedate pace. Placing her hand on Lord Winstead's forearm, she smiled up at him from under the rim of her saucy bonnet. "'Tis a fine day for a walk. How did you sleep?"

"Sleep? Not so much. I had some planning and thinking to do." He patted her hand before continuing. "I saw Halburt in London. It took me some time to locate him." He guided her toward the summerhouse.

"I hope you understand my leaving London."

"We're together now, dear, so it doesn't matter, as long as you are safe and happy."

They came to a pause at the foot of the shallow step leading to the latticework shelter. Winstead placed his hand at the small of Rosanna's back and guided her up the steps and through the doorway. The open-air room edged with faded blue padded benches held a hushed feel, and the smell of newly cut hay drifted in on gusts of hot summer air.

"Sit down, dear. I must tell you about Halburt."

"He's the last thing I want to hear about." She clutched her hands in her lap. The mention of the man's name and the grim look on Peter's face caused a sick flutter to land in her heart. Moving away from the marriage mart of London hadn't been far enough to get away from fortune hunters and the thought still made her shudder.

"You may be assured that he's been dealt with. He's moving permanently to one of his lesser estates. He'll be gone in a few days—by the end of the week, in fact. You'll not have him to fear, or worry about, any more. I made things clear to him, and he agreed that a move for his health would be a very good thing."

"Thank you. He has been a pest. I will be extremely pleased to see him gone." She leaned back a bit and braced her shaky hands against the seat cushion. "Let's talk about something else." She fluttered her fan in front of her face, then closed it again. Elation rose in her core at the thought of him proclaiming his love. Would it happen today?

"Yes, let's do." Peter sank down onto one knee, directly in front of Rosanna.

He took her hands into his dry, warm grasp. His hands felt hard and slightly rough, not soft like hers.

"My dear, you are my heart's desire. I must make you my own, and I must be yours. The Lord has clearly brought us together." He bent his head and placed a light kiss on her hands, first one, then the other. His lips were soft and warm.

Dizzy joy swept through her head, sizzled down to her toes, came back up and settled in her midsection. She opened her mouth, but no words emerged.

"No, let me speak, dear." Peter laid his finger over her lips for a moment. "Make my joy complete by agreeing to be my wife. We can be married in two weeks, if that's enough time for you?"

"Darling, I'd wait much longer if necessary, but two weeks sounds just right to me. I'd love to make your joy complete. Yes, I'll gladly be your wife." She tingled in anticipation as Peter stood, and then pulled her to her feet. He wrapped her in his strong arms.

The strength of his arms staggered her senses, and a sweet weakness crept over her. He put a gentle hand on the back of her head and moved in to kiss her lips. When his lips met hers, she felt as though she'd swoon from the waves of love and sensation, but he broke off the delightful kiss after a moment.

Releasing her with reluctance, he rummaged in his waistcoat pocket. "Ah, here it is. The Winstead betrothal ring." He lifted her left hand and slipped a filigreed band topped by a square cut sapphire onto her ring finger, turned her hand over and lightly kissed her palm.

"It's so beautiful." Rosanna breathed out her admiration. She held her hand out to regard it at arm's length. "Thank you. I am honored to wear it."

"I love you, my dear. With all my heart. When I think of the way God has worked to bring us together, I want to burst with gratitude. A few short weeks ago, I lived as a recluse, carrying a heavy burden, with no hopes for a happy future. Now, I am to marry the loveliest lady in the land."

"I had a cold heart, closed off to love with no thought of ever marrying. Now I am engaged to marry a fine lord." Rosanna gazed deeply into his eyes trying to convey all her love and passion.

The betrothed pair sank down onto the bench into a long, warm embrace.

61

"Look, Peter, it's Miss Barton, and Mr. Clough. And they're holding hands." Rosanna, with reluctance, eased away from Peter, ending his welcome caress. She kept her fingers entwined with his, though, while waiting for the older couple who approached the summerhouse, hand in hand.

Peter whispered. "Rosanna, dear, my face is sore from smiling."

"Mine, too. It appears we're not the only ones smelling like April and May. Look at them." She whispered back. They turned toward the open arched doorway and watched the older couple's progress in their direction. Mr. Clough clearly had Miss Barton's hand in an intimate lover's grasp.

"I love it when you hold my hand—I don't want to ever let you go." Rosanna murmured these words and squeezed his hand. They half hid their clasped hands in the folds of her dress.

"May we join you? It's such a beautiful day." Mr. Clough presumed the answer would be 'yes', assisted Miss Barton up the three shallow steps, and guided her over to a padded bench near the wall.

Rosanna turned to Peter, not yet able to stop smiling joy had taken over her face. She squeezed his hand again before she spoke. "It's the most wonderful, beautiful day ever. Isn't it, Lord Winstead?"

Peter radiated happiness. "Miss Barton, Mr. Clough, we'd like you to be the first to know. Miss Cabot has made me the happiest of men. We have resolved any and all impediments blocking our way to the marriage altar." Peter released Rosanna's hand and laid his arm around her shoulders. He looked long into her eyes.

Mr. Clough gave a quiet cough after a few seconds passed, breaking the moment. "Miss Cabot, Lord Winstead, that's excellent news. Not that I didn't expect it. I had a strong sense that you two were meant for each other. The circumstances that brought you together reveal God's guiding hand. So pleased for you both."

"My dear." Miss Barton rushed to Rosanna and clasped her hands. "Love is so wonderful. Isn't it Mr. Clough?" She looked back over her shoulder at the vicar for affirmation.

"Lord Winstead, harking back to the other night, when you found the treasure? Yes, well, I have found my own treasure, and today I claimed it for my own." Mr. Clough drew Miss Barton back to his side and put his arm around her waist. He paused a moment, then spoke. "She, Pearl that is, is my treasure. My earthly life's reward. We, too, shall be traversing to the altar."

"Pearl?" Rosanna put her fingers over her lips to hold in her astonishment.

"Yes, Rosanna, that's my name. All these years of going by 'Barton' as your nurse, and lady's maid, then being elevated to companion and 'Miss Barton' you never knew my first name. Bertrand likes it." She looked up at Mr. Clough, as if for reassurance.

"I do indeed. So much so that I selected a pearl ring for my beloved." He lifted Pearl's hand to show her betrothal ring to the younger couple.

"It's a beautiful name and a lovely ring. You'll be Mr. Clough's companion on life's path. You've always been a treasure to me, but now you're his Pearl. How sweet. How perfect."

Losing her longtime companion would have been a real blow for Rosanna not too long ago, however, she had Lord Winstead now. The thought of spending the rest of her life with him, day after day together, made her toes curl in anticipation.

Rosanna gazed at Peter, recollecting her first chance meeting with him disguised as a common villager. No, there was nothing common about this fine man. He was never meant to live a secluded life of poverty, tucked in a corner of what should have been his own estate. His restoration to full stature with God and man had come about, and Rosanna's heart treasured this fact.

In just two weeks' time they would begin their lives as Lord and Lady Winstead of Honor's Point. Rosanna reflected with contentment, having found her heart's true refuge at last. Her cup of blessing was full...very full indeed.

ACKNOWLEDGEMENTS

I want to thank my editor, Susan Baganz, for all the dedication and effort she has given to this book. Thanks also to my husband, John, for all his encouragement. My running partner, Sandy, has also been a steady source of feedback, encouragement, and inspiration.

About the Author

Susan Karsten lives in a small Wisconsin town, is the wife of a real estate broker, and mother three, and grandmother of three. Her hobbies include fitness, quilting, and reading.

Her love for writing developed while in college where she earned a BS degree in Home Economics.

Child-rearing days having drawn to an end, Susan now invests time in fiction writing. Having written three Regency historical romances, she is in the process of writing another book. Her personal blog can be found at Graciouswoman.wordpress.com.

You Can Help!

At Pelican Book Group it is our mission to entertain readers with fiction that uplifts the Gospel. It is our privilege to spend time with you awhile as you read our stories.

We believe you can help us to bring Christ into the lives of people across the globe. And you don't have to open your wallet or even leave your house!

Here are 3 simple things you can do to help us bring illuminating fiction™ to people everywhere.

1) If you enjoyed this book, write a positive review. Post it at online retailers and websites where readers gather. And share your review with us at reviews@pelicanbookgroup.com (this does give us permission to reprint your review in whole or in part.)

2) If you enjoyed this book, recommend it to a friend in person, at a book club or on social media.

3) If you have suggestions on how we can improve or expand our selection, let us know. We value your opinion. Use the contact form on our web site or e-mail us at customer@pelicanbookgroup.com

God Can Help!

Are you in need? The Almighty can do great things for you. Holy is His Name! He has mercy in every generation. He can lift up the lowly and accomplish all things. Reach out today.

Do not fear: I am with you; do not be anxious: I am your God. I will strengthen you, I will help you, I will uphold you with my victorious right hand.

~Isaiah 41:10 (NAB)

We pray daily, and we especially pray for everyone connected to Pelican Book Group—that includes you! If you have a specific need, we welcome the opportunity to pray for you. Share your needs or praise reports at http://pelink.us/pray4us

Free Book Offer

We're looking for booklovers like you to partner with us! Join our team of influencers today and periodically receive free eBooks.

For more information
Visit http://pelicanbookgroup.com/booklovers